Revelation Special Ops

Book 1

The Elite

of the Weak

By

Precarious Yates

To Cathy,
May God continue
to ignite the flame
in your heart and
send you forth to
boldly preach His Word!
Love!

ISBN: 0615564739

ISBN-13: 978-0615564739 (Precarious Yates)

Acknowledgments:

My heart bursts with gratitude toward my Lord and Savior, Jesus Christ, my Life, my Love.

I want to thank my husband, Logan, who, in tenderness and wisdom, counseled most steps of this journey, holding my trembling hands.

Three women sewed time, editing skills and creative influence into this book, carefully reading each word. To my two critique partners, Sarah Tipton and Lindsay Franklin, and my amazing editor, Nicole Cober-Lake —thank you!

Thanks to my family: Peter and Kathy, Bill and Susie, Steve and Jesse, Jonny and Desirea, Mark, Ben and Amanda, Amy, Kathryn, the Smith/Holihan clan, and especially my daughter for dealing with an over-tired mommy.

Thanks to the following people who made publication possible:

M.L. & P.L.; M.L.F.; G.R.F.; S.P.S. & W.S.; W.R. & M.B.R.; S.P.R. & J.C.R.; R.A.U.; R.W.B.; J.R. & D.S.R.; D.H. & R.H.; C.C.

A special thanks to Lauralee Bliss, who came up with 'Special' Ops, then introduced me to all the amazing people at ACFW. I've learned so much and forged friendships that will last a lifetime.

And lastly, thanks to the teachers at IHOP (that's the International House of Prayer, not pancakes). Your teachings inspired this story.

Dedication:

To my sister Amanda, and to Olivia,

you inspire me more than you know.

To Shoshanna, and to the Lilies:

you know who you are...

Part 1

God chose the weak things of the world to shame the strong.

~ Paul

1 Corinthians 1:27 (NIV)

New York City, NY, USA

Sometime in the near future, maybe five years from now, maybe twenty-five.

Chapter 1:
The Packet

With a smile as wide as the Brooklyn Bridge, Hadassah skipped down the steps outside the house of prayer, and wove through the crowds to the subway station. She hoped to make it to the F line in time. And before any new earthquakes hit. Her heart pattered. Coffee with Dad on Thursday afternoons was her favorite, but she never let her excitement show. Not like this. With the packet in her arms, she knew what she had to say as soon as she got home. She needed the excitement to keep her on course, no matter what argument he brought up.

Wisps of her black hair tangled in her eyelashes. She didn't dare let go of the packet, not even to get these hairs out of her face, so she blew them away. *Why did I forget my hairpin? Mom's right—I shouldn't leave the house without it.* Another strong breeze, hot as the rest of the air around her, whipped through corridors made by the skyscrapers and pushed her along.

Crowds swelled. They always did at this time of day in New York, and every face carried a flicker of fear. The earthquakes never caused significant damage, but each quake felt like labor pains growing more and more intense. After all, this was New York, not California, and quakes weren't supposed to be an issue. But earthquakes were happening everywhere. So much for feeling safe on the East Coast.

She ducked her head and rushed to the shadow of the nearest skyscraper, hoping to hide from the searing sun as she made for the subway station. The shade brought no relief. With humidity this high everyone sweat, including the business women in flawless attire. And everyone wore the same fatigued and stressed look—stocks must have plummeted again. That would make the ninth business day in a row.

But Hadassah couldn't think about this—not now.

Hugging the packet in her arms a little tighter, she recalled every detail of its contents, glancing at its frayed edges. She never felt this confident, except about her love for Yeshua and for her parents. In her fervor, she scraped her thumbnail against the tip of her index finger while she waited for the train. The possibility that Dad wouldn't give his blessing whispered at the edges of her exhilaration, but she hushed this away.

All the training from Mom flooded her as she hopped across the gap from the subway platform into the car. Perfect balance, even when jostled by a large man in a blue silk suit.

As soon as Dad learns about Revelation Special Ops, he has to give his blessing. She bounced on the balls of her feet and gripped the metal bar as the subway car jolted back and forth. *A sea of faces around me, and I'm sure not one of them can guess what put this smile on my face. But they must wonder. No one smiles on the F line.*

When she walked through the door of her apartment, Dad looked up from the sea of books on the dining room table, his face glowing at the sight of hers.

"Haddy! Shalom!" He stood. "I love seeing you sparkle like this. What a gift you give to the world. I can't wait to hear what has you so happy. But—" He raised his hand just as she opened her mouth to blurt the news. "Coffee first."

"Do we have any Ethiopian blend left in the freezer?" she asked, still bouncing on the balls of her feet.

"I've already prepped the machine, all I need to do is press start."

"You mean you've made the coffee all by yourself?"

"Oy, vey! Seeing as I'm your favorite chef, I figured you'd trust my coffee making skills again."

"That pot you measured and brewed last year was proverbially undrinkable."

"Oy yoi yoi! I followed the directions this time. Besides, I know how to make coffee. If you remember, I was born before the press-two-buttons-and-it's-done machines, back in the days when we always measured water and grinds and fiddled with filters."

"It's okay, Dad, you don't have to remind me that you're old." She grinned and threw her arms around his shoulders, pressing her cheek against his ear. "How was the Rabbi's day?"

He shrugged. "Cerebral." Then he smiled again. "But blessed. All the research is done for my trip to the Middle East this winter, and now I can work on my sermon for Shabbat."

"What are you gonna preach on?" She popped a grape into her mouth and sat upon a stool at the counter while she listened.

"First John. Abba Father's perfect love casting out our fears. I'll be preaching to myself since we're sending you off to Liberia the next day."

In all her excitement about the packet she had forgotten. She was going to Africa for three weeks to work in the orphanage their congregation sponsored while her friends Isabella and Danny picked up their soon to be adopted daughter. "That's a great topic to prepare us, Dad."

He poured two mugs before taking a seat at the counter beside her. "Okay. Now you can tell me what this packet is all about. I've held my peace ever since the envelope arrived yesterday. Then you were gone before I woke this morning."

Hadassah sighed, pressing her lips together. "I know it's unconventional, Dad, but I want to do it. I feel like I was made for this." She slid the envelope to him. "Ever since you had Mack MacArthur come to the church four months ago, I can't think about anything else. All those kids sold as slaves across the globe—it's horrible!"

"I know, Haddy. I think about it a lot, too; so does your mom." As he opened the contents of the envelope his eyebrows narrowed at the "CONFIDENTIAL" stamp on the top and subsequent pages.

"Whenever I thought about what happens to children sold as slaves, I wanted to hit something. Or someone. You know me, Dad, nothing stirs my emotions—not like this. I felt like a fire had been lit within my bones. The fire is still there, stronger than ever, but I feel such peace now too."

His lips pursed and his forehead wrinkled as he read.

After a few minutes of trying to interpret his expression, all the while hoping it would change, she asked, "Can I apply?"

He looked up at her. "You're only sixteen, Hadassah."

"I'll be seventeen in two and a half weeks."

"The training starts in January; you don't graduate until June."

"I know, but I was going to talk to the principal about that since I'll have completed all my requirements by December."

"If anyone talks to your principal, it'll be your mom or me. You are more independent than any sixteen year old—"

"Seventeen."

"Still, let me be your dad a little while longer."

"You'll always be my dad. But I know I'm made for this. Think of all the self-defense lessons Mom has given me for how many years now? Both of you have trained me to take care of myself."

He rubbed his forehead with his fingertips and sighed. "Have you talked to your mother about this?"

"I was going to tonight. I just... I wanted to talk to you first because I have a feeling Mom will say yes."

"I do, too."

"Will you?"

Their coffee cups began to rattle on the counter, and they stared at them until the rattling stopped. She rested her eyes and mind in a long blink then took a deep breath. Dad glanced at her knowingly.

He looked through the packet further. "Huh. It's connected with Ronny Gibbons in Greensboro."

Ronny Gibbons was one of his favorite teachers. Her smile returned. "If you look at the fourth page, they discuss their guiding principles."

He raised his eyebrows as he stared at the page. "I know. I'm looking at those right now."

"They teach the exact same things you do, that the church will be on the earth during the tribulation and we need to prepare now. I love the quote there about preparing."

"I see the one you mean, 'We'll prepare ourselves, not by stockpiling weapons, but by building our relationship with God through watching and praying—'"

"'—We'll prepare by setting our faces like flint, to love no matter the cost. We'll prepare by partnering with Jesus to release the oppressed from their bonds of slavery. The greater the darkness across the world the brighter the light of Christ will shine through us.' Isn't that awesome, Dad? It sounds like one of your sermons."

"It also sounds like Ronny Gibbons. I like what they say about recruiting the elite of the weak."

With a bittersweet smile, Hadassah quoted it from memory. "'Weak because of a broken heart for the slaves and hostages around the world, and weak because the plight of one person is significant enough.' That's what convinced me I want to be a part of Revelation Special Ops."

"Do you think you'll have the stamina for the training? It says it'll be similar to the Marines or the CIA." Then he rolled his eyes and shook his head. "I forget who I'm talking to, of course you'll have the stamina. And the ability to get into and out of—what did they say here?—high security facilities." He rolled his eyes again and sighed. "You're just like your mother."

She grinned. "I know. Does that mean I can go?"

"That means I'll consider it. I want to talk it over with your mother. She may want you working with her instead since she does similar work here in the City."

"When I was in the prayer room a few months back, praying about this problem of young girls sold as prostitutes, I wept for three solid hours."

"I remember."

"I couldn't tell if it was rage or God's own tears boiling inside me. And you know me, Dad, I never cry."

"I know."

"That was the night I found out about Revelation Special Ops. To this day, I don't remember who told me, but I knew it felt right."

"And I'm still considering it, but I don't think I can say 'yes' yet."

***

Dinner was filled with all the parental concern Hadassah had hoped to avoid.

Mom's years with the Mossad, the Israeli foreign intelligence, left her permanently scarred with skepticism. "It doesn't give a contact name, just an address." She set the packet down on the table beside her plate and stared at her food. "Whoever this is, he's former intelligence." She shook her head, took a small sip of her Kosher wine and looked up again. "I'm not saying no, but I won't have you send in an application based on mere feelings."

Hadassah swallowed her marzipan cookie before she finished chewing, then chased it with a swig of water. "That's fair. I guess I can understand."

"Let's see how things go in Liberia first. We'll talk about sending off this application when you get back." She gave the quickest flash of a smile Hadassah had ever seen.

Dad grinned as if he read his wife's thoughts. "What is it?"

"Languages. They ask how many she's fluent in and provide ten spaces to fill."

Hadassah sighed. "I can only fill five of those." Her gaze fell to the writing desk in the corner of the room, which held boxes of worn flash cards.

Mom let out a rare impulsive laugh. "Don't forget sign language and Morse code. But I'm sure they'd accept you anyway."

"You know, it's strange to be in the same room with you two ladies. You could have a whole conversation in Italian right now, and I'd have no idea what you'd be saying."

Hadassah leaned over and gave Dad a kiss on the cheek. "Ti amo, Papà."

Chapter 2:

Minister of Justice

Hadassah opened her eyes, contentment filling her as she stared through the mesh of mosquito netting, through the open window and out into the African sky. She stretched on her mat and prayed in the dawning light of her seventeenth birthday. After her second week in the orphanage, she had grown used to the baby smell, the unrelenting heat, the never-ending sound of crying.

Except this crying was no baby, and neither was it any of the other teens who had joined the mission trip. The cry, full of ache and disappointment, reminded her of a verse somewhere in Proverbs about hope deferred making the heart sick. She threw on clean clothing and transferred her belongings from the pockets of the jeans she wore the day before. She had a feeling she'd need everything: the chewing gum, the money, the amazing cell phone Mom gave as a birthday present before she left, and the mini transmitter and iPod her cousin, Yitzak, gave her at the airport. She shoved half of her money into her sock then pulled her hair back and stuck in her hairpin before stepping out of the mosquito netting.

Isabella was inconsolable. She stood leaning her hands atop the kitchen table and breathing small breaths in between heaving sobs. Her husband, Danny, gritted his teeth, seething with anger and anxiety even as he kissed his wife after each stomp back and forth across the floor.

"What happened?" Hadassah asked, but was blocked by the orphanage's head administrator.

"Don't bother them now, Miss Haddy." The administrator set her arm like a bar across the doorway. "Go with your friends to the market in Monrovia while we fix it here."

"Danny, tell me what happened."

The administrator grimaced. "Go on, Miss Hadassah. The van will be leaving for the market soon."

"I'm not leaving until I find out what's happened to my friends."

Isabella controlled her sobs enough to look up at her husband. "You can tell her."

Danny's jaw tightened. "Ariella's gone missing during the night. Bella's convinced someone kidnapped her."

Ariella. She had rocked ten month old Ariella to sleep yesterday afternoon—perhaps the best part of her trip so far. And the little girl was supposed to go home with Danny and Isabella. To calm her sudden surge of emotion, Hadassah breathed deep. Her mind became focused. "I'm so sorry, Bella."

Isabella groaned. Her eyes looked as if they'd burst from their sockets if she cried any harder. "What can we do?"

The look of fear on her placid friend's face cemented Hadassah's resolve.

Danny shook. "I'm going to call the Minister of Justice again."

"Go along, Miss Haddy. You kids'll only make it worse for them." The administrator reached out to grab her arm, but Hadassah bowed and ducked out the side door.

The van held only three of the eight other teens who came to work at the orphanage. Maybe she had time to make the phone call. She pulled out her cell, walked down the long, dusty driveway and dialed the number before she could change her mind.

"Haddy, are you okay?" The sound of Dad's voice, filled with all the concern she could imagine, almost distracted her.

"I'm fine, Dad, but Bella's not. Can you put Mom on the phone?"

"Okay." Dad sounded confused, almost hurt as he handed the phone over.

"Is this about Danny and Bella's baby?" Even in the middle of the night Mom sounded professional.

Hadassah explained what she knew then dove into her plan. "They want to take the team to town to give Danny and Bella space. I'm going to find out what I can while I'm there."

She could hear Dad in the background. "Don't let her do that, Eva. Give me the phone and let me talk to her."

Hadassah could imagine Mom's hand rising in a request for silence. The silence might have lasted only a few seconds, but it felt like hours.

"Don't put yourself in jeopardy, sweetie." Mom's tone was as matter-of-fact as always. "That's the last thing Danny and Bella need right now."

"I can do this, Mom. You've trained me well."

Dad's protest in the background became muffled by the unmistakable sound of Mom's hand covering the phone.

"I'll be in touch, Mom." She hoped they heard. "I've gotta get on this van with the team. I love you. Tell Dad I love him."

"Wait. Keep your phone on and text me as soon as you're in town. We love you, too."

"I love you, Hadassah," she heard Dad say before she disconnected.

Most of the kids in the van gossiped and cliqued the whole way over, as if grappling for coping strategies. Hadassah slipped her headphones on and scrolled through her iPod to a mix which would quiet her mind while she stared out the window. Where was the Capitol district with the Minister's office? Someone had pointed it out last week. Why hadn't she paid more attention?

The van driver dropped them off on United Nations Drive at the Water Side Market which meant she had quite a walk before she got to any of the government buildings. She waited until the van left and her friends dispersed by twos and threes before seeking out the Minister of Justice's office.

Pictures of the Minister of Justice lined the walls of the foyer: the Minister with numerous dignitaries, as well as a few victories of justice plastered across headlines and framed in gilt.

"I'm sorry, Minister Rhodes is out of the office," the secretary informed her without looking up from her paperwork.

"Any idea when he'll be back?" Hadassah couldn't believe her boldness.

The woman waved her hand dismissively toward her. "Xavier takes his coffee at this hour. You may lodge an inquiry and he can see you in a few days."

This can't wait a few days. But instead of growing frustrated, Hadassah flashed a quick smile and looked for a picture of the Minister to imprint in her memory.

As she stepped out onto the street again, her phone buzzed with a text. Mom. She opened the message and saw a picture of a thin-faced man.

HIS NAME'S AUGUSTUS LAVO. PIRATE. SOMALI. LAST SEEN IN MONROVIA. SPOKE W/ A FRIEND @ EMBASSY. TRYING 2 CONTACT MIN. OF JUSTICE ABOUT HIM. NO SUCCESS. B CAREFUL.

Hadassah made her way toward the Water Side Market, avoiding all the places where she saw the kids from her youth group.

***

"'Xcuse me, miss, 'xcuse me!" the child gasped as he tugged at Hadassah's shirt.

The boy in mismatched sneakers had been following her throughout the market for five minutes begging for money. His attire, an oversized shirt of a hip-hop star who was famous several decades ago and shorts he tugged back to his waist, clamored for a hand-out. All the while, Hadassah slipped through the crowds from one market stall to another to steal a closer look at two men sitting beside the rail of the outdoor café. If only she could hear what the men were saying. Neither the phone nor the iPod Yitzak gave her would pick up their voices among the throng of the market. The mini transmitter would help, but this sat unactivated at the bottom of her pocket. She pondered how to get a bug close to these men.

"'Xcuse me, miss!" the boy continued. "Just one dollar, please. Just one dollar."

One American dollar would go far in Liberia even though it was weak against most of the other currencies in the world. But she had converted all of her money at the airport when she arrived two weeks ago. And she wasn't supposed to give the boy any of it. Yet every glance at the child's face forced Mom's admonishment, "Never give them money," further from her mind.

She reached into her pocket, but instead of pulling out money, she rubbed the tiny transmitter between her fingers. As the boy tugged her shirt for the umpteenth time, her plan fell into place.

She reached her hand into her other pocket and took out the pack of gum, glancing at the boy and smiling. Crouching down, she extended a stick of gum toward him. "Would you like a piece?"

His saucer eyes stared at the gum as he nodded. They both popped pieces into their mouths at the same time.

"Would you do a job for your money?"

The boy grinned as if he was glad for the employment. "Most anything, Miss!"

She took the gum from her mouth and stuffed the tiny transmitter inside, just like Yitzak had instructed when she was back in New York.

"Run this over to the café and stick it to the rail near those two men, but don't let them know what you're doing. If no one sees you do it, I'll give you twice as much as an American dollar." It was an awful risk, but so was this entire plan.

The boy was invisible. He was so good, she pulled out the equivalent of three dollars before turning on the receiver in her iPod.

"Will your buyers be paying Babylonian silver for the package?" she heard the scrawny, thin-faced man ask the Minister of Justice who sat across the table from him.

The Minister leaned across the café table and frowned at his companion. She hardly heard his whisper. "Enough for you to afford my silence."

The boy appeared again, his hand outstretched and his grin wider than before. Hadassah slinked behind a clothing stall before giving him money—she didn't want the men at the café to notice—then she slipped back through the crowds from market stall to market stall. While she adjusted the volume, her little employee had run off with his wages.

She edged to a closer stall, allowing her youth to mask her as she gained a clear view of the men. Unlike most kids from her youth group, she liked looking young, and knew various tricks to escape notice or mask emotion. She rehearsed Mom's favorite maxim in her head, *Blend in, keep a secret, slip away unnoticed.*

Here in Africa, thousands of miles from New York City, blending in and masking emotion required more effort. Especially in this heat. Only a handful of light-skinned faces dappled the market stalls, and no one sweat as much as she did. She scanned her surroundings.

That's when she caught the glance of a young man not much older than she was. He looked Chinese, but with spiked hair dyed blonde at the tips, super sleek sunglasses, and earphones in, he could have been a member of her youth group. Except unlike the members of her youth group, he looked like someone she could talk to. But he disappeared again, following a black man who was too light-skinned to be from Liberia. Americans. She was almost sure of it, but she had no time to find out.

As she waited for the Minister's conversation to get even more interesting, Hadassah pulled up Mom's text to view that photo again.

There was no doubt. This thin-faced man sitting at the café was Augustus Lavo.

"My workers are looking for a larger cut this time." Mr. Lavo squirmed in his silk suit as if he sweat rivers beneath the fabric, as if he knew how ridiculous it looked on him. "I hope there's enough for *me* after I pay everyone."

"There will be plenty. Enough for you to afford immunity, too." Xavier Rhodes,The Minister of Justice sneered. Hadassah imagined he had been a rugby star before his days in politics. "Tell your peons: if they want pay, they work for it. Hold on, it's my phone again." He looked at the face of his phone and smiled.

Mr. Lavo gave a snide grin. "Good news?"

"Pictures of my daughter. She has her violin recital this afternoon."

"Sorry I'll miss that."

Minister Rhodes lowered his voice to a growl. "If you want your life as well as your immunity, I suggest never mentioning my daughter." He hissed as his phone rang. "It's those missionaries from the orphanage again. Whoever gave them my cell phone number is going to pay big."

She had been practicing her doe-in-the-headlights expression so everyone in the market would presume she was a tourist. While perfecting the look, standing at a market stall beside the café and inspecting a small wooden elephant, she listened to the Minister of Justice growl into his cell phone. He mopped his forehead and sipped iced coffee. His companion stared at the melting ice at the bottom of his glass and rolled his eyes at the Minister's tirade.

"What would I want with it—eh? I have four already. I think *you* have it... Oh, yes, I do... What would I have to gain from a missing baby?"

The baby's a girl, not an 'it,' Hadassah wanted to say, but she hid her thoughts behind the veil of tourist as she primed her phone's camera and discretely snapped pictures of the Minister with the other man.

"Do you know how hard this government has worked these past five years to raise this nation up from the dust?" the Minister continued. He paused and stared at his coffee as if it was to blame and then at his sneering companion. "Do you know how hard *I've* worked to make this country what it is today? Do you think we'd just throw it all away? Tell me—how do you know it didn't walk off when no one was watching? ... Maybe it *crawled* off, then... Fine, I'll set an inquiry this afternoon... Of course I care. I especially care about *Liberia's* children. ... I said I would set an inquiry... I've had enough of your conjectures. One more word out of you and I'll have my office reopen investigations into your..." he pulled the phone from his ear and looked at the face of it. "They think they come with better ideas to save our country. If they helped our country with more of their American dollars, maybe I'd listen to their tirades."

"Don't they know it's all about the highest bidder?" the smaller man whispered in a low voice Hadassah barely heard.

Minister Rhodes's face turned the color of ripe pomegranate as he stared at Mr. Lavo.

"Don't they know children disappear all the time over here?" Mr. Lavo squirmed again in his black silk suit.

"I'd keep those Somali lips shut if I were you," Minister Rhodes snapped back. He leaned in close again. "Unless you wish to tell me how your men nabbed a crawler. Especially one bound for the US by the end of the week. Newborns or walkers. We're going to have to return it before you leave in the morning and one of your men will have to take the fall. This is the last time we meet in public, Mr. Lavo. Oh, and your rate for my silence just increased. Insolence!" He hissed. "Incompetence. Idiocy. I've had more than I can stand." He flagged the waiter. "Hey, Steven, my check please!"

Mr. Lavo leaned in close to the Minister. "I wouldn't insult me again, little Minister of Justice." All the timidness had left his voice.

Xavier Rhodes turned on the man as if he was a cobra about to strike. "Do you want to say that again?"

"I have a direct line to Vladimir Therion."

The Minister of Justice loosened his fist as his stare turned to one of horror. "I have a direct line to him as well, so your threat won't work. You just do what you need to do. Our conversation is over."

Hadassah set the wooden elephant down on the table at the stall. There was no sign of her little employee, but as many as fifteen other kids crowded around her with outstretched hands.

Chapter 3:

The Chase

Thrusting her shaking hand into her pocket, Hadassah took out the pack of gum and began to hand out pieces to the kids until no more was left. *How did I not anticipate this?* she wondered as they closed in around her. She was supposed to come to Liberia to love on these kids, but all she wanted right now was for them to go away. She held up her hands as if to reclaim her personal space. "I don't have any more. I'll come back later with more."

The crowd of children looked up at her with distrustful faces and dispersed again.

Watching the Minister of Justice and Mr. Lavo leave, Hadassah took out her phone and keyed a quick text to Mom.

DWNTWN, SAW 2 MEN TALKING: 1—POSS KIDNPPR—LAVO. 2—MIN OF JUSTICE. I PLAN TO FOLLOW 1.

She set her phone to vibrate and could just see Mr. Lavo ahead of her, worming through the crowds. As she weaved her way closer to him, her phone vibrated with a returning text. Mom.

FOLLOW 1. KEEP DISTANCE 100 FEET OR MORE. HIDE FACE IF POSS. WAIT 4 NXT TXT.

She couldn't wait. She had to call her. "Is Dad mad at me?"

"No, sweetie, he was just scared. He's on the phone with Danny at the moment. Stay safe and don't do anything unless I tell you to. Now, go buy a scarf to cover your face."

As Hadassah threaded through the lunch hour crowds after Mr. Lavo, she glanced to her left and right for a vendor who sold scarves. Then she spied the perfect booth. *What did Mom say? Oh, yeah. Make sure to barter.*

"This?" She used a thick Yorkshire accent to mask her American one.

"Fifty," the vendor told her.

"Forty?" Hadassah suggested.

"Forty-five."

Hadassah grew nervous. Mr. Lavo was out of sight. She reached into her pocket for the money, but none of the bills were there—all of them lifted from her. Must have been one of the street kids. Frustration rose as she realized she'd never be able to catch up to Lavo. At least the kids had left her phone. Then she remembered the stash of money she always kept in her sock. She sighed, reached down to pull out her last wad of bills and handed two of them to the vendor.

"One more," the lady told her.

"Forgive me." Hadassah replied while she scanned the market again. She spied Lavo but would have to move fast. She handed the lady another bill and slipped away into the crowd.

Walking briskly along, she twirled her hair into a French twist with one hand while she pushed her hairpin through with the other. She wrapped the scarf loosely about her head and face without missing a step.

Her phone buzzed with another text.

IF U RUN IN2 TROUBLE/DISCOVER SUMTHING, ICE TXT ME.

The ICE text was Mom's favorite aspect of the phone. As soon as Hadassah sent a text through the In Case of Emergency list, Mom obtained exact coordinates of her location, then could access a satellite visual as well.

Her phone buzzed again.

STAY 100FT OR MORE BHIND HIM. HPE U BROT UR HAIRPIN. UNSCREW END 4 XTRA CAMRA.

Mom was always full of surprises. Yup, she texted back. She was gaining on Mr. Lavo now. He dragged his feet; maybe he dreaded his work, or grew lazy, or terribly confident.

Then the man stepped into a champagne colored Mercedes Benz SUV, and Hadassah feared losing him altogether.

Maintaining her thick Yorkshire accent, Hadassah addressed a young man sitting on a motorbike in the taxi station. "Excuse me."

The young man turned and beamed a smile at her. "How may I help you?"

"Are you a taxi?" she asked. She hoped she could keep this up—English accents were the hardest for her. "I need to follow a man in a car."

"I can follow a car, young lady, but it'll cost a little extra. Will he not drive you?"

"He was my boyfriend and he broke my heart, sir." She turned on the waterworks. "I came all this way and he breaks my heart. I've got to talk to him again before I leave." Deceiving people like this always made her feel ill. "Please."

"Okay, okay, climb on, young lady." The young man donned a helmet, masking his whole face.

"I need a helmet."

"You don't need one, young lady. I'm a safe driver."

"How much for yours? I'll pay you for it."

"For mine? A lot extra," he replied.

"I'll pay it." Cringing as she gave this promise, she tried to remember how much money she had left in her sock. Probably not enough, but she couldn't think about that just yet. She wiped fake tears away, took the scarf off, wrapped it tight around her waist and tucked in any strings. When he handed her the helmet, she took out her hairpin and slipped on the helmet. It concealed her face completely. "Follow that car please, sir, but not too closely."

"Which one?"

"The SUV, the Mercedes GL550, please."

"Oh, sweet young lady, please tell me he is not your boyfriend." The young man shook his head. "He is a bad, bad man."

"I know he's a bad man! I came all this way and he breaks my heart. I'm going to give him a piece of my mind, so if you please, sir, follow the SUV."

The young man revved the bike's engine and then pulled out into traffic. He treated other cars as his personal obstacle course. Hadassah gripped the small handles to her right and left, struggling to keep her balance while her knuckles whitened and her palms sweat.

"He's a bad, bad man, young lady," the driver said again after they crossed Mesurado Bridge and were following the Mercedes north on United Nations Drive. "You don't need a man like him. You need Jesus. You need Jesus, young lady."

Hadassah smiled at this remark, although no one but God Almighty, Yeshua Himself, saw the joy on her face. How much could she tell him? She hated lying or staying in character around a brother or sister in the Lord.

But he didn't let her get a word in edgewise. The rest of the way he continued to preach the gospel to her and his words raced through the breeze to her ears like a cup of cold water under all that hot African sun.

"Slow down," Hadassah shouted when the SUV turned down a dirt road toward a thin jungle. "Let him have more space. I don't want him to suspect it's me."

The driver complied and widened the gap to 300 yards between the vehicles, then he resumed preaching the gospel to her, explaining how Jesus would bear all of her hurt, heartache and shame. She listened as if this was beautiful background music while she surveyed her surroundings for any sign of a landmark or anomaly. Another vehicle followed the motorbike down this road. Although it relieved her in one way, she made sure to keep her guard up. It could be anyone. He could work for Mr. Lavo.

Augustus Lavo drove his Mercedes another three or four miles before he slowed and turned down a long driveway leading to a warehouse surrounded by a barbed wire fence.

"Drive further," Hadassah told the motorbike evangelist. "I'll tell you when to stop."

She looked behind and saw the other car still following. Her nervousness swelled when the motorbike had to swerve around all the bumps and ruts in the road and the car began to catch up.

"Pull off here and let him pass." Hadassah unintentionally left aside the English accent and resumed her Brooklyn accent.

He braked to a stop and waited for the car to pass. The car sped past and bumped all the way down the road until it was out of sight. Hadassah sighed and stepped off the back of the bike.

"You can leave me here." Her smile jittered even more than her arms as she handed him his helmet. "Here. And thanks for telling me about Jesus. I love Him too."

He gave her an incredulous stare. "Augustus Lavo is a bad, bad man."

"He's exactly the man I need to find."

"Please think again. My cousin Andrew works for him, and he has cut himself off from the family ever since. I worry for you, young lady. Here is my card with my phone number if you need a lift back to the city. My name is Joseph Blessing."

"Thank you, Mr. Blessing. Here is 150. I wish I had more to give you."

"It's more than I would have asked for. Do you need me to stay and wait for you?"

"No, thank you, Mr. Blessing. That would make it more dangerous for me."

"You aren't here because he broke your heart, are you? You are here to help bring him to justice."

She nodded.

He smiled at her. "Your voice changed when we got here, that is how I knew. Don't worry, I am not angry, I understand now. I will pray for you. He is a bad man."

She turned toward the bushes. "God bless you, Joseph Blessing. You have been a blessing to me."

"Wait," he called out to her. "I will give you something." He reached into his small saddle bag. "Bug spray for the mosquitoes. Do you have a flashlight?"

"I have a flashlight, but I could use the bug spray."

"Take this bottle of water too. And may God go before you and His angels surround you."

She smiled back. "Thanks." The sound of a car driving down the road shook her into watchfulness. Hadassah slipped behind the undergrowth for cover just in time.

Chapter 4:

Evidence

It was a black Audi bumping down the dirt road . It stopped at the motorbike and the man at the wheel leaned out the window. "Hey, you! What do you think you're doing down this road?"

"I'm a taxi driver," Joseph Blessing told the him. "I was looking for a house."

"There are no houses out here. And your bike stinks."

"I will move in a minute, sir, as soon as I find my directions to the house."

"No one comes down this road unless they do it on purpose," the man snarled. "Were you traveling alone?"

"Yes, sir," Joseph replied. "As I said, I was looking for a fare. I took a wrong turn."

"Go along, then."

After Joseph Blessing turned his bike and left, the Audi drove back toward the warehouse.

Hadassah chewed the side of her tongue until she saw the dust settle. She stood up, wrapped the scarf about her belly under her shirt to hide its bright color and to mask her girlish figure, then she crept along the undergrowth parallel to the road, careful not to make a sound. Crouching behind bushes and discarded slabs of corrugated metal, it took her almost forty-five minutes to cover the mile toward the warehouse. The sun, oppressive with its heat, arched toward mid-afternoon.

When she reached the edge of the clearing, she crouched behind a sheet of rusted corrugated metal. The holes in the metal provided a direct line of sight. Barbed wire lined the top of the chain-link fence all around the warehouse, but the fence didn't surround the entire building. In the gaps ran two lines of barbed wire. This would deter most people—not many seventeen year olds had the benefit of a mom who had been a spy with the Mossad.

Eva Michelman had been trained by some of the best in the industry, and she passed the training along to her daughter beginning the morning after Hadassah's Bat Mitzvah ceremony. Or at least their version of the Bat Mitzvah ceremony, now that they followed Yeshua Ha'Mashiach. Getting past barbed wire was one of the first lessons.

"Notice the gaps between the barbs," Mom had said when they practiced behind an abandoned industrial park in New Jersey. "There's a lot of space between these barbs if you know what to do with it. That's why I gave you the hair pin for your Bat Mitzvah gift."

Hadassah still remembered Mom's grin that day, less suppressed than usual, and the smile she gave in return before climbing back and forth through barbed wire until sunset.

But crossing barbed wire here would have to wait for cover of darkness.

After observing the fence, Hadassah noticed the trash cans—huge metal barrels overflowing with flies. That was one thing Mom always said: people incriminate themselves by carelessly discarding evidence. Hadassah needed a picture of those barrels and the trash inside.

She counted the four armed guards outside the warehouse covering two entrances: the west-facing front and the side facing north. She assumed there would be four more guards on the south and east. They carried shotguns. Old ones. Must have been from the 1940's by the look of them.

The phone buzzed in her pocket and she nearly jumped out of her skin. At least she had turned the ringer off. The text was from Mom.

TXT ME ICE.

She sent off the text, wondering what Mom would say when she saw the satellite footage.

The next time her phone buzzed, it didn't scare Hadassah quite so much; the incessant buzzing of the flies drowned out a lot of noise.

I SEE WAREHOUSE VIA SAT. WHERE R U?

HIDDEN. EAST NORTH EAST, Hadassah texted.

GLAD. STAY HIDDEN. HERE'S THE SAT VISUAL.

When Hadassah opened the 3D satellite image, it matched her suspicion: eight guards total along the perimeter. She zoomed in on the holographic image and memorized all the details she saw.

TAKE PICS OF TRASH BARRELS, Mom sent.

I know, Mom. But she constrained herself from texting it.

Hadassah took out her hair pin and unscrewed the tiny, pen-shaped camera. The specs she read etched into the side of the camera declared its high resolution. Exactly what she needed for these shots.

The first photos she sent were of the compound with the guards out front. As she uploaded these photos onto her phone, the sound of a baby crying from inside the warehouse cut through the thick afternoon air. Then she heard another. And another. Their sad chorus grew louder and louder until it drowned out the sound of the flies. Hadassah guessed there were well over fifty babies by the sound; their swelling cries tugged at every gram of her heart and made her belly feel like water. Guards milled about restlessly in the noise. Then all eight of them gathered at the north entrance of the building and moved toward the front gate, further and further from the warehouse.

As soon as the photos of the outside of the warehouse were delivered, Hadassah used her phone to record a video of the babies crying. It was so loud. Can u hear? she texted along with the video. Mom answered within a minute.

LOUD & CLEAR.

With the guards congregated at the front gate, Hadassah saw a possible route to the trash barrels. The brush covered her from their view, and one of the bushes beside the fence and next to the barrels protruded through the chain-links enough to conceal her activity. Or at least she hoped. She looked again at the surroundings. All clear.

Jogging along in a crouched position, she was careful not to make noise above the hum of the flies, though the crying from the warehouse still drowned out even that.

As she drew closer to the trash barrels, the smell overpowered her. The Water Side Market also had an intense human smell, but it had been mixed with spices. There was no spice here. Her stomach of steel lurched. Did baby diapers fill these barrels? Holding her sleeve across her face, she peered over the edge. She gagged and blinked; the stench stung her eyes and the back of her throat. Soiled diapers, both cloth and disposable, filled the barrels to the brim, and none of them were folded to conceal the contents. The sight of the flies masked almost everything else, except the maggots. She also saw a few old bottles and some dirty clothes.

Heady from both the heat and the stench, Hadassah crouched low again, praying and holding her nose shut, hoping this would keep the rising bile down. How could she bring herself to stand? She prayed for grace, for strength, for a temporary absence of the sense of smell. *Gotta do this fast.* She took a deep breath through her mouth and held it. Click. Click. Click. In the end she took six pictures, including one with the warehouse in the background.

With a constant eye on the guards, she crept back to the hiding place under the corrugated metal, where she downloaded the pictures to her phone. As she waited for each download, Hadassah realized she'd have to see the inside of the warehouse, even though she didn't want to after the sight of those barrels. And how would she take pictures? All the windows of the place hung fifteen feet or more off the ground. While formulating her plan, she spied several small holes where the wall was rusted away. All of those holes were big enough to fit the camera through—assuming the holes penetrated to the other side. She'd wait until dark to see if any light came through.

The downloads seemed to be taking forever.

Twilight grew and small streams of light filtered through those rusted holes in the warehouse. While waiting for the right moment to come, she sent off more photos.

The cries of the babies increased as if calling to her for help.

I may have enough – Mom texted back – Any more and we'll def have the police & army there tonight.

I'm going to take pics of inside warehouse – she sent to Mom – Tell me current satellite on guards.

Darkness deepened. She filled her mind with various exit strategies to avoid thinking about anything else.

Her phone finally buzzed again.

The guards r all @ the gate. If u go, go now.

Using her hair pin, Hadassah fastened the lower string of barbed wire to the ground while she held up the top wire and slipped through without a snag. As soon as she stood again she looked for the guards—still at the gate, still unaware of her. She crouched low, like a lioness, and ran. When she reached the warehouse she knelt on one knee, ready to sprint away if need be. The clamorous crying still masked any sound she made.

Threading the camera a quarter-inch into the hole, she angled it left and right, snapping picture after picture. She debated downloading the photos while sitting beside the warehouse, but had taken so many risks already. Still, she needed to glance inside the building in case the photos didn't catch the right evidence. Pressing her face against the rusted wall, she peered through the hole.

Her eyes confirmed what her ears and nose observed: babies throughout the warehouse, anywhere from fifty to seventy of them—some with diapers, some without—were all screaming, confined in shabby cribs. Some of the cribs had two or three children apiece. She couldn't tell which one of them was Ariella in all that confusion.

But there was Mr. Lavo, stripped down to a white tank-top, which looked out of place with the silk pants of his suit. He chewed a thick cigar between his big teeth and thick lips as he paced the floor and typed into his phone. Even with the warehouse as big as it was, Hadassah could smell the smoke off his rancid cigar. And he never once looked at a child, but he dropped bottles into a few of the cribs as he walked by. She caught herself scraping the tips of her fingers with her thumbnail. Instead of succumbing to nervousness, Hadassah took two more pictures, this time holding the camera to her line of sight.

Turning toward the night and running back to the barbed wire, she tried to remember how many photos she had taken. How much memory did she have left? And how much battery? The pen camera couldn't have a battery anything like the phone.

She retrieved the hair pin and raced to her refuge under the rusted metal. The rustling sounds in the jungle and screams of monkeys in the distance, some of them louder than the crying babies, began to disturb her. Fear started to pulse within her. Mosquitoes hummed their high pitched song, perhaps even singing about the malaria they carried. She debated using the spray.

It was hard to calm her breathing and heart rate while watching the photos upload. The bottled water Joseph Blessing gave her was warmer than her body temperature and did little more than saturate her parched tongue and make her empty stomach queasy.

The devices were taking longer than ever.

A blinking orange light on the pen-shaped camera told her the battery was running low. The thought *mission failure* crossed her mind, and she tried to shoo it away like the many mosquitoes surrounding her. One text to Mom and she could have a helicopter extraction. Instead, she unwrapped the scarf from around her waist and used it to wipe the sweat streaming down her forehead.

When she saw the uploaded photos, she knew she didn't dare blow her cover. These little ones needed help, and she had that help in the palm of her hand. She needed to send the pictures.

Hadassah hid her phone under her arm to mask its light. Those footfalls, too heavy and clumsy to be an animal, were now accompanied by voices. There were two of them. At least she hadn't used the odoriferous bug spray yet, even though the mosquitoes increased by the minute.

"It was a man, Dez, I swear it," one of the men told the other.

"You sure you saw someone 'ere?" Dez asked.

"I ain't lyin'. I tell you I seen a man," the first guard answered. "He slipped through the barbed wire."

"You've been awful jittery today. Remember what Lavo told us. One of us is gonna take the fall tonight. You better be right, Mr.

Blessing, or you better watch your back."

Mr. Blessing! The taxi driver's cousin.

"I tell you I seen what I seen," Mr. Blessing said.

"Well, 'e's too late. Lavo found the 'ighest bidder. We leave before dawn, and there's no one who can stop us. The delivery truck should be 'ere any minute."

Chapter 5:

Such a Time As This

Hadassah's breath grew even more shallow. She had to send the pictures soon. Wrapping the scarf over her phone to conceal the LED light, she manipulated the applications and prayed she'd tapped the right place on the screen. Sweat seeped out of every pore, and her hands felt slippery.

The men's footsteps fell right beside her hiding spot and they shined the flashlight all over the metal.

"See? What did I tell you?" Dez said. "Nothing 'ere. It must 'ave been an animal."

How long had it been since she breathed normally? Her head spun. *Don't fall asleep here.* The terror alone was exhausting.

The men lingered awhile as if Dez wasn't as skeptical as he let on. "You stay 'ere to watch for 'im, Mr. Blessing. That is if you ain't scared of the black mambas."

Black mambas? What are black mambas? Then she remembered. Only one of the deadliest snakes in the world. *Why did I get myself into this?*

"I ain't scared o' nothin', Dez," Mr. Blessing replied.

"If you shoot 'im when you see 'im, then you might not take the fall tonight."

As soon as she heard Dez walk off, her phone vibrated with a return text. Using her scarf to shield the light from curious eyes, she chanced a glimpse at what it said.

Mom again.

GOOD WRK. I HV ENUF. GET AS FAR AS U CAN. POLICE & ARMY R COMING. ICE TXT 1 MILE OR MORE FROM THERE.

OKAY, Hadassah texted back.

The fact she sat in an African jungle at night, miles from any friend, paralyzed her muscles. While she tried to calm rising anxieties, the headlights of a truck pulling into the driveway shone across the metal where she sat. There was lots of yelling. Then it was dark again, but the yelling grew louder. Was Mr. Blessing still close? There was no sound of footfall, no light.

His voice startled her. "I know you are here," Mr. Blessing said. But he sounded different from when the other man was around. He sounded kind, but such kindness might be a lure. "I hope you are here for good and not for evil. I mean, I hope you are here for God and not the devil. There is too much of the devil here already."

With all the yelling and noise around the truck, no one from inside the fence would have heard his words.

"If you are here for good and not evil, please say something," the man continued.

She glanced through the holes in the metal and saw what she thought was his silhouette.

Hadassah's heart beat in her mouth. Her staccato breathing was so loud she must have given herself away already. But she couldn't bring herself to say a word. The taxi driver had said his cousin cut himself off from the family. Numerous reasons for this flooded her mind.

"My name is Andrew," the man said. "If you know something, please tell me."

She was so afraid she decided to risk it. Maybe he was as kind as he sounded. "The army and police are on their way."

"You are a girl!" Mr. Blessing burst out in whisper. "And American. How can I believe you about the army?"

"I don't know," she replied, unable to keep the fear out of her voice. "There *is* too much of the devil here, but God is here too."

"I can help you. Will you take my help?"

Her phone buzzed once more.

I C U VIA HEAT SATELLITE. ONE OF LAVO'S MEN STANDS NEAR. POLICE & ARMY R ON THE WAY. U MUST LEAVE AS SOON AS U CAN.

Hadassah wasn't sure what terrified her more, the guards or the possibility of black mambas and other wild animals in the jungle.

She began to dig her thumbnail into the tips of her fingers. "I will take your help. I need to leave." She fought back rising tears.

"When I count to three, run for the trees toward the northwest, right behind us. I will shoot toward the trees, but not at you."

"How can I believe you?"

"Because God is here too, little friend. If we meet on the other side, after the police and the army come, my name is Andrew Blessing."

"I spoke with your cousin, Joseph, today. He misses you."

"Little American girl, you bless me with this news. But now is your chance. Now or never."

The route she used to get there seemed the safest and the wisest, and she took it at a run with prayer pulsing inside each heartbeat: *please get me out alive, God, please get me out alive.* Even though she anticipated it, the gunshot made her jump. Her feet landed solidly; she continued to run and counted the 2,000 footsteps to measure off a mile.

Every rustle of an animal, every screech of a monkey, every squawk of a bird caused her to start. Even the leaves on the trees looked menacing. She was so afraid. She was so afraid she began to feel nauseous. Fear tried to convince her she didn't care if she got caught. But when she remembered that predators smell such emotions and follow the smell to their next prey, she thought of Mr. Lavo at the warehouse; he was an animal the way he treated those children. This excusable dread would victimize her if she didn't get rid of it.

How did that verse go? There is no fear in love, but perfect love casts out fear. When she was a child her dad prayed the verse over her when she awoke from nightmares. And his sermon two weeks ago. *Perfect love casts out fear.* But terror crowded all her thoughts.

With those 2,000 steps all counted out, she scanned the trees for a place where she could sit and send off the ICE text. The branches of one tree hung wide, low and sturdy, like a cradle of unbreakable boughs. She swung her tired body up and clung to the surrounding branches to brace herself. How she wanted to sleep! But she didn't want to fall off: the boughs were wide enough for a couch but not a bed. At least she had her phone. She sent out her text right away.

The night passed like a walking-through-gelatin-dream at first, and Hadassah sucked on the tips of her fingers which were sore now from scraping at them all day. Her heart raced and her body shook as much as a mouse in the talons of an eagle.

Mom sent a text saying a friend of a friend in the American Embassy would extract her, but they shouldn't talk until they knew the raid was under way. Hadassah didn't feel up for conversation anyway with as embarrassed as she felt about her fear.

As she waited in the darkness, Hadassah repeated the scripture verse from 1 John over and over, like a prayer, like a reminder, like a shot in the dark to the heart of God. She needed Him as Father so badly. She needed His perfect love to cast out this fear.

Suddenly, the feeling of dread left her and in its place she felt the presence of the Lord. Her heart swelled with gratitude. The more she thanked Him, the more she felt His presence.

"Thank you, thank you, thank you, Abba Father," she whispered. Both Mom and Dad taught her to call the Lord by the same name Yeshua did, by the Hebrew name meaning 'Papa' or 'Daddy'.

Helicopters whirred overhead, and the sound of trucks, perhaps army trucks, bumped and thumped down the road beside where she staked out in the trees. She prayed the police and army arrived in time, before the men left the warehouse with the babies. She prayed Andrew Blessing would be kept safe.

Shouting and gunfire escalated in the distance; the animals grew quiet, as if in response.

In the darkness, in the jungle, as the raid of the warehouse took place a mile away, she perceived the presence of the Lord stronger than she ever had before. Stronger than when she gave her life to Him at the age of ten. Stronger than when her dad preached on the book of 1 John two weeks ago.

And as God spoke to Hadassah's heart in what Dad called the internal audible voice, her heart filled with another kind of fear—an awe invigorating her, challenging her, setting her heart into stillness. Dad had preached on the internal audible voice of God before, and this sense of awe accompanying it. "A beautiful fear," he called it once. She agreed. And it came with a promise. She would never be afraid again, at least not like she had been tonight.

"Hadassah," she heard.

"Speak, Abba," she said in her heart, *"for I am yours."*

"You were born, My daughter, for such a time as this," He said within her. *"Watch for the Cooper and watch for the Hop. When you see them—go there, go there, GO THERE!"*

She passed the next two hours leaning on His everlasting arms, never once wondering why Mom's friend from the embassy took so long.

The night grew cool and damp. She began to doze again when a car drove up the road and stopped beside where she sat in the trees. The car door's slam jarred her to wakefulness.

"Hadassah!" a woman with a thick accent called out from the road. "Hadassah Michelman, are you here?"

"I'm here," Hadassah said. Her mouth felt so dry.

"I am Manuela. I was told to pick you up, but I was afraid you would not be here."

Hungry, parched and stiff, Hadassah edged her way to the ground, happy to see the flashlight Manuela waved about.

"I am glad I finally got to you," Manuela said. "The army had the road blocked off for hours. And this is not a safe place to be trapped for hours." The woman shined the flashlight around the jungle. "See, look!"

There in the tree, ten feet above where Hadassah's head had been, a three foot black mamba encircled a branch. The snake stared at her with its beady eyes, angling its head back and forth as its silvery brown body writhed and coiled about the branch.

"You are like Daniel in the lion's den," Manuela said. "I bet you an angel's up there holding that mamba's mouth closed. But let's go. I'll take you by my place first so you can get cleaned up. I will give you some fresh clothes as well."

"Thank you," Hadassah said. She climbed into the front seat of the Jeep, where a bottle of cool water waited for her. After a slow, deep drink she closed her eyes, and sleep overtook her despite the Jeep bumping over all those holes and ruts.

In the evening, when Manuela took Hadassah back to see the rest of the missionaries at the orphanage, every one of the kids from the youth group had a thousand or more questions for her.

"You would not believe what has been happening," Isabella said when the questions let up. "They've found our daughter. They found Ariella! It's been all over the news stations since late last night, and we received a call this morning. The police have her and will be bringing her here this evening."

Hadassah smiled with her friend's joy. "That's amazing. Praise the Lord!"

"So what did happen to you?"

"I got lost." It was easier than she thought to lie to her friend. To all of her friends. Especially considering how sick she felt.

Though she wished she invented a better excuse.

New York, NY, USA

Three days later

Chapter 6:

Debrief and Dinosaurs

Her flight home, including all the transfers, took almost 30 hours, and Hadassah came in to JFK airport some time after midnight. Dizziness and nausea rocked her the entire trip. After she saw Mom in the terminal and held her for a full minute, Hadassah relaxed.

"Where's Dad?"

"He's at home, waiting for you."

"Is he really mad at me?"

"No, but he didn't want to get emotional in front of the team. Both of us thought it'd be better. And he's getting food ready for us."

"I wish I was hungry. I miss his cooking." She sighed another laborious breath. "But I'm sure he's angry at me."

Mom hugged her again and whispered in her ear. "Look at how many children's lives were saved. He's so proud of you."

Hadassah smiled as she dragged her weary body to the car. New

York City, once her comfort zone, seemed so foreign after Africa. The glare of street lights off the sea of cars looked extraordinarily artificial, and she wanted to be overseas again. She had no memory of her fear in the jungle, but thought about the prospect of joining Revelation Special Ops. *Will Dad say yes? Have I proven myself?*

When she walked through the door and glanced at Dad, she rested into one of his bear hugs and listened instead of trying to say anything.

"Oh, my Haddy. My wonderful, brave, foolish Hadassah." His tears stopped him from saying anything more. He held her face in his hands and kissed the top of her head.

For the first time in who knew how long, she allowed the tears to escape her eyes as she held onto Dad, enough tears to soak the front of his shirt.

She didn't remember eating more than a bite of Dad's delicious roast chicken. After crawling into her pajamas, she climbed into bed. One aspect of her comfort zone was welcoming—the memory foam still remembered her and enveloped her aching body. As soon as she had tucked herself in, Dad knocked on the door.

She propped her tired body up on an elbow. "Come in."

"I know it's been years since I've done it, but I'd like to pray with you tonight. I hope you are not too old for this." His eyes still glistened with tears.

"Not at all, Dad. I'm just so tired."

"Well, you rest and I'll pray." He sat on the edge of her mattress and held her hand.

As tired as she was, she couldn't concentrate on the words of the prayer, but rested her soul in the presence of the Spirit. No sooner did he say "Amen" than she fell asleep and didn't wake until midday the next day, feeling physically weak but refreshed.

There was a text notification on her phone. Mom. How long had it been there?

MEET ME @ OFFICE B4 3PM 2DAY. COINS IN JAR.

The clock read 1:12pm. She wouldn't have enough time to wash the airplane smell off if she lingered even a moment.

She didn't mean to take an eight minute shower, but she felt so drained, and water pressure was a precious gift she had forgotten to be thankful for. Hadassah grabbed enough money from the jar for an OJ from the corner store as well as subway fare, and she raced to catch the M train to Mom's office.

When she stepped through the door at 2:53pm, still sipping her OJ and regaining her composure after battling crowds, she allowed nostalgia to wash over her as she soaked in the familiarity of the place. Photos of missing and found children and teens lined the walls of the foyer and covered the four cubicles beyond the secretary's desk.

Eva Michelman worked as a private investigator in tandem with police to find any child or teen who had been missing. She would even take cases 23 hours before the police would, often within the hour of a child's disappearance. Both her fee and her success rate were better than almost any other in the city.

Instead of greeting Hadassah, the secretary paged Eva over the intercom. "Your daughter is here."

Mom would usually page back, 'Send her in.' This time, she came out herself, and every employee in the front office rose to give Hadassah a standing ovation.

Mom raised her hand until everyone in the office grew quiet again. "I've never seen someone do a solo operation like that before. And you did it in Africa. Nice work."

"Thanks, Mom." Hadassah felt warm inside, and hid her blushing cheeks between her shoulder and her hand.

"Oh, and happy birthday, four days late." Mom brought out a chocolate cheesecake. "Mazel Tov."

Hadassah shared it with the office staff until there were only crumbs. She knew Mom was making a big deal out of what happened in Africa; Eva Michelman never splurged on an office party so much as to buy a cake this good. There were too many other expenses. Such as the back office, which cost Mom nine years of investment capital.

Following Mom, Hadassah passed through the bank-safe-thick door and fireproof walls of the back office. The five small air ducts on the walls and ceiling, too small for any adult to fit through, always spurred a chuckle in her whenever Hadassah saw them. But what Mom spared no expense on was the equipment. She had three computers, two of which could access satellite footage from American and Israeli spy satellites. And then there was Yitzak's station.

Yitzak, her cousin and eight years her senior, worked in the corner of Mom's back office, and Hadassah wondered if he still kept fourteen- to nineteen-hour days here like he used to. His thin frame, hunching over his desk, seemed as permanent a fixture as the hanging lamp; before him the desk was littered with jewelry, watches, computer chips, soldering irons and various gadgets in process, almost finished, or lying open for further inspection. He looked melded to the soldering iron in his hand as if he hadn't left his seat for coffee since that morning.

Yitzak carefully set his latest project onto his desk and looked up at her. "Nice of you to come back alive." He grinned. "How'd you like the iPod?"

She nodded. "And the transmitter. Thanks. Couldn't have done it without you, Yitz."

"That's all the gratitude I need. You wanna see my latest project?"

Mom sat in her office chair, straightened a few of her papers and cleared her throat. "Maybe later, Yitzak. How was your birthday cake, Haddy?"

Hadassah smiled. "It was delicious. I felt woozy and disoriented when I woke up today, but I'm feeling better already."

"I felt woozy and disoriented after my first trip to India. You better get used to it if you still want to join Revelation Special Ops."

Hadassah allowed another wave of warmth to fill her.

"Dad wants to take you out tomorrow to celebrate your birthday. If you're not too tired."

"I hope I'm not too tired."

"Yitzak, work on the new surveillance camera later. You need a coffee break and some sunlight while I meet with Haddy for debriefing."

The debrief was tough for Hadassah, but she kept her face and voice as placid as she could while relating the details and reliving the whole episode. She almost cried when she recalled the sight of the warehouse. When she recounted meeting Andrew Blessing she fidgeted, remembering her fear. Yet all the while, Hadassah looked forward to telling Mom what God had said to her.

"While I huddled in the trees and waited for Manuela, I prayed earnestly because I had never been so terrified in my life—of wild beasts, of those men, for all those babies. And I heard God say the strangest thing in the midst of my heart. But He spoke so loudly I almost thought He was right beside me. As soon as He spoke I wasn't afraid anymore—of anything." She grew quiet and returned in her mind to the moment in the trees.

"What did He say?"

Hadassah smiled wide, the first burst of emotion she had allowed to slip. "He said I was born for such a time as this."

"Like Esther. The other Hadassah."

"Right. He also said to watch for the 'Cooper' and to watch for the 'Hop.' And you know how you hear people say, 'Don't go there!'? Well, I heard God say in my heart just as emphatically, "Go there, go there, go there!" And I felt such peace. Two more hours passed before Manuela called my name and shined her flashlight toward me. During those two hours my heart sang songs of praise to the Lord. And I'm here now—He preserved my life."

"Manuela told me to tell you a proverb of her people, 'The daughter of a lion is also a lion.'"

"Tell her thank you for me."

"I'll forward the e-mail so you can tell her yourself."

"What do you think about the Lord's word to me, about the Cooper and the Hop?"

"Don't go looking for this Cooper or the Hop. Wait for the Lord to reveal them to you."

"I can't stop thinking about it."

"Pray about it, Haddy, but don't try to make it be one thing or another. Remember, understanding grows at a snail's pace."

Hadassah sighed in sudden melancholy. "Bobeshi used to say that all the time. I miss her."

Mom scraped one of her thumbnails across the tip of her index finger, then folded her hands together quickly and set them on her lap. "I didn't tell you. Mr. Lavo was killed during the raid."

"Any word about Mr. Blessing?"

"None."

Hadassah pressed her lips together and sighed again. "So, what do you think about my joining Revelation Special Ops?"

Mom nodded, but if Hadassah hadn't been looking at her she would have missed it. "I think you'll do better in a team than on your own. You might not lose half your money."

Heat rushed to her ears and cheeks as she cast her gaze to the ground fixing her stare on the wire covered floor. How did Mom manage to keep so many wires looking so neat?

Mom interrupted her listless thoughts. "That is if you still want to join this Revelation Special Ops."

"So are you saying yes?"

"Perhaps you should do an assignment or two with me first."

She gave Mom a wide smile. "When can I start?"

"I'm going to let you get some rest and settle into your senior year before I send you on any assignments."

"I forgot, only six more days until I start. I hope they don't have another 'What did you do with your summer?' essay question on the first day."

Mom chuckled. "What would you write?"

She shrugged. "Oh, a short anecdote about how I dispersed a human trafficking ring in Africa and slept alone in a jungle ten feet below the most poisonous snake in the world. All sorts of believable stuff."

Mom shot her the get-serious face, then chuckled again. "I'm glad you can joke about it after the fact. Have you been struggling with nightmares at all?"

She shook her head. "I've been too tired to dream. Were there any more earthquakes while I was gone?"

Mom shook her head. "Nothing serious. Don't forget to wake early tomorrow so Dad can take you out for your birthday."

***

The next morning, it took a fourth knock at her door for Hadassah to wake. She looked at the clock; it was already 10:30am. This was the second morning in a row she had slept in. The jet lag woke her at 1:28am, and she tossed and turned until almost 6:30.

"Are you okay?" Dad asked.

"Oy vey!" She jumped out of bed and scrambled about her room. "I forgot to set my alarm."

"I thought we'd go out for breakfast. Then I could take you to the aviary at the Bronx Zoo."

"Really?" She stuffed her tired body into the closest clean clothes. "I'd love that. Sorry I slept in. Give me three minutes."

"This isn't the army, Haddy, you can take your time."

"Trust me, Dad, three minutes and I'll be at the front door."

***

During breakfast at her favorite diner, where the eggs and bagel tasted different after a few weeks out of the country, she and Dad both noticed the cover of the same newspaper.

"Did you see what it said in the headline of the *Post*?" Hadassah asked.

"I did. Scientists in Babylon have cloned their first dinosaur." Dad winced as if the words assaulted him even as he spoke them.

Not knowing what to make of his reaction she stored it away to think about later. "I wonder what kind of dinosaur it was."

Dad ambled ponderously to the stand and purchased a copy of the paper.

After reading the first two paragraphs Hadassah looked up at him again. "Was there anything about this in the *Times*?"

"Not even a blip, but I'm sure if this is real there will be an article soon. And I hope the *Times* won't be as sensational."

Hadassah lowered her voice. "I heard the strangest thing while in Africa. The kidnapper was talking to the Minister of Justice about receiving payment in Babylonian silver. I thought the Kingdom of Jordan was overseeing the rebuilding of Babylon, so wouldn't they have the dinar just like Jordan does?"

Dad glanced up at her. "Both Iraq and Jordan are involved in the construction of Babylon. Jordan's Prime Minister, Fahd Afsal, is overseeing most of the work, as well as some elusive, Scandinavian businessman named Vladimir Therion."

Hadassah gasped when she heard the name. "How do you know all this?"

Dad gave a shrug. "Your mom has friends who've been there for years. They even brought back evidence of the new Hanging Gardens. The place is supposed to be impressive, so I wouldn't be surprised to hear they have stores of silver and even treasure troves of gold."

"Mom didn't say anything to me when I mentioned Vladimir Therion's name to her."

"You know your mother and the secrets she keeps."

Hadassah rolled her eyes. "Always. I don't know how you can stand it."

Dad gave a rare, knowing smile to her. "See?" He pointed at the newspaper. "The first dinosaur is a brachiosaurus."

She scanned through the whole article. "This is disturbing, because who knows when they'll start cloning the T. Rex or velociraptor?"

Dad sighed and closed his eyes in response.

A tingle ran through every one of her limbs. "If they're doing all this in Babylon, do you think the End Times have begun?"

"I don't know. But it looks like it might be very soon."

"But do you think Yeshua has started to open the seals yet?"

"I think if He hasn't opened the first seal already, it'll be in a few years from now instead of decades away."

This time, when the tingling ran through her limbs, she shivered. "Do we start asking Him to open the seals yet?

Dad reached his strong hands across the table to hold onto hers then nodded. "Also, given this news about Babylon, we need to stand even more with our brothers and sisters in Israel."

"Do you think the nations will surround her again and try to destroy her?"

"They have since she formed 3,500 years ago. But hopefully they won't for a few more years."

"Then can I go to Israel yet?"

"Soon, Haddy... I'm still preparing my heart for that day."

"Why are you always so uptight about me going to Eretz Israel?"

He glanced at his plate, then at the wall. "Because."

She stared hard at him.

"It won't work. I learned how to ignore that stare nineteen years ago, after my honeymoon with your mother."

She continued to stare at him.

"Your mother will kill me if I tell you. You know this, right?"

"C'mon, Dad. I'll take the blame. What is it?"

"You have an Israeli passport. You have citizenship. You'll have to serve in the military if you go there."

"Not till I'm eighteen, though, right?"

"And I know you. You'll fall in love with Eretz Israel, just like I did, and you won't want to leave."

"Then why did *you* leave?"

He pushed his plate forward and looked at her. "It just got too violent. I moved us over here after Hamas began murdering children in their beds."

She furrowed her brow at him. "So I lived there too?"

"For about a year and a half. We moved back to Brooklyn before you turned four."

"Wow. I wonder if some of my memories aren't from movies or pictures, but from my time in Israel."

"Probably."

What other secrets would he tell if she asked the right questions?

***

The World of Birds at the Bronx Zoo was one of Hadassah's favorite places on earth. With elbows leaned against the rail, she stood beside Dad and drank in the sounds while her heart grew quiet. In the presence of those birds she felt she could approach one thought at a time, or nothing at all. Sometimes she stared at each beautiful creature in turn and tried to figure what sound it made. Sometimes she let the symphony meld. The older she was, the more those less exotic birds enraptured her, the ones with brown or gray plumage and sweet songs: the wood thrush, the wren, the song sparrow, the mourning dove, the nightingale.

There was so much to sort through about Africa, her Israeli citizenship and her application to Revelation Special Ops. Today she wanted contentment. She yearned for it. Closing her eyes she distinguished one birdsong from another. There was the wood thrush, there the nightingale, there the song sparrow.

"It's 4:30," Dad said. "We've been here five hours."

"I've taken your whole day."

"I gave it to you. I hope you feel rested."

"I do. How about you?"

"I've been praying. Do you still want to join this Revelation Special Ops?"

"Your teachings as much as Mom's make me certain about Revelation Special Ops. You always talk about how we need to lay our lives down for Yeshua, for His gospel and for others. You've sown this in my heart for years. I need to live it."

He nodded. "I agree with you, and so I'll give my blessing to your application. You were made for this sort of work."

The birds suddenly grew quiet. The bench beneath them trembled, and they looked at one another until the quake stopped.

"My daughter, this is not the hour for me to hold you back. But don't forget what I have taught you about Yeshua. Don't forget what He teaches us about our Abba Father."

She reached over and took hold of his hand. "I won't, Dad."

As soon as she got home, she completed her application. Despite her exhaustion she stayed up until 11:00pm to finish it. Each answer she filled out revitalized her further. She woke at 6am the next morning and skipped all the way to the mailbox.

Chapter 7:

Assignment and Departure

The first month of school passed quickly. Some of her classmates, the ones who had seen the news coverage of the incident in Africa and knew she had gone, asked if she had run into trouble while there. She told them about the miraculous return of Isabella and Danny's baby, without the details of her involvement, and some other benign stories from the orphanage. She grew a little nervous in early October after Isabella posted the story on her blog and on Facebook. Isabella mentioned Hadassah in the story, how she went missing and came back the same day as their baby. Both Mom and Dad assured Hadassah there wasn't enough information for anyone to make the connection.

As the semester drew on, Hadassah wondered if she'd ever hear back about her application or go on another assignment. She pined for more reconnaissance work.

On a Friday morning that she had off from school, four days before Dad was scheduled to leave for Pakistan, Mom called her into the office.

"You ready to help me on a job?"

"Always." She was about to flash Mom a smile but caught a stressed look in her eyes.

"It's bad this year." Mom shook her head. "Bad."

Concern crossed Hadassah's face. "What's bad?"

"The number of children who have gone missing in the City since the beginning of the school year. I had three new clients this morning. Someone has organized a seedy operation, and I'd like your help to figure out who."

"Do you have any leads?"

Hadassah took an envelope from Mom which had pictures of eight men and two women.

"Each of these people is innocent until we prove them guilty. So please, help me prove someone guilty. Maybe even two or three, if we find enough evidence. There's a smaller envelope which has a picture of each of the teens. If we can get a photograph of any or all of these children with any of the men or women I gave you photos of, then we'll have enough to feed to the boys in blue for warrants."

"Are there any other investigators on this case?" Hadassah asked as she committed the faces in the pictures to memory.

"Three detectives from NYPD, but we'll be going to a location no one else has looked into." Mom handed Hadassah a sheet of paper with an address.

"When do we start?"

"Tonight. I'll be going right inside the club; you'll need to take photos from outside in the back of the place, since this club checks ID some nights. But I've observed the back door, and there's not much by way of security."

"What do you mean by 'not much,' Mom?"

"Two men, but you should be able to escape their notice if you keep a low profile. Here's satellite footage of some of the girls going out back for cigarettes and fresh air. I haven't been able to get a close-up on any faces. While you're out back I'll go inside the club as an evangelist. Maybe one or two will repent of their wicked ways."

"We can always hope." Hadassah looked over the satellite footage of the night club. She noticed an air duct running between the club and the building next to it. "What's in this building next door?"

"You know, I'm not sure." Mom lifted her eyes and called toward the other corner of the office. "Yitzak."

"Yeah?" He set down the bracelets and ear pieces he was placing the final touches on.

"Find out what's in the building east of the club."

After a minute of browsing the web, he answered, "It appears to be vacant at the moment. But it looks like Giuseppe DiNapoli owns it."

Mom cringed. "Oh. This is not good."

Hadassah stared at the photo, hoping it would yield a different option. "You can't get me in?"

"I didn't say that. But *he* won't open the door for you."

"Oh, wait, look at this," Yitzak called over his shoulder. "The building's up for sale."

"Who's the agent?"

"God is good, Aunty Eva. Jacob DeSalvoso, from Warehouse Realty."

Mom closed her file and dropped it on the desk. "God is good. Jacob's the one whose son we found in a drug house in Connecticut two years ago. I've had to boost our security since then, but it was so worth it." She paged her secretary. "Lena, get Jacob DeSalvoso on the phone for me."

"So can you get me in?"

Eva winked at her daughter. "He'll turn the key if I ask him to."

***

A cold front moved in over the Northeast that November evening, promising an early snow in the city. This weather felt colder to Hadassah after the heat of an African summer. Stomping her feet and shivering, she tried to look as inconspicuous as possible while she waited for the realtor to show up. But he was late. Along this street, in the section of Queens Hadassah never traveled alone, the night clubs bloomed with patrons, the drug houses loomed with despair, and the warehouses owned by the mafia clenched secrets even the police wouldn't want to know. The African jungle at night was probably safer than this neighborhood. At least Mom was with her. Eva knew how to blend in better than most, and even wore a green wig for the occasion. She dressed Hadassah for the assignment: spikes on her leather clothing, blue streaks in her hair, heeled boots elevating her to six feet.

"Ms. Michelman," Hadassah heard behind her.

She turned about to face this man, maintaining her professional facade. "Yes."

"I'm Jacob DeSalvoso. Nice to meet you." His covert skills were terrible. "I want to show you around this side of the building."

As she followed him she kept in full character in case anyone from the street took notice of them.

Before rounding the corner, she caught Mom's glance. Eva Michelman waited in line to gain entrance into the club, looking for all the world like a punk rocker instead of the evangelist, private detective, or abolitionist she was. She tapped her wrist to remind her daughter she planned to keep in contact through the bracelets and ear pieces Yitzak had made. Hadassah turned the ear piece on as soon as she was off the street.

"This is the entrance you'll use." Mr. DeSalvoso unlocked the door and held it open for Hadassah. "The building's still in DiNapoli's name, so his people have access here too, but I told him I was showing it this evening. I doubt anyone will show up. Still, we'll need to keep the light use minimal. I'll come in with you at first, so we can keep up the pretense. Oh, and I need to show you to the air duct, which is on the second floor. I hope there are no earthquakes while you're inside."

"Yeah, me too. After you show me you can turn the lights out again—I brought a flashlight with me."

Once DeSalvoso had left, Hadassah set her boots on the floor beside the entrance of the duct so her movements would be muffled. She began to make her way through the long, narrow and very cold shaft. The thump-thump-thump of the bass from the club masked every sound she made and rattled the duct in a way that made her a little nervous.

She could tell when she reached the other side because the draft wasn't so brutal and the metal wasn't so painfully cold on her hands. Up ahead some light streamed through a vent; she inched her way along.

From the vent, she looked down on a small, dirty and dimly lit room where she saw two girls. The closest girl sat at a dressing table staring into a mirror and smudging make-up on her left cheek as if covering a bruise. The other girl lay disconsolately on the couch, staring at candle wax melting onto a coffee table. She poked at the hot wax every once in a while as if this was the most excitement she had had in a week, then passed her finger back and forth through the candle's flame and gave a delayed wince.

A tremor of a quake rattled the make-up at the dressing table and shook the candle until it tipped out of the candlestick and fell onto the shag carpet. The girl on the couch chuckled and stared at the flame for a moment before sitting up and slowly stamping it out with her stiletto heels. All the while, the girl at the dressing table ignored her. It had been a year since people reacted to an earthquake of this size.

Hadassah angled her thin camera through the vent and took a picture of each of the girls.

When the door to the small room burst open, both of the girls stiffened, sat upright and hardened their expressions.

The man's frame filled the doorway. He was well dressed in a dark blue silk suit and neatly shaven, save for his thin mustache. But he must have overindulged at every meal, because his stomach entered the room before he did. Since she remembered his face from the envelope of photos, Hadassah took out her phone to record a video of whatever was about to take place.

"You." The man pointed to the girl on the couch before shutting the door behind him. "Get up, you lazy girl. I've had another complaint. Your Uncle Tony is never supposed to have complaints."

"So." The young girl sneered as she slowly pushed herself from the couch. "I'm sorry," she said languidly.

"You're here to please my customers." Uncle Tony stood close enough to her that his spit sprayed her face when he said 'please.'

The girl's stare of contempt filled the room with an electric hatred. "I thought I's here to line yer pockets."

He glared at her then appeared to calm himself. "In exchange for pleasing my customers I give you room and board, and occasionally some of the good stuff." As he said this, he held up a small bag filled with chalky powder. "I thought your little friend here would serve as an example for you girls. This is what happens when we hear about dissatisfied customers."

The girl in front of him suddenly softened her seething glower. "How 'bout givin' me a li'l bit o' that, Uncle Tony," she whined. "Then I can do some work."

"Do you take me for a fool? Get back to work first, then you can have some." He turned and scoffed at the other girl. "What are you looking at?"

The girl at the mirror cringed. "Nothing." Hadassah barely heard her over the music, but she saw her stifle a tear.

As soon as Uncle Tony left, the girl who had been standing in front of him defamed his character thoroughly before crashing to the couch again.

"Why do you let him sell you off like that?" the girl at the mirror asked. "That dope's ruining you."

"Shut up. I know what I'm doing, okay? Letting yourself get beat up by Uncle Tony might be your way of finding an escape, but it's not mine. Besides, this stuff helps me deal with how awful his customers are."

The other girl turned her head and cried softly. "You used to be so beautiful before all this, Brianna."

"Keep on cryin' to your Jesus, Shaniqua, I'm sure He'll be eager to help girls like us." Brianna slammed the door as she left the room.

Hadassah stopped the video recording and fished in her pocket for pen and paper. She scrawled: *Those who sow in tears will reap in joy.* Did she dare to give away her position? But another glance at Shaniqua convinced her to send it down. She gently fed the paper through the vent and let it drop. The girl saw it as it drifted down, but waited for it to land before she picked it up off the floor.

"I can't read," the girl said aloud after glancing at the paper, as if speaking to the angels or to God Himself. She stared at it again for a while, then tried to sound out each syllable. Suddenly her eyes welled with tears. "Thank you, Jesus, thank you for this sign. I know you'll be coming for me!"

Hadassah waited until the girl left the room before she dared to crawl back through the cold and out of the vent. It cost her about half an hour, during which she sent the video off to Yitzak at Mom's office.

She heard Mom's voice in her ear piece.

"Are you okay, Haddy?"

"Fine," Hadassah whispered back. "Edging my way out now."

"Someone's gone into the warehouse, and it's not DeSalvoso. Lights are now on. A truck's just pulled up out front and it looks like they're moving something in or out."

"I need to get out of here. The socks aren't keeping out the cold and my feet are freezing."

"What about the boots?"

"I left them at the entrance of the air duct so I wouldn't make too much noise."

In the next few minutes, her feet ached with such cold it could have been the precursor to frostbite.

"The lights are out now," Mom told her.

When Hadassah edged out of the air duct her toes and feet felt like lead as she stood again. She shined her flashlight on the ground. The boots were gone. They were given as a loan from Lena, Mom's secretary, for the assignment. Whoever took the boots would know she was in the ventilation system. And might be waiting for her.

"Can you call our driver and ask for a closer extraction? Maybe a block from here," Hadassah whispered into her com-link as she picked her way through the dark warehouse to the side door.

"Why?" Mom barked.

"The boots are gone."

"What? You can't be serious."

"I'm sorry. My feet are so cold."

"Done. She'll be there before we are."

Hadassah searched about for the door. "Please wait for me."

"I'm almost to the alley now."

Hadassah halted when something clanked in the offices below her and a light turned on. A door closed, blocking most of the light and sound. With the outside door she needed only ten feet away she bolted. Once she was under the street lights' orange glow again, she saw DeSalvoso and Mom converging in the alley, giving glaring at one another as if each was more protective of her than the other.

"Mr. DeSalvoso," Hadassah said. "I don't know if you've met my mom, but she needs to be your potential buyer." She smiled at both of them, then ducked behind one of the dumpsters before the warehouse door opened again.

"Hey, DeSalvoso," the man at the door of the warehouse shouted. "Is she the one who you were showing the warehouse to?" He glared at Mom.

"Yes."

"You know the boss doesn't want to sell to no punk rocker types, right?"

"Yes, he made that quite clear."

"I hope I don't have to tell the boss you've been wasting his time."

"No, sir, not wasting his time at all. In fact, she's just getting ready to go."

"Tell her to take her boots with her." The man hurled the boots down the alley.

Mom caught one of them in mid-air. "Thank you." But he didn't wait around to hear her say it.

"Well, fancy that." Hadassah laughed. She slipped the boots on before stepping out from behind the dumpster. "I think it'll take till morning to feel my feet again."

Mom scanned the alley. "Let's get out of here."

The next afternoon, when she met for the official debrief, Mom wore the smile Hadassah always looked forward to.

"We collected plenty of evidence, Haddy. The police have a warrant and will be going in tonight. Well done."

"Will you do me a favor, Mom?"

"Sure."

"Will you let me know if Shaniqua and Brianna make it out?"

On Tuesday morning, when Hadassah was in between classes, she received the text. The raid was successful and all the girls were either in rehab, a safe house or back home. Then came a second text.

SHANIQUA IS HOME W/ HER FAM, BRIANNA IN REHAB.

Hadassah sang a private Hallelujah in her heart all the rest of the day.

***

When evening came she tagged along with Mom to drive Dad to the airport for his trip to the Middle East.

Dad lingered in the hug. "I'll be back after New Year's, Haddy."

"I know. I just wish you weren't gone for Hanukkah." She forced any show of emotion out of her voice. "You make the best latkes in Brooklyn." She grinned, but then revealed her apprehension. "I'll miss you so much."

"I know, I'll miss you too. Both of you." He had an unusual excitement as he gave them a last hug and she couldn't help her smile.

But as soon as he walked down the departure terminal, she began to cry. She couldn't explain her emotions and swallowed them hard until her throat ached and the well of tears dried.

"I understand." Mom's tone wasn't as flat or professional as usual. "Sometimes I have a hard time, too, when he leaves."

Chapter 8:

Early Graduation

School lunchtimes always bothered her. Hadassah would have been glad for any excuse to pass the time and not think about Dad, but instead her skin crawled. New Year's had already come and gone, and thirty-six hours had passed since Dad last called or e-mailed. She had stopped drinking coffee the day he left.

Half the students in the small cafeteria clamored for the spotlight, the other half yearned to be anywhere besides here. She belonged to the second group for many more reasons than her inability to mingle with this crowd.

The crackle of the intercom speakers and the voice of the principal calling a student to see him pricked her ears to attention. There were always trouble-makers called to the office, even at this private Christian school, but she kept a low profile. Maybe if it was her name they called, she could avoid reading her award-winning essay in next period's Religious Education class. Mrs. London's request was like lemon juice in the wound of her anxious heart.

Josh, who was either the meanest boy on the planet or the worst flirt in existence, knocked her on the shoulder, making her spew that last bite of felafel sandwich. "What'd you do this time, eh?"

Jake the pothead chimed in. "Nothing, of course. They're probably calling her in 'cause she won the Nobel Prize for Kiss-ups or a full scholarship to Freak University."

"Or maybe she's graduating early and leaving all you lame-o's in the dust." Farrah could always be counted on to stick up for those on the bottom of any pecking order.

Hadassah wiped the food from around her mouth and stared absently at her fellow students. "What?"

Jake nudged her this time. "They called your name, Tsigele."

Why was the word for 'little goat' the only Yiddish term of endearment Jake knew? Every time he called her this, it made her more determined to tell the principal about the stash of weed in his locker. But then she'd have to explain how she broke into Jake's locker to get her science book back. So she decided against vengeance and slipped further into her favorite facade of clueless-brainy-girl. "Thanks. I think I have a doctor's appointment."

"You're such a liar." Jake sneered. "And a bad liar at that."

She hated how he pointed out this fact. It made it more difficult for her to be a wallflower. Instead of arguing and proving his point even more, she waved at them in mock shyness and sauntered toward the teachers' table for a hall pass.

The empty hallways gave her mind plenty of thought space, and the dialogue in her head was loud. *Why would anyone want to see me?*

She tried so hard to stay under the radar, to remain unnoticed, to keep all the secrets. Isabella did blog about the incident in Africa, but her friend still didn't know what role Hadassah played. And the operation in Queens—well, Mom was the only one who knew, aside from the realtor, but he didn't know her real name, or hair color, or what her face looked like without make-up. *No one knows me.* She was so good at concealing the truth, keeping the secret, telling a good story. Then why would anyone call for her? *Maybe it's about Dad!* Her heart skipped a beat, and she hushed those thoughts before hope and despair waged war.

As soon as she walked into the principal's office, her mouth dropped open. Mom stood beside the principal's desk wearing her black and silver suit, black and silver like her hair, black and silver like her eyes. *Mom never leaves work early for anything except...* She hushed this thought just before choking up.

Mom gave a deeply maternal smile. "Everything's in place now for your early graduation."

The principal extended his hand. "Congratulations, Ms. Michelman. We'll be mailing your diploma to you, as your mother requested."

Hadassah couldn't help bouncing for joy on the balls of her feet, or grinning ear to ear. "So you heard back about my application?"

"We'll talk in the car." Mom's flash of a smile kept Hadassah's countenance from falling. "But yes, you've been accepted. Do you need help clearing out your locker?"

Hadassah shook her head. "I emptied it before Christmas break, so I just need to hand in the key." She looked over at the principal and dropped the key on his desk. "By the way, you might want to think about a new system for next year. Those locks are way too easy to pick."

Mom suppressed a chuckle behind her hand.

The principal stared wide-eyed at the key and then at this honor student.

"Don't worry, I didn't pick anyone else's locker, just my own." If only that had been true, but she never found any evidence in Jake's locker to turn him in to the police. "God bless you, Mr. Leary."

***

As soon as they stepped into the car, Mom gestured toward the Old Navy bags in the back seat. "New clothes. Some of your old clothes as well as your Bible and most of your books are in suitcases in the trunk."

"Wow. You've been busy. Are we going somewhere?"

Mom nodded while she turned the key. "North Carolina. Buckle up." She threw the car into drive, slammed her foot on the gas and zoomed out of the parking lot.

Hadassah pulled her seatbelt across her lap and clipped it on. "Are you going to tell me what's going on, Mrs. NASCAR? Or are you just going to juggle me around the car and leave me hanging?"

"I got a phone call early this morning from a man named Aaron Cooper, from the North Carolina House of Prayer, or NoCaHoP."

Hadassah jumped in her seat and smiled wide. "No way! The Cooper and the HoP. Do you know how super crazy cool that is?"

"Just wait. He said you've been accepted to Revelation Special Ops."

Another smile bloomed across her wide-eyed expression. "Crazy. Wow. What else did he say?"

"I'll tell you soon, Haddy. It'll be a long drive tonight."

"Why aren't we waiting for Dad to get back?"

Mom's silence disquieted her.

"What is it you're not telling me?"

Chapter 9:

The Phone Call

Eva Michelman sat in the back office sipping her caramel cappuccino while the phone rang. *This is a strange hour for a phone call.* But Lena in the main office would get it. Her mind still hummed with the City's constant traffic, and she longed to pray as she always did at the start of the day. Then her secretary's voice came over the intercom.

"There's a call from a North Carolina area code. He says his name is Aaron Cooper and he wants to talk about your husband, your daughter and something called R.S.O."

She nearly dropped her cappuccino. "*What's* his name?"

"It's Aaron Cooper, Mrs. Michelman."

She set her drink on her desk and pulled the phone closer. "Put the call through."

"Hello, Mrs. Michelman, I'm from Revelation Special Ops, and I have your daughter's application in front of me. But there are two reasons I called you, ma'am, and I wanted to speak with you about your husband first. You are the wife of Pastor Asher Michelman, right?"

Her mouth tightened. She picked up the receiver. "I am."

"Was he on a team with Pastor Cho and Pastor Gallagher in the Middle East?"

Eva waited a full ten seconds before responding. Her heart would burst if it beat any faster. "Among others, yes. Have you heard from any of them?"

"I did. Do you have a secure line?"

Her chest tightened and she swallowed hard. "It's secure."

"The whole convoy was ambushed yesterday in Baghdad after they got off the plane from Karachi, Pakistan."

"Can you confirm this report?"

"Pastor Cho was on the phone with his son, Matthew, when their vehicle was surrounded. Also, I don't know if you're familiar with Sun Xi."

"I knew she was on the team."

"Her daughter, Hyun, is a member of R.S.O. as well, and Hyun was on the phone with her mother when their vehicle was attacked."

Eva focused all of her resolve to keep her voice from cracking. "I'll call you in a few minutes, Mr. Cooper." Then she turned to Yitzak who worked steadily at the corner desk. "I need a few minutes alone, Yitz."

She closed the door behind him, locked it, collapsed on the floor and sobbed until she stopped hyperventilating.

Within a minute of composing herself, Eva had the phone to her ear again. "Mr. Cooper? You said you were from Revelation Special Ops. Have you accepted my daughter into your program?"

"She's an impressive young lady."

"You don't have to tell me."

"Did you train her in any of her skills?"

"Many of them. You'll be surprised how driven she is." She liked this man already, but she wasn't about to let him know. "Is she accepted into the program, Mr. Cooper?"

"Maybe you can clear something up for me. I caught a blog post a few nights ago about the Kaufmans' adoption in Africa. Wild story, eh?"

Eva sipped her coffee. "Yes, Mr. Cooper, it was a wild story."

"Well, ma'am, I've been praying about this incredible miracle in Africa—all those children who were rescued from trafficking. Sixty in total, right?"

"Yes, Mr. Cooper."

"I read that your daughter went missing for the better part of two days. I'm glad to hear she was okay."

"Me too."

"I wasn't going to accept your daughter because she is under eighteen. But after I read Mrs. Kaufman's blog, I knew she'd be a good fit with us. I have reason to believe your daughter helped rescue those babies."

Eva began to pray.

"Mrs. Michelman? Are you still there?"

She opened her eyes again and typed 'Greensboro' into Google Maps. "I'm here."

After another long silence, Mr. Cooper spoke again. "I also had intel from a friend named Andrew Blessing pointing to your daughter's involvement in their rescue."

"How do you know Mr. Blessing?"

"I spoke with him in Monrovia before the raid. He was working undercover and was about to blow Mr. Lavo's operation wide open."

"Please tell me about your background, Mr. Cooper."

"I worked for the FBI and CIA in my twenties and thirties and I was full time staff with NoCaHoP for a few years. Last year, Pastor Gibbons released me to start R.S.O."

I didn't want to make this decision about Haddy without Asher. She sighed.

"We've accepted your daughter, Mrs. Michelman, but I understand if, given the circumstances, you want to keep her with you."

"I'll be driving her down tonight. I need to know she's going to be taken care of while I look for her father."

Mr. Cooper cleared his throat. "I understand. I like to interview potential recruits first."

Eva viewed driving directions on her computer screen. "Then meet us for an early breakfast in Richmond."

"How about Kelley's Street Diner?"

"Sure. I've been there once or twice before."

"I'll be there at 5:00am."

"It's in my GPS. That's a twenty-four hour joint, right?"

"Sure is."

"Make it 4:00am."

Chapter 10:

Need to Know Basis

Mom, don't give me a need-to-know-basis excuse again. Tell me what's going on." She fixed her gaze on Mom, who swerved onto an off ramp then back onto the highway to get around a car driving the speed limit.

Mom gripped the steering wheel tighter and grimaced. "Mr. Cooper had information about your Dad."

Hadassah's heart fluttered and she felt a sudden chill, even in the 76° air of the car. Her thumbnails dug into her fingertips. "What information?"

"He was kidnapped yesterday outside Baghdad."

Her whole body shook until it felt as if her rattling bones would break the skin. Once she began to breathe again, she looked at Mom. "Then why am I going to North Carolina? Why can't I stay with you and help find him? We need to find him, Mom."

"I need to make sure you're cared for, Haddy, while I look for him. Besides, I thought R.S.O. was something you wanted to do."

"That was before I found out about Dad."

"I'm meeting with people in Greensboro who know about the last moments before your dad disappeared. I may leave straight from North Carolina."

"Do you mean leave the States?" She swallowed her rising tears.

Mom nodded. "I don't think New York's going to be safe for very much longer."

Hadassah stared out on the sea of cars and blinked. Not crying made her throat sting. She swallowed again. Suddenly, as if on cue, she saw a billboard for coffee that triggered her heart. Thoughts tumbled through her mind like water from a breached dam within her and wordless prayers spilled with each silent tear that fell.

***

After seven hours of staring out the window while Mom weaved in and out of traffic, they pulled into an Omni Hotel in Richmond, VA. Mom encouraged her to eat something at the restaurant, but Hadassah had no desire for food.

"Tell me plainly, Mom, has God ever given you such crystal clear direction before you did something?"

"I know He did for your dad. He told your dad I would be his Eve a week before he met me, even though I had a disdain for Christians at the time."

Hadassah smiled for the first time since noon. She had never heard Mom's version of the story about how her parents met. "Was Dad a pastor then?"

"He was the assistant pastor at this tiny Messianic congregation in Manhattan. He invited me to the service and I attended so I could argue my point with him better. I had just moved over from Israel, and my heart had a thick shell after five years with the Mossad. And after living under my parents' orthodoxy, I had a skewed view of Eve. Your dad's teachings about Eve as the helpmeet healed something in my heart. Long story short, he heard the Lord clearly about me, and here you are to prove it."

Hadassah stared at Mom while pondering Dad's persistence. "So, what's this Mr. Cooper like?"

"He's a little hyper, but you'll like him."

Hadassah squinted at her mother. "Did you just say a little hyper?"

"You'll see when you meet him. Your dad would like this guy."

"Do you think Dad's okay?"

"I have to." She took a sip of water before handing the check and her credit card to the waiter.

Richmond, VA

Chapter 11:
Kelley's Diner

The beep of the alarm clock ricocheted off the walls in the dark hotel room, and while Hadassah thrashed the end table searching for the snooze button, Mom calmly sat up and turned on the closest light. They hardly spoke as they dressed, gathered belongings, and left before the clock read 3:45am.

The streets were busier than Hadassah had anticipated for a Thursday morning. No one seemed to sleep anymore in this mad world, and none of those prowling the streets at this hour looked as if they carried good intent. But Mom found a parking spot right in front of the diner, and once inside they followed a tattooed waitress to a booth on the second floor overlooking the street below.

"Mr. Cooper told me to keep an eye on you." The waitress handed them menus. Hadassah glanced at the angel wings tattooed on both of the girl's forearms.

Mom and I are the only people here without tattoos and the only diners who don't smell like breweries. She was surprised there was no beer on the menu.

"They come here to sober up before going home," Mom commented, eying a girl passing by who had more than a dozen piercings and a tattoo of a hummingbird on her shaved head. "The perk about this place is that no one will remember a word we say even if they do happen to eavesdrop."

"Is this the sort of place you expected to meet Mr. Cooper?"

"This isn't my first time here, Haddy, so I knew what to anticipate. We can go back to the hotel if you'd like."

"No. I feel more comfortable in this setting than in most other places. When I look at all these people I love them with Yeshua's love and I long for them to change."

Mom glanced over at her. "Don't let anyone ever preach that out of you."

As soon as Hadassah saw Mr. Cooper she knew it was him, although he wasn't anything like she'd imagined. He had the lean build and muscular prowess of an accomplished spy, but was short, only as tall as Mom. Also, he was black; although she didn't expect this, it was comforting to her. She knew he was a brother in the Lord before he opened his mouth. And Mom was right, Dad would have liked him.

He stopped at the booth and looked toward her. "Good morning. You must be Hadassah. I recognize you from your application photo. I'm Aaron Cooper."

Hadassah stood to greet him. "It's nice to meet you, sir."

"The pleasure and honor are mine, young lady." Mr. Cooper bowed slightly when he shook her hand, almost as if he was Japanese. "I didn't expect you to be so tall."

"She's taller than either of us." Mom flashed one of her quick grins as she stood.

Mr. Cooper took a seat across the table. "I'm sure we all have dozens of questions, but you ladies can go first."

Hadassah and Mom glanced at each other, but Hadassah began. "What will the academic part of the program include?"

"The recruits to R.S.O. will learn cultures of the world and protocols regarding hostage and crisis situations. You'll also take three Bible courses a week, studying a book of the Bible per course. Much of our teaching will be focused on End Times prophecies throughout the Bible."

Hadassah narrowed her eyebrows. "End of the tribulation rapture, right?"

"Mostly. Apostolic pre-millenialism. A big phrase to describe the same thing your father teaches."

"You're familiar with my dad's teaching?"

"I downloaded MP3's from your church's website on the book of Revelation and listened to them while driving up here."

"It'll be a relief to be surrounded by people who don't subscribe to the 'we'll get out of here before it gets bad' theology my school taught us."

"We teach that the saints will be on the earth *during* the tribulation until the seventh trumpet, and will be partnering with the Lord by praying for the release of judgments when the timing is right."

The tattooed waitress stood beside their table smiling at Mr. Cooper. "Preach it, my brotha'. It's always nice to hear God's word in amongst all this late-night rabble. What can I get for ya?"

After they ordered, the waitress ignored them except to refill drinks.

Mom took a sip of her coffee, grimaced at the cup and set it down again on the scratched up diner table. "I know about your stint with the FBI and CIA, but why did you choose the North Carolina House of Prayer?"

"I grew up down the street from their old facility on Friendly Avenue. When I returned to Greensboro, I met Ronny Gibbons. He invited me to one of the evening prayer sessions—8:00-10:00 I think —and I stayed until 6:30 the next morning. The short answer is, I am where God wants me."

"And how long have you been at NoCaHoP?"

"I'm afraid I can't answer that in detail. CIA constraints. But it's been over five years."

Hadassah attempted to eat her eggs while Mom asked another

question. "How many will be in R.S.O.?"

"Seven have already been training for a year. Most of those coming on board now, like you, Hadassah, have had at least the amount of training our current team has. There will be fifteen altogether, including the nurse, the chef and the tech person."

Unable to suppress her curiosity any longer, Hadassah asked, "What are the ages of the other recruits?"

"Most of them are between the ages of eighteen and twenty-five. You'll be the youngest, Hadassah."

She smiled graciously, unsure how else to respond.

Mom drew her eyebrows close together. "What I haven't heard yet is how all of this is financed."

Mr. Cooper lowered his voice to a whisper. "There are several businessmen, whose names I cannot disclose. They have set up an account which already has enough to finance everything for the next four or five years. They've invested in several currencies and in silver, so there will be plenty of money. These business men neither dictate policy nor plan missions, but they believe in what we'll be doing and are parties we're accountable to. In other words, they make sure their money is used to expand the Kingdom of God. But Hadassah, please tell me about Liberia."

Hadassah gave him a brief rundown of her mission.

When she finished, Mr. Cooper nodded his head as if in approval. "I believe you met Andrew Blessing in Monrovia."

Her eyes widened and she stared back and forth between Mom and Mr. Cooper. "I did talk to him before the army came, but I didn't see him. How do you know him?"

"I'd known Mr. Blessing for years. And I also remember you from the market in Monrovia. Last time I saw you, I debated rescuing you from a swarm of street kids."

She remembered all too clearly. "Yeah, they stole half of my money and I felt really dumb for not anticipating their actions. But I remember seeing you. There was an Asian kid with you."

A grin crossed the man's face. "Just for that, I'm sure you belong with R.S.O. Matthew's one of the recruits, and has been training with me longer than any of the others."

Hadassah tried to suppress her smile. Then Andrew Blessing came to mind again. "What do you know about Mr. Blessing?"

"He made it out of the raid without a problem and told me the next day about the 'little American girl' who hid under a sheet of metal." Mr. Cooper's eyelids suddenly sank and his countenance fell. "Several weeks later he was killed. He's gone home to the Lord."

She willed her tears not to flow, but wasn't sure if she masked how sick she felt. "How did he die?"

"I believe the Minister of Justice, Xavier Rhodes, had his hand in it. It was a drive-by shooting at a church gathering."

The news fell like a snowplow into Hadassah's heart. She winced as if the weight was real. "I had hoped he'd be okay."

"Before he died, he sent a message to me saying, 'Look to the cargo ships and look to Babylon.'"

"What does this mean to you?" Mom set her level gaze on him. Hadassah could see the wheels turning in her head.

"I think they're trafficking humans on those cargo ships. Mr. Lavo was a big player in that business before he was killed. But tell me what other questions you have, Hadassah."

"Okay. Why do you want us studying the Bible for six months instead of helping kids who are hurting right now?"

He looked quite comfortable with her confrontation. "We need to know the Lord's voice before we go out into the field." He took a small Bible out of his pocket and placed it on the table. "This is how we acquaint ourselves with His voice. We hope to train and prepare recruits for the day when the events described in Revelation begin to unfold. The best way we can train you to be operatives is to exhort you to watch and pray, and to study His word."

"How do you teach the book of Revelation?"

"Our goal is to take Jesus at His word. When He says it's a symbol we take it as a symbol; when He doesn't, we don't. Mary of Bethany took Jesus at His word about His death on the cross, and she was commended by Him. We'll take Him at His word about His second coming. That includes the 150 chapters in the Bible related to the end of this age."

Hadassah raised her eyebrows. "Wow. I didn't know there were so many. Do you have a list of them?"

"Here's a whole list of suggested reading, which includes these 150 chapters. But I have one question for you, Hadassah. Do you know about the Bridal Paradigm?"

"I don't think I even know what you mean by paradigm?"

"It's a lens or point of view through which we view things, in this case the Bible and the world around us. The Bridal Paradigm involves reading and understanding the Word through the revelation of Jesus coming for His bride, the Church."

"Yeah, I don't think it's my thing." Romance was something both high school and New York had extinguished within her.

"We're not talking about romantic dates with Jesus or any notion along those lines."

"Well, that's comforting. But what does the Bridal Paradigm have to do with preparing for the End Times?"

"It has everything to do with preparing for the End Times."

***

While Mom followed Mr. Cooper's car during the three and a half hour drive from Richmond to NoCaHoP, Hadassah read most of the 150 chapters of the Bible relating to the End Times. Somewhere near half way through the suggested reading list, she realized she hadn't really read the chapters. She'd been scanning the pages as if memorizing them for a test rather than reading God's Word to hide it in her heart. When she began to view the passages in the light of the encroaching End Times, a new fervor for Yeshua welled inside her.

She watched the landscape pass outside the window: innumerable buildings and houses rested under blankets of snow. But the whole landscape: the cities, the trees, the farms, the sky, all looked different than before. *What will the fate of America be? Will war come to these shores before the End? And how on earth would the sky roll back like a scroll?* She glanced again at Mr. Cooper's suggested reading list. A note at the top of the page read, "Pray through the scriptures and write down any questions you have." *How did I miss these instructions before?* It must have been the excitement. She reread the material slowly, prayerfully. The radical faith of the saints stood out to her, laying one's life down as Jesus did: it was more about this than about doctrine.

Then she read the Sermon on the Mount. Turn the other cheek had a whole lot more significance. So did praying, fasting and giving to those in need. It seemed as if the need for these activities would increase in the light of the what was happening in the world. Questions she wanted answers for overflowed the pages of her notebook.

She turned to the second portion of the reading list—the Bridal Paradigm. There were only a few passages listed: Psalm 45, Hosea 2, Isaiah 54, John 3, Song of Solomon. Beautiful poetry and amazing words, but what was their significance in the light of the book of Revelation? *Why did Mr. Cooper say this had everything to do with the End Times?*

"You're awfully quiet, you know," Mom pointed out somewhere across the North Carolina state line.

"I've been studying the suggested reading. Frankly, after all the questions we asked Mr. Cooper, I still don't know what to expect."

"You may be waiting on people at first. That's what I did in Mossad for the first two months. Then you will have various levels of endurance training, according to Mr. Cooper, and enough academic work to make you feel as if you had chosen Yale or Princeton instead."

"I hope I can fall asleep without the constant lullaby of sirens."

"You've always adjusted quickly. I'm sure you will at R.S.O."

Hadassah shrugged and tried to put on a cheerful face. "And I don't know if I'll be able to make friends."

Mom smiled softly. "I know you're used to keeping to yourself. But remember to put yourself out there and show lots of interest in others. If you ask people questions about themselves, most are so self-absorbed they won't suspect you're keeping secrets from them."

"Do you think I can train myself to be an extrovert?"

"I used to be shy."

Hadassah laughed at the thought of Mom being shy.

"I'm serious. My personality changed a thousand times when I was younger, especially in the army."

Greensboro, NC

Chapter 12:

Paradigm Shift at NoCaHoP

When greeters opened the doors at NoCaHoP and ushered them inside, both mother and daughter fell silent. The presence of the Lord was palpable. Mom found a seat near a box of tissues where she shed silent tears and raised her hands to God.

Hadassah's whole body tingled as she tried to find a seat. She didn't mean to ignore the kind faces and waves of welcome, she just didn't know how to acknowledge them. The church in Brooklyn had many conferences and prayer meetings where the presence of God swelled to this level, but she had never felt it with this immediacy and with this much strength. She felt both afraid and safe. *So this is what Dad meant when he talked about the Shekinah glory.*

After half an hour she realized she had been sitting on the floor staring at a seat back, thinking about the Bridal Paradigm from John 3, Psalm 45 and Song of Solomon. It wasn't at all like Yeshua being her boyfriend. This was about her position as a partner beside Him, and the privilege of His favor and listening ear. She'd have open access to the throne at all times where she could ask Him to reveal

His love to her. The revelation of this privilege was overwhelming, like being told she owned the ocean and could do with it what she liked.

But there was more. It wasn't just an idea. He actually opened His heart to her when she asked. Sitting there on the floor of the prayer room, she burned with a warmth she hadn't felt since that night in the jungle. He tore the thick curtain of heaviness away, and the wind of His love blew in and refreshed corners of her soul she had hidden for years. He wasn't afraid of her emotions, the sadness, the anger, the fear, her love for Dad, her feelings of superiority toward others. She could run to Him instead of from Him, and He would transform her. Her heart burned further, as if the transformation were physical as well.

He liked her and she knew this would be the premise of all His other emotions. She would be able to draw on His tenderness toward her. Forever.

Another two hours passed, but she was unaware. She didn't move except to brush away tears.

Where was Mom? She lifted her gaze to scan the room. An Asian girl with coppery skin, sad, aged eyes and arms over her belly stood at the back and caught her glance; they smiled at one another.

Mom was out in the lobby talking with Mr. Cooper and Ronny Gibbons. At least he looked like Ronny Gibbons from the website picture. Hadassah followed Mom's beckon into the lobby.

"I'll be taking you to visit the other recruits and team members," Mr. Cooper said. "We were waiting for Priscilla, but she got here about 20 minutes ago."

She turned to Mom. "Will you be coming too?"

"I'll see you tomorrow. I'll be meeting with Pastor Gibbons and several others while you settle in."

Chapter 13:

Priscilla

Priscilla gave what smile she had left to the girl with the determined, tear-stained face. Of all the people in the prayer room, this girl with fly-away black hair sitting on the floor had been the one Priscilla felt most drawn to. Like they were friends before hello. But having kept quiet her whole train ride from Tampa, FL, to Greensboro, NC, Priscilla couldn't bring herself to say hello. Not in this solemn and holy room.

This had to be the girl Mr. Cooper had referred to as the youngest recruit at R.S.O. And this girl made her feel old, even though she was still two months shy of her nineteenth birthday. She wondered, as she had the whole train ride there, if anyone at R.S.O. would be able to relate to what she had been through in her short life.

The sound of rapid-fire prayers brought her thoughts back to the prayer room. The second girl stepping up to the microphone to pray reminded Priscilla of her sister, Filipa. It was her voice, high, sweet, so confident of God.

Filipa. Why did she have to go on that mission trip back to the Philippines? Priscilla closed her eyes against the flood of memories planting her back in Cebu City in the Philippines, in the brothel, in the corner of the always dark bedroom, all those years ago.

She loved it here in America, thousands of miles away from Cebu City's filth. Why did Filipa go back? Priscilla rehashed the night Filipa left, thinking of all the words she should have said to keep her sister from going, as if she could go back in time and make it different. Then Filipa disappeared along with everyone else on the mission trip.

Priscilla had hid in the prayer room at her church for the next three months and silently screamed at God. She prayed for her sister's safety. She cried until both body and soul felt dry.

Her adoptive parents wept with her and promised to do what they could to find Filipa. In their search they happened to contact Ronny Gibbons, who connected them with Aaron Cooper.

"Why is this happening all over the world?" Priscilla demanded of Mr. Cooper the day she met him. "If my sister's alive, sir, I know the sort of life she's forced to live. I know it better than I ever want to tell you." She jutted her jaw forward and ground her teeth as she remembered the sound of the gun shot twelve years ago. The brothel owner's sneer, her mom collapsing onto the bed as life ebbed away all too quickly, but the scene replayed in slow motion more often than she ever told anyone. "If there's anything you can do to help me get my sister back, please tell me. My parents won't let me go alone."

"With good reason." Mr. Cooper's sad smile held the compassion she longed for and a determination she related to. "With R.S.O. you wouldn't have to go back there alone. But we'd need to train you before we send you anywhere."

"Sign me up to R.S.O. and I'll go with you." She focused her gaze on him, then all her anger and frustration began to melt when she saw that Mr. Cooper had a plan instead of mere condolences.

"It will take about a year to train everyone."

"A year! She might not be alive by then."

He seemed so patient with her emotional outbursts. "It's up to you if you want to join us. If you don't, then we can keep in contact and try to find your sister for you in a year."

"No. I said whatever it takes and I meant it. Sign me up."

Priscilla's dad, always the pacifist, objected at first, but said he preferred this option far above the army, the other place Priscilla determined to go if she found no solid leads about her sister.

Her mom wanted to drive her all the way up to North Carolina, but Priscilla insisted on the train.

"I need time to think," she told her parents when they stood with her on the platform in Tampa.

The twenty-five hours on the train definitely gave her time to think. But when she had to transfer with all of her bags in Raleigh, she wondered whether she should have taken her dad's offer.

Mr. Cooper's wife, who picked her up from the Greensboro station, was a short, light-skinned black woman who exuded plenty of no-nonsense attitude. She stood beside the station, only ten feet from the train tracks, with sharp eyes and a generous smile as she held the sign reading 'Priscilla Rogers.' As soon as Priscilla made eye contact, Mrs. Cooper rushed over and offered to carry the baggage encumbering her.

"When my husband told me you were definitely coming, I told him I'd come getcha." Mrs. Cooper flashed another of her welcoming grins. "I'm going to be on staff with R.S.O. now that I've retired from the Department of Social Services, because I know y'all will need someone to hold your secrets with you."

"I don't think I'm ready to talk about stuff on that level yet." Priscilla lowered her eyes from this woman's tenderhearted gaze.

Mrs. Cooper clicked her tongue and shook her head. "Yer gonna be a hard shell to crack, ain't ya. No worries. Most of the folk my husband recruited for R.S.O. are similar to you. My husband, too. I think you'll be a good fit here."

"Why do you say that?"

"I can tell you keep a secret real well."

Priscilla's attempt at a smile failed. She loaded her bags into the back of Mrs. Cooper's hybrid SUV. "I can tell you were a social worker."

"You've seen quite a few, haven't ya, darlin'."

She shrugged, then gave a small smile when Mrs. Cooper opened the door to the front seat for her. "Thanks."

"I promise I won't pull any social worker tricks, but I wanted to let you know I'm available."

Priscilla crossed her arms over her belly. "Thanks."

Greensboro looked so different from Tampa. There were no palm trees, for one. For another, it wasn't very green, despite its name. Yet there were a few groves of evergreens in the middle of the city. She never would have seen this in Tampa.

As soon as she arrived at NoCaHoP she stepped from Mrs. Cooper's SUV and stretched her legs.

"The last recruit is praying in the main room," Mrs. Cooper told her. "Feel free to pray as well for a few minutes."

But she hardly needed the permission. The yearning of her heart pulled her close to the Lord's presence.

She stood in the back of the prayer room with arms folded over her stomach, eyes cast at her feet and a whisper on her lips of the only Name which brought her peace. Jesus. After a minute she chanced a scan of the room, curious about who the other recruit was. The girl's piercing brown eyes seemed to hold lots of secrets too. They both smiled.

Peace and urgency filled her as she raised her face toward heaven and began to praise Jesus and thank Him for safe travels. He'd protected her from so much already... But she felt too antsy to stay still. She loved this sense of God's presence, yet she didn't want another moment to go by before she could start her training, since Mr. Cooper said she'd be the most untrained of all the recruits.

When she stepped out of the prayer room, the tall, lithe girl who had been sitting on the floor now stood in the lobby talking to Mr. Cooper, Pastor Ronny Gibbons and some other lady who was probably the girl's mom.

"Priscilla." Mr. Cooper interrupted her thoughts which were spiraling toward a heavy shyness. "I want to introduce you to Hadassah. The two of you will be coming with Mrs. Cooper and me to meet the others."

Priscilla tried to give a firm handshake to this recruit. Instead, when she encountered Hadassah's unexpected strength, her hand went limp.

"Nice to meet you," Priscilla mumbled, but couldn't remember if Hadassah said anything in return. She wrapped her arms around her middle again and stared at her knees. Why were they always wobbly in the presence of new people?

The whole car ride from NoCaHoP to the house where the recruits were staying, Hadassah and Mrs. Cooper dominated the conversation. Hadassah evaded most of the questions Mrs. Cooper asked. This young girl kept turning the questions around—not in a sarcastic or unkind way, but as if she wanted to listen more than she wanted to talk. Priscilla always admired this trait in other people, but never seemed to emulate it well.

Mr. Cooper found the right question for Hadassah. "So, I saw you praying for about two and a half hours in there… what was the Lord showing you?"

"Well, I was meditating on the suggested reading list, and asking God some of the questions I had written down on the long drive here when He began to reveal the Bridal Paradigm to me."

"Really?" He grinned. "I knew He would, but I didn't anticipate it this soon. Did He show you how important the Bridal Paradigm is for the times we're living in?"

"Not so much. He just told me over and over how much He loves me." The corners of her mouth raised in a smile.

Priscilla had been meditating on the Bridal Paradigm a bit on the train and longed for this same assurance from the Lord.

"Make sure you write it down," Mrs. Cooper said. "You too, Priscilla. Write down everything the Lord says to you. I'll be handing out journals to everyone tonight."

If only He spoke so clearly to me.

The house was smaller than a true mansion, but reminded Priscilla of celebrity homes in Tampa. It stood at the end of a long driveway which was lined with a low stone wall and pristine landscaping. The porch was wide and long, a place to watch thunderstorms roll in. Black trim crisscrossing white plaster gave the house a Tudor look, but it was obviously less than ten years old. She had never been inside a place like this.

Three women she suspected to be R.S.O. recruits sat on the large porch swing and on the carved wooden bench sharing a laugh. One of the women was Chinese with soft features and the athletic contours of a soccer player or gymnast. The second was a black woman who looked ageless. She could have been sixteen or thirty with a face like that. Priscilla saw her chuckle graciously and place a gentle hand on the forearm of the third woman.

This last young woman was as pale as a lab rat, as if the only rays she ever soaked up were through a laptop; but IQ seeped from her pores—she would still be smarter than 99.9% of the world if she lost half her brain cells in a sneeze. This woman was the jester among the three, judging by the laughter of the other two.

Priscilla could hear them even while she sat inside the running car. She had expected much more seriousness and wanted to hide at the sound of that laughter, despite the bright and friendly eyes of these women.

Chapter 14:

Icebreakers and Blessedness

Hadassah wanted to love this laughter as soon as she heard it. Such contagious laughter. It almost made her forget her heartache.

"Mrs. Cooper!" the pale young woman shouted when they all got out of the car. "Are these the last two recruits?"

"They are," Mrs. Cooper told them. "Lisa, Hyun, Tameka, come meet Priscilla and Hadassah. Would you take them inside to introduce them to the others?"

Hadassah took the opportunity to practice being an extrovert again. Since she was closest to Lisa, she smiled wide at her and began with her hand outstretched.

"Hi, Lisa, it's so nice to meet you." She shook Lisa's thin hand as confidently as she dared. "This place is huge. How many are staying here?"

Lisa skipped up the stairs. "We won't be staying here. We've only come here to gather in one place before we head out to what everyone calls the Lighthouse. That's the new place and none of us, except the Coopers, have been there. Oops, I'm forgetting Mr.

Murray, but he's there already. Oh, yeah, how many of us—there are sixteen, well eighteen with you and Priscilla here. Enough to make this place feel small, even though it is huge! The ladies are sharing rooms on the second floor. Here, follow me."

Tameka chuckled behind them. "Just don't ask Lisa about any computer programing ideas. She will have you doubling over with laughter while you're trying to walk up the stairs."

Hadassah detected a West Coast accent from Tameka's succinct tone. "How long have you been with NoCaHoP?"

"I've been here almost four years now, but only when on leave."

"On leave?"

"I was in the Army."

Hadassah's mouth fell agape—Tameka looked so young.

"A few others here are former military, too," Lisa said. "Take Dave—he's the guy with a buzz cut and the mean scar across his nose and cheek—he's a former Ranger."

"Army Ranger?" Hadassah asked.

Lisa nodded. "And Christina was a Marine. She's the short one with the long blond braid down her back. Between Christina and Dave I don't know who's toughest around here."

Glancing at everyone who gathered in the large living room, Hadassah saw several of the guys in the midst of the crowd, showing off to each other with handstands. Some of them, especially that Asian kid, were really good. She drew her shoulders in and slumped her head, trying to think of another question. "Are there any who are former intelligence?"

"Besides Mr. Cooper?" Tameka took the stairs two at a time. "Hyun Xi, who you met outside, was CIA before retiring to be with R.S.O."

"Retiring?" With a small gasp, Hadassah turned briefly to glance at Hyun, who was helping Priscilla carry her luggage. "She doesn't look a day over twenty-two."

Lisa chuckled. "She's a bit older, but none of us want to ask her a third time."

"I hear Mrs. Cooper," Tameka said. "We're probably going to do another icebreaker game, since you and Priscilla have arrived."

***

"One more icebreaker, y'all," Mrs. Cooper told the crowd. "Then we're going to have pizza for dinner. Mr. Cooper told me there will be a teaching tonight, but he hasn't told me who the teacher is."

The crowd milled around in boisterous curiosity, but grew quiet again when Mrs. Cooper raised her hands.

"The game's called Lollipops. I've got a bag of lollipops and each flavor will have 4 matches. Your goal is to form a group without duplicate flavors. The first group to form tells their name, age, where they're from and one fact about themselves; the second group to form tells name, age and two facts. And so on. Okay, ready? Go."

The scramble, the laughter and the mingling of faces and names—Hadassah had had other notions about Revelation Special Ops. This fit none of those.

She ended up on the second team. Then she saw him—the Asian kid who ended up on the first team—and remembered his face from the market in Liberia.

"Yo, dudes, I'm Matthew Cho." His wide smile beamed. "I'm eighteen. I grew up in Greensboro. And, uh, let's see—I've gone spear fishing off the coast of South Korea where I caught a shark."

South Korean? She was sure he was Chinese, but that didn't matter. Up close, Matthew was the most good looking young man she had ever seen, with spiky hair, flashing eyes and strong hands moving confidently as he talked. She was startled by how attractive he was. And after witnessing his agile and wiry frame do those handstands earlier, she was sure he could spear a shark. But she was ready to write him off for this boasting.

More than a few from the crowd exclaimed, "Ooh!" She didn't.

"I'm Hyun. I'm still not telling my age, Mrs. C, but nice try." She giggled as everyone, including Hadassah, laughed. "I grew up both in Virginia and in Shanghai. I qualified to compete in the Olympics but chose to work for the government instead."

"What event?" someone called out.

"I'm in the first group, so I only have to tell one thing."

When it was time for the second group, Hadassah was swept up into the camaraderie in the room. "I was called Tsigele by a boy the other day. For those of you who don't know, that's Yiddish for 'little goat.' Oh, and I only like flat, lukewarm soda."

"Eww!" someone from the crowd shouted out, accompanied by loud laughter. Feeling jittery in the spotlight, Hadassah shuffled her feet and laughed nervously.

"I'm Tameka and I'm twenty-three. I grew up in Pasadena, Cali, I like *cold* and *carbonated* soda," she giggled and winked at Hadassah, "and I don't like bananas in the morning—but I do like them in desserts."

"My name's Dave, I'm twenty-eight. I'm from Minneapolis. I love jumping out of airplanes, I like the desert in the dead of night when it's real quiet but you hear the rustling of the animals in the sand, and once I wrestled an alligator in the swamplands of Georgia."

There was a resounding "Ooh!" throughout the room at that one.

"Hi, I'm Christina, and I'm twenty-nine. I grew up all over North Carolina, mostly in Greensboro. I love working out, I like hiking, I really like fine foods but I eat straight from a can when I need to, and, let's see, I certainly can't beat Dave's story, but I did eat a scorpion when I was in China."

Another "Ooh!" This time Hadassah joined in.

"I'm Lisa, and I'm twenty. I'm from Austin, Texas. I used to design Facebook games, I'm trying to design a computer screen that emits Vitamin D, I love almonds and pistachios while I work, and I work best during the hours of 1-3am." Lisa rattled this off so fast

Hadassah would have missed it if she hadn't heard half of it earlier.

"I'm Amelia and I'm twenty-four. I'm from Georgia, except I never wrestled an alligator. But I will be the main chef when we get to the Lighthouse, so I suggest being kind to me because I choose who peels the potatoes." She laughed. "Actually, I'm joking, I don't get to choose, but I do love to cook, and I love variety and challenge, so I hope y'all have adventurous taste buds. But don't worry, it's all edible, all delicious, and rarely deep-fried. So, Christina, you and me will be best friends."

Mr. Cooper announced that pizzas were on the way. But they all had to wash up and meet in the common room about schedules first.

"Tomorrow being Sunday, you can either rest here, for those who have had long travels, or you can pile into the van with us and go to church. We're leaving for the Lighthouse next Saturday morning.

"Between Monday and Saturday, you'll head out in teams of two and serve the staff, students and volunteers at NoCaHoP. You'll also work with some of the mercy ministries. Each team will get a list of duties first thing every morning until we leave. And yes, you are allowed to gripe, but only to me, to my wife, or to God. If I hear you griping among yourselves everyone will get an extra list for the following day. Rough, I know, but I encourage you to be praying for one another instead of griping or worrying about who might gripe.

"Stick around after the teaching since we'll be going over the rules of R.S.O."

"Pizzas are here, y'all," Mrs. Cooper said.

During dinner everyone speculated on who this teacher would be, but Mr. Cooper gave no hints or clues.

While Hadassah helped with clean-up, Tameka stopped and looked out at the common room. "Our guest speaker's here. Oh my! It's John Mark Gregory. They brought in John Mark Gregory."

Hadassah craned her neck to catch a glimpse of him. "I've read one of his books, but I never heard him preach before. Have you?"

"Only in large conferences. Come on, girl, they're gathering in the common room now."

Pastor Gregory tottered with his cane as he walked to the front of the common room. But when he looked each one of them in the eye Hadassah no longer thought of him as a teetering old man.

"Friends, brothers and sisters in Christ, beloved of the Lord," began John Mark Gregory, "I count it a privilege to bring this word to you as you launch into training. I am stunned as I stand before you, observing how the Holy Spirit is faithful to His promise. He's bringing the Bride to maturity before Jesus returns. Not since the days of the apostles has His Church been filled with such character, resolve and willingness to serve and be unknown. But you *are* known: in heaven, in the Lamb's Book of Life, in the heart of the Father.

"Yet I tell you, and urge you in Christ, this is the beginning of maturity and not the fullness. Yes, we have seen so many of the signs fulfilled in our lifetime. Beloved of Christ, the Gospel is being preached to every tribe, every tongue, every people, every nation right now!" His eyes glistened with tears. "He is coming soon. It may be in the next few years, maybe in the next thirty or forty." His elderly body shook with a joy which made him look twenty years younger.

"I want to speak to you this evening about your blessedness. You have each experienced the Kingdom of God, and been filled with the Holy Spirit.

"You are blessed because you are meek—every one of you. The word meek has received some bad press in the last century or so. Meekness is not weakness, even though *we* are weak. Meekness is not mousy. Of all the ways Jesus chose to describe Himself in the Gospels, He chose two words: 'meek' and 'lowly'. He created the universe—He is as strong as they come, but while He walked this earth He chose to empty Himself and put His strength *under* the Holy Spirit's strength so he would glorify the Father and the Spirit in everything. He was not timid. And neither are you. Inasmuch as you voluntarily submit your strength to His strength, you are blessed, you are meek, and you will inherit the earth.

"But you and I are weak, friends. God still chooses the weak things of this world to shame the strong. You are an elite group of young adults, but you realize your weaknesses: you are the elite of the weak. You are blessed because you realize that any strength you have is His.

"Blessed are you peacemakers. Spies are sometimes thought to be peacemakers, but you are of a different spirit than the spies of this world. Our war isn't with flesh and blood, but with powers and principalities. Releasing captives is an act of peace, and it wages war against these powers and principalities; these will strike at you through people. Your enemy will tell you that you are not a peacemaker. Releasing captives is the work of a peacemaker, so listen to me when I tell you that you are sons and daughters of God. You are blessed. Listen for the Lord's voice when He calls you sons and daughters. Listen and believe it now, before the time of testing comes upon you.

"Blessed are those who are persecuted for righteousness' sake, for theirs is the Kingdom of Heaven. And I promise you, as many of you know well, those who do righteous works in the name of Jesus will be persecuted. In this age, all works of righteousness face persecution.

"But Jesus goes on: people will curse you, insult you, tell lies about you and say all manner of evil things about you because of your testimony of Jesus. People you rescue may do this, so their gratitude cannot be your reward. But we can rejoice and be glad because our reward in Heaven will be great.

"Let's stand and thank the Lord for the blessedness He gives us."

Tameka came forward and played a song on the piano while everyone prayed. As soon as she began to sing, Hadassah reckoned she had the sweetest and most captivating trill of a voice. Like a song sparrow at dawn. Like a wood thrush on a pristine evening. Like a nightingale through a dark night of the soul.

As she sat meditating and asking the Lord to reveal Himself, Hadassah became aware of a fire within her heart. Within her whole body. This neither alarmed nor frightened her, but she felt as if she was the only person in the room and God had His spotlight—and His fire—on *her*. She didn't realize her body rocked back and forth, and neither did she realize she was praying aloud. In Hebrew. Then in French. Then in Spanish. Then a language came from her mouth she didn't know. But she continued to pray, relishing the bonfire in her heart. His Shekinah glory.

Chapter 15:

Hyun

Hyun collected her books and papers, her mind still processing what Pastor Gregory had said concerning her blessedness. She would have refuted every claim, except it was Jesus who said it first. And she made it a point to agree with Jesus. Especially after her last year with the CIA.

Aaron Cooper laid a firm hand on her shoulder. "You doin' alright, girl?"

She flashed her spy glare, the one she had perfected years ago on assignment in Taiwan. "I'm just fine. It doesn't bother me to be the oldest one here, if that's what you're asking; it's invigorating to be around this crowd."

"That's not what I meant."

"I don't want to talk about my mom right now."

"Will you soon? I'm putting together a meeting this week. Everyone here who's had a relative go missing."

"I'll talk then. But not now."

"I understand." He lowered his voice further. "Tell me what you think of Priscilla."

"You're the one who recruited her."

"I know, but aside from Larry Murray, you're the best judge of character I know."

She sighed and rolled her eyes. "You gleaned this from working with me for only five months?"

"Five months in the Middle East can reveal a great deal about someone."

"Since you ask, she's got a lot of anger issues, but it looks like she's dealing with them head-on instead of ignoring her problems. You'd be hard pressed to find someone so scarred and angry who has her level of loyalty and truth of character."

"I take it she told you about her childhood."

Hyun shook her head. "No. I can see from looking at her. You'll need to give her lots of TLC, but she may be one of the best operatives at R.S.O. when all is said and done."

"See, girl? You rock when it comes to character judgment. No wonder the CIA didn't want to let you go."

Hyun cringed. "They were a little more eager than you might think."

"What about our youngest recruit?" Aaron nudged her as he glanced at Hadassah.

"That's Pastor Asher's daughter, isn't it?"

"Hadassah."

"Does she know about her dad yet?"

"She does. She'll need a bit of TLC too. Her mom's leaving from here to try and find everyone."

Hyun shut her eyes and steeled her emotions.

Aaron's stare was upon her when she opened her eyes. "You want to go with her mom?"

"I called the State Department all day yesterday and got the run-around. No one wants to touch disappearances in the Middle East for some reason. It takes a lot for me to get angry, but I might snap soon."

"You didn't answer me."

"Pastor Gibbons sent me a text already. I'll be meeting with Mrs. Michelman tomorrow during our free day. As of right now, those are my only plans, aside from working with you and R.S.O."

"But you never told me what you think of Hadassah."

She chuckled softly. "You know how to find them is all I can say."

"Whatcha mean by that?"

Hyun gave a half smile. "I mean, well done on the recruiting end. She's a spy if I ever saw one. Give her a few months and she'll be schooling the lot of us. And I can't wait 'til she meets Larry Murray. She'll be your other best operative."

"He's got all their files, so I'm sure he knows what to expect. Are you okay to train alongside them?"

"What's my other option, teaching? No thanks."

"I was hoping you and Christina would mentor the younger girls."

"I could. One step at a time, Aaron."

She glanced over at Hadassah while Aaron turned to talk to Dave. The girl was lost in prayer in the midst of a swirl of activity. Hyun sat down again, placed her Bible and notebook on an empty chair and began to pray. Of everything Aaron had offered when he told her about R.S.O., he should have said she'd have a focused prayer life again. It would have been his best selling point. A smile swept across her face as she began to perceive God's presence. Tameka's song echoed in her heart and she lifted it up silently in praise to her King.

She glanced at her watch. Only five minutes had gone by. She loved when five minutes felt like an hour, as if she had been briefly invited into God's reality of time. With a few whispers of "I love you," and "Thank you," to the Lord, she began gathering her Bible and notebook again.

"I'm very curious about you, Hyun." Hadassah stood beside her with right hand outstretched. "I'm Hadassah, by the way. I'm having trouble remembering everyone's name."

Hyun shook her hand and smiled candidly. "You remembered mine."

"I also remember what you said about the Olympics, and I was wondering what event you qualified for."

"We never did have another questions game, did we? I qualified for gymnastics, the uneven bars."

"Nice. Did you love it?"

She shrugged. *Maybe in the beginning, but that was so long ago.* "I remember performing on the bars before the judges and trying to figure out what use I was to the Lord. They told me I qualified, and I wanted to go home and cry—I knew in my heart the other girl was supposed to go instead of me. I withdrew my name the following morning, then finished my bachelor's and headed off to Langley to work for the CIA."

"Did you know Mr. Cooper while you were with the CIA?"

"I did. He's the reason I retired from the agency and moved to North Carolina. He told me what he was doing and I said count me in. I loved the work I did at the agency, but they kept asking agents to compromise their faith for the sake of country. The reason I love this country so much is because I *can* pursue Christ here without compromise." She chuckled to herself. "I never told these things to anyone beside the Coopers and Pastor Gibbons. You have a real disarming way about you, Hadassah."

"Thanks. I feel like I'm so much younger than everyone else. Do you think I'll fit in?"

"I hardly know you, but I know if Mr. Cooper recruited you then I am honored to be on your team. You have confidence without arrogance. It's a rare find."

Hadassah blushed and looked down. "I guess New York didn't rub off on me too badly. Mr. Cooper's gathering everyone again. Have you heard these guidelines already?"

"I have, but it'll be good to hear them again. These guidelines are a major reason I signed up."

Hyun smiled when Hadassah took the seat right next to her.

Aaron raised his hands for everyone to quiet down. "Many of you have heard our purpose and guidelines, but I want to repeat them for the new recruits. None of you will ever have a normal public life again. And not one of you will have fame here on earth, at least I really hope not."

Hyun laughed out loud, even though no one else did.

Aaron smiled and nodded his head at her before continuing. "We have a mission at R.S.O. born out of many hours of watching and praying, and our work will be unlike most anything on the grid of the church, or most of history. You still have five more days to run for the door, but here is what will be required of you if you stay.

"At R.S.O., we are not to defile ourselves with sexual immorality. If you did in the past and you repented before the Lord, then you have a clean slate because of the cross. But at R.S.O. we can't allow that mistake. We need to be set apart as holy if we're to do His work. Especially this work. I know there are guys and ladies together here, but honor one another, honor the Lord and honor yourselves.

"Second, each person needs to follow the Lamb. Yes, we have to work as a team, but we cannot rely on our teammates' relationships with the Lord to boost us while we're in the field, we need to have our own. Each one of us needs oil for our own lamps. We need to stand before Him individually and as a team and follow Him in and through all the places He goes. This will be the biggest way you build up trust with one another. And believe me, we need to trust one another.

"The last guideline will run contrary to everything you may think our program would entail. There is to be no lie on our lips; we're to be blameless. I'm not going to let anyone slide on this one: we won't tolerate lying. We will discuss and act out various scenarios during training at the Lighthouse. Some of us may have been trained to tell lies and deceive others. It's time to bring heart and mind before the Lord. He alone can eliminate our inclination to lie.

"Some of you may recognize these regulations from the book of Revelation and yes, these are the descriptions of the 144,000. Am I saying you'll be one of those 144,000? I don't know if that's a literal number, but I will tell you this: these are the standards of the Lamb, our Lord of Glory, so they are the standards for R.S.O. That's all for tonight. I hope you have a restful sleep."

As she trudged upstairs and readied her bed, Hyun noticed Hadassah several times. The girl's terse movements confirmed to her that Aaron's guidelines had dredged up more questions than answers. Even though she was exhausted from worry and wrestling with past issues stirred up by the guidelines, Hyun stepped over sleeping bags and around cots to talk to Hadassah.

"So, what did you think of what Mr. Cooper said?" Hyun asked as she sat on the remaining patch of plush carpet beside Hadassah's sleeping bag.

Hadassah looked up at her with a smile then cast her glance down at her sleeping bag again. "I liked it, I guess. There wasn't much to disagree with for a person who's given her life to Yeshua— I mean Jesus."

"I love how you call Him Yeshua."

"It's just..." Hadassah stared off at the wall.

"What is it?"

"The whole thing about there being no lie on our lips. I mean, I agree with it, especially about not lying to each other or to people who love Yeshua, but I can't stop thinking about the midwives in Egypt." Hadassah looked up at Hyun again. "Do you remember the ones from the first chapter of Exodus who lied to Pharaoh about the baby boys and were commended for it by God?"

"I know the story."

"Am I justifying myself by thinking of them?"

Hyun sat in stunned silence as she listened to Hadassah tell about her conversation with the taxi driver in Liberia.

"Was I wrong to pretend I was a naïve English tourist? I mean, I did it so I could save those children. But this is just one of many examples. And I've been lying about things I don't even need to lie about, like tonight when I said I like warm, flat soda. I don't even like soda, so I don't know why I mentioned it."

"When Mr. Cooper said some of us were taught to lie, I think he meant you and me."

"But I don't think my mom taught me to lie. She tells people things on a need-to-know basis, and she always wears a disguise of some kind when on assignment. I don't know. Maybe I got it from all the spy movies and books."

Hyun chuckled softly. "I like those too. But let me tell you a story. The last year I worked at the CIA, I was strongly encouraged to lie about everything, even inconsequential things, and was told on several occasions that if I didn't, I would endanger the lives of other operatives in the field. My lies enabled a mole in the Agency, one of my superiors, a traitor who bombed the US embassy in Lebanon and carried out two terrorist attacks in and around Jerusalem. His was the only character I ever misjudged, but looking back, I'm sure my steady stream of lies clouded my vision."

"Wow. I needed to hear that."

"It's a hard pattern to break, especially if you've been lying about inconsequential things."

"I guess I have been justifying myself."

"Don't discredit what you did in Africa, though. That was a righteous work, and there aren't enough righteous works in the world today. Open this area of your heart to the Lord's scrutiny. He dealt with our lies at the cross, and He alone will give us a clean conscience."

Chapter 16:

Christina

Christina opened her eyes at 5:45am on Monday morning, just as she did every morning to grab thirty minutes of solitude before everyone woke. Except this morning drowsiness assaulted more than ever. Most of those girls stayed up chatting far too late; thankfully they all slept silently now. Well, all except Lisa, who continued to snore like a chainsaw.

Four minutes in the shower, three minutes to dress and brush teeth, three minutes to brush and braid hair. This would give her twenty minutes alone in the common room. Christina tiptoed around the sleeping girls with Bible and journal in hand. She'd exercise first, and if no one else stirred, push-ups and sit-ups would be done before 6:05. Exercising alone was a rare privilege.

She caught Amelia's glance as she finished the last of her sit-ups. The woman, still dressed in pajamas, began to prepare breakfast for everyone. They smiled briefly at one another before Christina returned to her exercises. Tomorrow she'd start with reading her Bible first.

After quickly reading through Psalm 8 and Proverbs 3, she set aside her books to help Amelia fix breakfast. It always amazed her to watch what this woman could cook for an impending mob with just a few ingredients.

The former soldiers—Tameka, Dave and Robert—were the first to trickle toward the kitchen, joined by Hadassah, which surprised her. The youngest of all proved to be a morning person. Maybe Hadassah wouldn't be R.S.O.'s first drop-out. After all, she did say something to Hyun the other night about Liberia. But Christina couldn't see any similarities between herself and this young girl, besides both being early risers.

"Would I be able to make some tea?" Hadassah asked her.

Christina smiled. Sometimes she liked to be proved wrong about people. "Be my guest. But can you make a pot? I think I'd prefer tea over coffee this morning."

"No problem. Thanks for making breakfast."

"Oh, that's Amelia's specialty. I just dice and sauté, dice and sauté."

Hadassah giggled as she filled the tea kettle and set it to boil on the stove.

***

"I'll be sending you out in teams of two," Mr. Cooper told them over breakfast. The sun shone bright through the sliding doors leading from the common room to the back deck. "No switching partners over the next five days. If you have a problem with your partner, feel free to speak with my wife."

Mrs. Cooper's smile indicated she wouldn't change anything for anyone. No one stirred.

"Go ahead and finish up your food," Mr. Cooper continued, "but as I call your names, come get a list of the people you will be serving today. Christina and Hadassah, please come get your list…"

On the way to the prayer room, Christina read over the list, trying to think of reasons not to complain about her partner. "All our tasks seem to be cleaning," she told Hadassah. "It also looks like everyone lives in the same neighborhood of low income housing, so once we get there we can walk from place to place."

"I love walking, but I'm not the best cleaner. Are you?"

Christina suppressed another desire to complain. "I had to be. The Marine Corps has strict rules on it."

Hadassah laughed. "You can give me orders and I'll try to keep up. What rank were you in the Marines, by the way?"

"High enough to pull rank when need be, but I don't talk about it here, because here we're all the same rank."

Every house she and Hadassah cleaned had at least three children, and one house had as many as ten. Some of the mothers were massively grateful and looked frazzled right down to their fingertips; others were mildly grateful and highly particular.

Christina cleaned the kitchens, common rooms, laundry rooms, and any extra rooms, and left the bathrooms and kids' rooms for

Hadassah. This young girl tried to keep up with any orders and suggestions, but always needed help to finish.

"I guess I should have spent as much time learning to clean a house as I did learning to crawl through an air duct," Hadassah confessed when they stopped for lunch. "I hope my cleaning was up to standard."

Christina tried not to scowl; Mr. Cooper had asked her to mentor these young girls. "It wouldn't be up to standard if we were roommates. But you can blame the government, because I was much messier than you at your age."

After lunch, when they returned to cleaning, the maggots in the trashcans of one house pulled at Christina's gag reflex.

Hadassah happened to show up in the kitchen just before Christina's lunch revisited. "Do you want me to take over?"

She tried hard not to gag again. "If you really want to."

"I don't mind. I grew up in the City, so I'm used to gross stuff. Anyway, I've been slower than you all day long. It's the least I can do."

Christina stood back and breathed with her chin up in the air to try to avoid the smell of the trashcan and to coax her lunch back down. When she glanced down at Hadassah, she noticed tears steaming down the girl's face and splashing onto the maggots in the trashcan.

"You okay, Hadassah?"

"I'm okay." She wiped her tears off on her shoulders and upper arms. "I was just remembering an assignment."

She looked at the young girl, who was kneeling on the kitchen floor, crying and scraping maggots out of a trash can. She smiled empathetically. "Sounds like you've already been an agent. Is that what you did over in Africa?"

"You heard about Africa?"

"I heard you and Hyun talking two nights ago. You weren't the one who helped free all those babies in Liberia, were you?"

"Sort of, I guess. My mom helped me."

"Was she over there with you?"

"No, she gave me a satellite cell phone before I left so I could call her."

"In other words, you rescued those babies by yourself."

"I can't take so much credit. I took surveillance photos and videos which give the government's army permission and reason to raid the warehouse. If you saw it on the news, that was thanks to my mom. Also, one of Mr. Cooper's friends was there in deep cover, but I didn't know that until later."

"So you were the catalyst. You took those photos and videos. How old were you?" Christina asked.

"It was on my seventeenth birthday."

"No way! Wow. I couldn't have done something like that when I was seventeen."

"Would you mind holding the bag open while I scrape out the rest of this mess?"

Christina complied. "You're Pastor Michelman's daughter, aren't you?"

Hadassah looked as if she'd cry again. "Did you know my dad?"

"I've heard your dad speak four or five times at our church, and I loved his teachings, especially the ones on 1 John." Christina looked at the ceiling and grew quiet. She said more than she had intended. "I can't believe I'm almost twice your age. Don't get me wrong, girl, I'm honored to have you here with us."

"Thanks for saying so. After listening to Mr. Cooper give the guidelines last night, I see how much I messed up while on assignments. At least according to God's standard."

"Girl, we've all messed up according to God's standard. If only I could say I messed up doing half of the good you did over in Africa. I'm just glad for God's grace and mercy. And for the cross."

"Me too. I'm almost done here."

"Thanks for braving the maggots. I owe you big time." Christina kept her eyes away from the bag and trashcan while she spoke.

A rumble and a rattle of the dishes told her another earthquake had come, as small as the others recently, but just as unnerving. Hadassah's eyes grew wide and she stood stock still until the shaking ended.

"I didn't know they were here, too," Hadassah whispered.

"They're everywhere, girl. Birth pangs."

Hadassah cringed. "That means the big ones will come soon."

"Unfortunately. Along with the wars and pestilence."

"Do you think His judgments really need to be so severe?"

"Do you think the world would wake up otherwise? I hope it will, but people have been wandering around like drunkards for far too long. They won't wake from their stupor without serious shaking. I want to be here to tell them what they can awake to."

Hadassah smiled. "Yeshua. I think I want to do the same."

"Good, 'cause that's why we're here."

Christina's appetite returned by dinnertime. And she liked this young girl a whole lot more than she did at the beginning of the day. When they arrived back at the house, she couldn't help but eavesdrop on Hadassah's farewell to her mom, that Jewish woman who could intimidate with a mere glance.

Eva Michelman pulled her daughter into an embrace. "I'll be in touch with you through Mr. Cooper."

Hadassah leaned her head on her mom's shoulder. "Please tell me as soon as you learn something."

"I'll e-mail you." Her mom held her tighter. "As long as I know you're safe, I can do what I need to do."

"I'll write too, Mom. I'm going to miss you so much." When tears began to roll down this girl's face, Christina looked away.

"I know, Haddy. I'm going to miss you too. I bought you a few gifts today, but don't open them until you get to the Lighthouse."

***

The following day, Christina and Hadassah worked as office assistants for the leaders of NoCaHoP.

Christina stood at a desk and straightened up the stack of papers she finished collating. "Your mom seems like a really interesting lady."

Hadassah's countenance fell. She thumbed through a stack of teaching notes she needed to organize. "Yeah, you can say that again."

Christina smiled. "She loves you a lot too."

"She's never given me a reason to deny it."

"Grr! Another paper cut." Christina shoved her finger against her clenched teeth then wiped it on her jeans.

"I know. I just got my fifth."

"Shall we go find some bandages?"

"Sure."

On the way back to the van, with bandages on every finger, they discussed how they preferred cleaning since it kept them physically active.

"I hope Mr. Cooper doesn't treat our request as griping." Hadassah fidgeted with her bandages.

"Me too. Maybe we can just show him our hands."

Chapter 17:

The Missing

Hadassah stared out the window as the van took them in a different direction. That night, instead of going back to the house right away, Mr. Cooper arranged for her and a select group of other recruits to meet at New Life Church, one of the churches affiliated with NoCaHoP.

With the popularity of the prayer house and Ronny Gibbons' teaching, Hadassah expected this building to be much larger, at least large enough to accommodate 500 people, if not several thousand. The occupancy sign reading "110" surprised her. The place began to look full with just eleven people.

"I guess Pastor Gibbons likes it small," Priscilla remarked as they wandered the room.

Hadassah stared at the murals meandering around the walls, windows and parts of the ceiling. Pictures of creation interwove with Noah's ark and the story of Abraham. Next she saw some pictures of the Exodus story and the journey through the desert to the Promised Land. She scanned along, observing the whole history of ancient

Israel painted on the walls of the sanctuary, when her eyes caught a depiction of Paul and Silas in prison in Macedonia. An image of Dad's face replaced Paul's. She blinked back the sudden flux of tears until she saw the artist's original painting again, but the parallels between Dad's sufferings and Paul's wouldn't let go of her.

Mrs. Cooper moved chairs to form a circle in the middle of the floor. Hadassah found a seat next to Christina, and ignored the flutter in her heart when Matthew took the seat to her left.

Mr. Cooper sat beside his wife and looked at each face as if to pass on encouragement. "Tonight I'm going to ask you to do one of the hardest things I'll ask all year, but I've gathered you here so you can lay it all on the table together. I want everyone to share who in your family is missing and where he or she was last seen. I hope sharing like this will raise some clues to the surface. I know many of you will be surprised by who knows who. Maleek, will you start us off?"

Maleek's gaze was fixed on the floor. "Yes, sir. My half-brother, Carlos, was with a team in Puerto Vallarta, Mexico. He had just turned eleven when he was kidnapped. We had an argument the night before he left, and I hate to think of how I spoke to him."

Zacharias nodded his head at Maleek, then slumped his broad shoulders and stared at his own large feet. "My sister, Ileyah, went missing in Cairo, Egypt. The last time I saw her, I did not share her faith in Jesus."

Priscilla stared at the floor and waited before speaking, as if she wanted to hide all her emotions first. "My sister, Filipa, was with a team of missionaries when she went missing from Bacolod City in the Philippines."

"My uncle, Pastor Jorgé, and his wife were missionaries in Puerto Vallarta," Pedro said.

"My dad, Pastor Lim Cho, was in Iraq," Matthew said. "He was fresh off the plane in Baghdad and on his way to do a healing service at a new house of prayer twenty minutes south of Baghdad City. Their vehicle was surrounded by insurgents somewhere en route." Gone was Matthew's usual playfulness. Gone was his joking manner. He held his mouth tight and looked at no one in particular. Witnessing his despondency made Hadassah forget her own. Wait— he said Iraq.

The sanctuary fell silent. A thick sort of silence, as sanctuaries sometimes have late at night, but rarely with so many people there. Hadassah scraped at the bandages on her fingers and finally looked away from Matthew. Every eye was on her.

"Oh." Her face colored with embarrassment. She glanced again at Matthew's eyes. "My dad, Pastor Asher Michelman, was also in Iraq." She looked tentatively over at Christina.

Her friend smiled sadly at her. "My dad, too. Pastor Isaac Gallagher."

Hadassah's glance at her friend turned to an incredulous gaze. This woman who she had been working alongside for the past two days was the daughter of Pastor Isaac Gallagher? Pastor Gallagher would often stay at her family's apartment for the weekend and teach at the church in Brooklyn. When she was ten, he had stayed with her family for a week. She recalled detail after detail about that week. He was one of the teachers at the conference when she came forward during an altar call and gave her life to the Lord. But he wasn't the preacher that night. Who was that other preacher?

Hadassah looked at Matthew again and it all came back to her. Matthew's dad, Pastor Lim Cho, was that other preacher.

A clear memory from that week flashed through her mind. It was dawn, and Pastor Cho knelt beside the pull-out couch in the living room, reading his Bible by flashlight and weeping. She wore her favorite footed pajamas and stood on the landing in the half-light peering around the corner, afraid to bother him yet so curious about this behavior. Over breakfast when Hadassah mentioned this, Pastor Cho explained how God had been showing His love to him. When Pastor Cho preached at the conference that evening, Hadassah gave her heart and life to the Lord. She wanted to experience God's love too.

Five months had passed since she last saw Pastor Cho. He had spoken at her church three months before he left with Dad for the Middle East. But here was his son. Matthew didn't look very much like his dad, but he talked like him. Instead of smiling and crying like she wanted to, she attempted Mom's stoic look to hide the pounding in her heart.

"My dad was in Iraq too," Paul said. They were still going around the circle, and the mention of 'Iraq' brought Hadassah right back to the moment. "Alex Howell."

"You mean the prophet, Alex Howell?" Hadassah asked.

"That's him," Paul replied sadly.

She also remembered Alex Howell, who had come to her church three times a year when she was younger. Paul looked so much like his dad, and he had the same quiet demeanor.

Hyun's face looked more stolid than usual. "My mother, Sun Xi, was also taken hostage in Iraq. I was on the phone with her when her vehicle was surrounded. There are still no news reports about this attack and no answers from anyone in the State Department."

In the necessary but awkward silence following Hyun's words, a mix of anxiousness and sorrow clung to the air Hadassah breathed. Maleek's knees bounced up and down. Matthew, with both elbows on his knees, gripped his hair in his fists. Christina rubbed the end of her long braid against the palm of her hand and stared stoically at the wall. Priscilla fixed her gaze on the carpet and gripped the sides of her chair until her knuckles turned white. Scraping at the edges of her bandages, Hadassah chewed the side of her tongue and fought tears, each breath taking every ounce of strength in her.

After a few minutes of silence, Mr. Cooper spoke again. "R.S.O has a mission beyond finding your family members, but I wanted to let you know we'll be making this a priority. I have friends who are hunting down details on each one of your relatives. Let us pray."

After Aaron finished speaking, Hadassah had no desire to talk about it further. Not tonight. But she felt closer to everyone here after sharing like this. And her mind churned away theories connecting all the disappearances.

Chapter 18:

Paul

Closing his Bible and his eyes, Paul sank deep into prayer. Since the death of his mom and the disappearance of his dad, he felt like an orphan, and last night at the church reminded him of this. He drank in the promise from Jesus again, "I will not leave you as orphans, I will come to you."

At least he had Matt as his partner for the week.

As soon as he thought of Matt, he looked up and saw his friend walking through the doorway of the guys' room.

"Yo, dude, you're gonna waste away if you keep skipping breakfast." Matt chuckled as he rummaged through his bag and pulled out a sweater.

Paul glanced down at his thick stomach line. "It'll take skipping many more meals before anything like that happens. Is breakfast done?"

"Scraped clean, dude. There might be an apple left, but I doubt it, since Adam and Dave are in the house."

"Did Mr. Cooper hand out the list for the day?"

"Yup. We're building a handicap ramp in the Mount Olivet community."

"Is that the new community with all the house churches?"

"There are way too many house churches springing up to keep track of them. But Mr. Cooper gave some clear directions for building this ramp, so it won't take all day."

***

Matt's hammering beat in time with Paul's heavy thoughts about the disappearances.

"So, whatcha think of the new recruits?" Matt asked, interrupting Paul's heady processing.

"Aye, they're fine, I'd say."

Matt burst with laughter.

"What?"

"You. Yer still talking like an Irishman when you haven't been there in how many years?" Matt's attempt at a brogue was embarrassing.

"Seven. But I spent half my life there."

"Okay, but 'fine' doesn't tell me what you think about them."

"Who?"

"You're avoiding my question, bro. I know you're a prophet like your dad."

"But I never use it for gossip."

"Fair enough. And a good rule to live by."

Paul looked up from his hammering. "You thinking of someone in particular?"

"Hadassah."

"Pastor Michelman's daughter? Sure, she's cute as a button, but did you see her mom? She was terrifying. Chances are her daughter will end up the same."

"I know." Matt grinned.

"I didn't know you liked that in a girl."

"To be terrified by a glance? I love a challenge."

"Don't you remember what Mr. Cooper told us the other night? We're not supposed to look at the girls if we want to stay with R.S.O."

"I know, dude. I ain't gonna blow my only chance to find my dad and to work with R.S.O. because of a girl. But I've never met anyone like her before."

Paul looked up at his friend and grunted.

"Yo, I'm serious about R.S.O., so don't think I'll blow it now."

"Then get those dreamy eyes out of your head."

As if the wood weighed no more than a few sheets of paper, Matt carted over three large slabs of plywood and laid them on the frame. "I got to meet Pastor Michelman before he left with my dad."

Glancing up and down the ramp, Paul pondered where he would begin nailing down the plywood first. Then he looked up at his friend. "Yeah, Pastor Michelman was a great speaker."

"Would you stop talking about them in past tense? They're alive and I'm gonna find them: your dad, her dad, my dad, Hyun's mom, Christina's dad. And you're gonna help me."

Paul picked up the nail gun and fired a few shots, securing one of the slabs to the frame. The air compressor kicked on and whirred louder than his thoughts, calming the thunder in his heart. He nailed the next slab to the frame, firing the gun over and over until the compressor's whir lulled to silence. Thankfully, having the prophetic gift didn't mean he saw the future clearly. Maybe Matthew was right. But hope wrestled with the fear that he really was an orphan. "Who do you think is responsible for all the disappearances?"

"I take it you think it's one person, too."

"Or some diabolical league. Nine days have passed and we still can't convince a government official anywhere to take the disappearances seriously. This is America, where missing persons are supposed to matter. It's like there's this big cover-up."

"Careful, dude, you're starting to sound like a conspiracy theorist."

"You mean I'm starting to sound like you?"

Matt measured off the last piece of plywood. "Or Mr. Cooper. But is that so bad? Did you hear the news about the Prime Minister over in Jordan?"

"You mean Fahd Afsal? No, what?"

"He took power late yesterday after a plane crash killed the king and his family. You know he was the Minister of Aviation before his appointment as Prime Minister, right?"

Paul almost doubled over, as if the news was a kick to his stomach.

Matt grimaced and looked up at him. "You thinking what I'm thinking?"

"That it wasn't an accident? My goodness, the one morning I skip reading CNN's website." He shook his head. "But do you really think this Prime Minister wielded so much power before this coup to have orchestrated the attacks in Iraq last week?"

"He just killed his king, dude."

This time Paul grimaced, shut his eyes, then relaxed his fist. "Okay, so maybe I wouldn't put it past him. I'm surprised Mr. Cooper didn't tell everyone over breakfast."

"He didn't tell everyone, but he did tell a few of us second years. And if you remember, you skipped breakfast, bro."

"But you think the kidnappings are linked to this Prime Minister?"

"Who else?"

"Iran. Syria. Russia. China. Libya. Need I go on?"

"What about the pope?"

Paul shook his head. "Leo XIV? He's been the pope, what, six months? And he's not much older than we are; he never should have been chosen as pope. I think scheming of that scale might be beyond him."

Matt shrugged. "Or it might not. He rose to power awfully young, and through what scheming?"

"Yeah, he does have a weaselly look to him."

Chapter 19: Jealousy

When she woke early on Friday morning, Hadassah sat up in her makeshift bed and pulled her Bible into her lap. Everyone was still asleep, except for Christina, who had stepped out the door only a moment before. Hadassah stared at the cover of her Bible and whispered a prayer past the grogginess consuming her brain. It had been a long week. She desired more than ever to read and pray as much as possible before everyone woke.

She opened her Bible and switched on the tiny book light, illuminating the first page she opened to. Psalm 119 stared at her, in all its long, majestic musings on the beauty of the law. Her eyes swirled, glancing at this longest chapter in the Bible. They came to focus on the next Psalm, 120, a short one she had hardly read before. She fixated on the second verse: "Save me, LORD, from lying lips and from deceitful tongues." The writer of the Psalm probably had a different meaning in mind, but the lying lips she wanted salvation from were her own. It had taken all of her concentration this week to keep from lying, and she couldn't keep it up. *There has to be a better way.* She focused her thoughts into a prayer. She would have skipped breakfast, except she didn't know what to anticipate for the workday.

During the rush for food, Hadassah sat at the far end of the common room staring at her plate of stewed apples and scrambled eggs while she ate. Both heart and mind lagged with exhaustion.

"So, how many languages do you speak?"

She looked up to see Matthew standing beside her. The pace of her heart suddenly quickened.

"You looked so lonely all the way over here, I figured I'd finally come over and talk to you."

She covered her mouth with her hand to hide both her smile and her bite of food. "Hello."

Matthew used his foot to kick a chair into a spin and sat down with the back of it against his chest and his arms perched atop the metal frame. "I'll get the boring stuff out of the way while you're a captive audience. I only speak four languages, but I'm learning Arabic and Farsi. Paul, Zeke, Pedro, Maleek and I have been training with R.S.O. for a year, but I've known most of those dudes for forever. And I've known Mr. Cooper for years. He started training me before the idea of R.S.O. came about. Both my dad and my mom insisted. My family's been friends with the Coopers for nine years, which is literally half my life. Okay, my boring life is all discussed. Your turn, yo."

She swallowed a mouthful of bagel. "I'm still eating."

"Alright, then. So, I heard you've been to Liberia. I went there with Mr. Cooper last August."

She lifted her gaze to meet his. "I know. I saw you in the market in Monrovia."

"I wish I'd seen you."

"Did you meet Andrew Blessing?"

He cast his glance down at the carpet.

In that awkward silence which followed, she wished she hadn't have asked.

He looked up again. "One more year till God releases us to bring His justice and freedom to people. Are you looking forward to it?" His sudden grin filled her with mirroring determination.

Nodding in agreement, she swallowed her last bite before she should have. "I am. I feel at home working out there, not inside walls." She smiled.

"Hey, do you think we'll ever be on assignment together?"

She caught herself smiling and nodding, as if this was all she knew how to do.

"And I might even be able to keep up with you out there, girl."

This time she gave a coy grin. "Oh, you think you're that stealth?"

He nudged her shoulder playfully with his elbow. "Yeah, you're right, probably not."

She wanted the conversation to continue, but the van going to the prayer room was ready to leave.

Hadassah and Christina spent half the day cleaning up the prayer room and healing rooms at NoCaHoP. Matthew consumed her daydreams, even the ones about rescuing Dad. For this reason she spent her afternoon break soaking in the presence of the Lord. This time alone with God refreshed her.

She was falling in love with Yeshua. As she sat in the prayer room, she longed for His return more than she longed for anything. "Come, Yeshua," she whispered until love for Him flooded her being. She couldn't imagine a better gift than to love the Lord.

On the way back to the house for their last night there, Mr. Cooper informed everyone that not many of them could look forward to a hot shower.

"Too many are too grimy," Mr. Cooper said. The largest group of recruits had cleaned in the low income housing neighborhood.

"I don't mind taking a warm shower," Lisa said. "I mean, if it's a burden on anyone to try to figure out who goes first."

Matthew nudged Lisa with his elbow. "It's not a burden to me, dude."

Watching him joke around like this, a fascination for Matthew welled up in Hadassah's heart. She was quite sure, after hearing the guidelines spelled out three times already, that boyfriend and girlfriend relationships between recruits were discouraged. But no one ever made her feel the way he did, none from her church in New York and certainly no one from high school. Hadassah wanted to know more about him than about anyone else she had ever met.

Was Mrs. Cooper safe to talk to? Would the Coopers kick her out of the program? *Management of emotion is the best way to deal with this.* She could control fear while on assignments, why not this?

All night, during a long, dark wrestling through prayer, she attempted this strategy of management. At least Matthew didn't show any more interest in her.

By 3:00am she had tossed and turned more than she could bear and quietly crept past all the sleeping, snoring, dreaming girls. Nightlights in the hallway helped her find the stairs in the huge house. Not a creak all the way down the hall nor on the stairs. She sighed. She wanted some time completely alone; the presence of people, either sleeping or awake, clouded her thinking.

The flickering amber glow on the walls of the kitchen told her at least someone was still awake. She stopped at the foot of the stairs and listened. She didn't want to disturb anyone—perhaps they sought solitude as well—but if no one stirred, she would blow out the candles. Not a sound. She made her way into the kitchen, stood over the two candles and inhaled deeply to blow them both out at once.

"Don't blow out the candles yet." The urgent whisper was Christina's voice.

"I'm sorry." Hadassah searched the darker part of the common room for her friend. "I didn't think anyone else was awake."

"I was getting ready to go to sleep."

"Yo, me too." This second voice was Matthew's. Hadassah felt her head and heart spin in opposite directions. The surge of jealousy she fought lingered like a silk scarf wrapped tight around her neck.

"Tomorrow will be a long day." Christina sighed. "I know I won't be able to sleep in the van all the way to the Lighthouse."

"Mr. Cooper will be handing out eye masks to everyone so no one knows how to get back there if we bail out early," Matthew said. "You'll be able to sleep, girl."

"Oh, the things you contrive, Matt," Christina whispered back.

Matthew laughed one of his louder laughs, the kind that bounced off the walls so the whole room laughed with him, and his eyes trained on Hadassah in that dim light. He winked at her then looked back at Christina. "You think I'm joking? Well, just wait and see."

Christina chuckled. "You going to bed, Mr. Insomnia?" She placed a hand on his arm as she spoke.

At this gesture of familiarity, Hadassah's rising jealousy crawled across her skin like a scorpion.

"Oy vey!" He winked at Hadassah a second time. "I suppose. If I can. Who knows? I may get an hour or two yet."

"How about you?" Christina asked her.

She peeled her gaze from Matthew, dreading the idea of looking straight at Christina. "I can't sleep." At least this was honest.

"Are you anxious about tomorrow?"

"Probably." She couldn't tell, under the mountain of other emotions, if this was the truth. What did she tell herself about emotional management?

"I gotta find the guys' room." Matthew's voice cracked and pitched as he spoke. "Good night, Hadassah." His smile at her danced nervously across his face. "Yo, thanks for talking, Christina." He turned and nearly crashed into an end table, playing off his misstep with a fluttering laugh.

"Any time, Matt. Come on, Hadassah, let's go upstairs."

"I will." But she didn't move. Not when Matthew left, nor when Christina blew out the candles, leaving Hadassah to rely on starlight and a sliver of a moon. She groped in the dark for a seat, but when she found the couch, she sat on the carpet instead and stared out the sliding glass doors upon a clear night sky. It reminded her of Liberia, except this sky wasn't as clear with the city lights of Greensboro tinging it orange.

Christina placed a gentle hand on her shoulder. "You okay?"

In her exhaustion, Hadassah merely groaned her response and scraped at the tips of her fingers.

"Are you sick?"

"I don't know." This blow to her heart felt like sickness. If she allowed herself she really could get sick.

"Were you thinking about Africa again?"

Can I say yes without lying? She looked up at the stars again. "Yeah." She gave a little cough to clear her throat of the desire to stay silent. "I was remembering the night I spent in the tree waiting for my mom's friend. The stars were different."

"I remember one night in Afghanistan when I got disconnected from my regiment and had to hole up in a tiny cave until dawn. It's a frightening thing to be so lost and alone in a foreign country."

"It was beautiful at the same time." Feelings of competition rose within her.

"I'm amazed you were able to find beauty in the situation. All I felt was terror, huddled all by myself until the sun came up. I have a lot to learn from you, Hadassah."

Hadassah hated feeling patronized. She gave no response.

"I hope you don't think Matt and I were doing anything we shouldn't."

She mustered up as much truth as she could. "I didn't know what to think."

"He needed to talk. I can understand if it looked strange, walking in on the two of us talking by candlelight at three in the morning but I assure you it wasn't at all what you think. He wanted to talk to someone who wouldn't gossip."

"Are you saying this because you hope I'll keep it secret about you and Matt?"

"You're my friend, Hadassah, so I won't manipulate you. And second of all, he's eleven years younger than me, and like a brother at that. All I'm saying is I keep secret what my friends tell me."

Jealousy still gripped Hadassah's heart despite Christina's reassurances. "It's okay," Hadassah mumbled, even though it wasn't. It might be again one day, so it wasn't entirely a lie. Out of the corner of her eye she saw the gleam of starlight off Christina's teeth. The woman had such perfect teeth, while Hadassah's... she should have had braces but opted out. Now she wished she hadn't.

"Here." Christina handed Hadassah an iPod. "It's retro, but it still works, and it has a good mix. I have the whole library of Nicole C. Mullen's music, if you like her. I know a lot of it's older, but it's classic. And here's an album of some hymns beautifully redone by Abigail Zsiga—I like this album when I'm yearning for stillness. You can look through the lists if you want. I know when I'm anxious or upset the music calms me."

"Me too." She didn't want to take the iPod, but figured she had been offensive enough already. "Thanks."

She stared at the pale LED screen and shuffled through the library. The playlist names intrigued her: *broken heart, cradled, in the mist, on a red dawn, racing thoughts* and *when it snows*. She chose *cradled*, for she wanted to be. The sound of Misty Edwards's voice on the first song evoked a tear. "Simple Devotion" was one of Dad's favorite songs. She prayed for Dad within her throbbing sorrow. In the arms of God, her Abba Father, she felt cradled indeed. Although her heart ebbed and flowed with a chaos of emotion, she felt a stillness in the core of her being. And although her body shook, as if in echo of her emotions and as if she was outside on this cold

January night instead of inside this warm house, she grew aware of the Lord. She tried her best to steer away from anger and accusation. And her fingertips felt as raw as her heart. She rubbed them against her teeth as she tried to reel in her thoughts. In her heart stood a throne and the Lord, her Lord, sat upon it.

"This hurts," she told Him. "This hurts so much. How did all this happen so fast?"

***

Mrs. Cooper woke Hadassah from the common room floor at 5:30am. "I thought you were hurt or sick, honey. If I didn't see those earphones on you I'd have feared the worst."

"Sorry," Hadassah confessed. "I couldn't sleep upstairs. I kept thinking all these negative thoughts last night."

Mrs. Cooper sighed. "I should've made myself more available. I suspect you weren't the only one to feel the barbs of the enemy last night. We have an enemy in the unseen realm, honey, and he ain't happy about what y'all are gettin' ready to do. Never mind slave owners who find out you're busting in to free their captives. But right now, girl, you can help me make the coffee and toast the bagels." She giggled. "That'll be warfare enough for the morning. And perhaps you can share your trials with me so I can pray for you."

"I'm not... I don't really know how to explain it. Does the enemy make you like someone you're not supposed to?"

"Ah." Mrs. Cooper looked at her in a delicate and motherly way. "You talkin' 'bout one of the young men here, ain't ya?"

"Matthew," Hadassah whispered.

"What was that, love?"

Hadassah didn't know if she had the courage to repeat his name. "Oh, one of the guys here, yeah." She began to scrape at her raw fingertips again.

"It sounded like you said Matthew."

"I did." She surveyed the room again to make sure no one else overheard. She was angry and smitten at the same time and wanted to untangle her emotions privately rather than under scrutiny.

"If y'all were a little older, and the nature of R.S.O. was any different, I'd say to try and see how it works out, especially with a young man of God like Matthew. But, honey, I can't encourage it at all. If not dating seems too much of a burden, then by all means we'll help you get back to New York today."

"I can't go back to New York even if I wanted to. But I'd like to stay here if I can."

"Then I'll pray with you."

Hadassah stuffed bagels into the toaster slots. Of all the advances in technology over the last century and a half, why were toaster slots always too thin for bagels? *And why do I think about these things when asked about my emotions?* She reeled her thoughts back.

"I'd like that." Her body shuddered as she fought the lump in her throat. A single tear escaped. Then two. Then two more. She wiped them off on her shoulder and tried to butter a few of the bagels popping up. Tears in her throat and heat on her fingers dosed reality to her.

Mrs. Cooper placed a comforting arm around her shoulders. "Your tears aren't weakness, Hadassah. You're the first of the new recruits to be this honest with me. Lord, I ask: Would You strengthen this young woman in her inmost being? Would You set Your angels around her to protect her? Would You teach Hadassah how to guard her heart, where You sit on the throne? We ask this in the precious Name of Jesus, Amen."

Other team members began to show up in search of coffee, lured, perhaps, by the scent of toasted bagels. Hadassah rubbed the rest of her tears off on her shoulder.

Mrs. Cooper put an arm around her. "Sugar, you just make sure you run to God and not from Him whenever you're strugglin', okay?"

Hadassah lowered her eyes. "Thanks, Mrs. Cooper."

"Pass it on, honey, pass it on. Y'all could use a flow of encouragement in the ranks."

Andrea shuffled toward the percolator with eyes half open. "I could use a flow of *coffee.* I love you to pieces, Lisa, but you snored like a freight train last night, and knowing we'd be leaving early—I don't think I slept five minutes."

Lifting her eyes, Hadassah saw Priscilla show her first small smile since the girl arrived. The sight of this smile yanked her out of brooding.

Lisa stretched her arms high and wide. "I slept enough to feel beautiful. You should all try snoring—it works wonders at keeping me asleep through the night."

Tameka gasped. "One snorer is enough. I hope the rumor is true about Mr. Cooper doling out eye masks in the van."

"We could use ear plugs as well," Hyun commented dryly amid a chorus of cheers and laughter.

"I will tell y'all this," Mrs. Cooper said, "you ladies have an hour to clean the upstairs, gentlemen, the downstairs. Make sure y'all have your belongings out to the vans by 7:30am, or it'll go to Mrs. Gibbons' charity come Monday. Grab bagels and coffee and go, go, go people!"

"That's what I like to hear," Mr. Cooper said, "the Missus taking charge first thing in the morning and lighting a fire under everyone." He filled his coffee cup and lifted it toward his wife before taking a sip. "Go, Mrs. Cooper."

With the house cleaned and the vans packed, Hadassah gathered with everyone to pray before leaving. Then the weary group piled in wherever they found space and readied themselves for the journey. Hadassah found an empty seat between Paul and Priscilla, whom she had hardly spoken with since she arrived five days ago. She was glad for the reprieve from jokes and socializing after the morning rush, since her wrestling with anger and jealousy had intensified over bagels and coffee.

Mr. Cooper came by with a box of eye masks for everyone. Thankfully this rumor was true—she wanted an excuse to hide at least half of her face. Settling down in her seat, she forced herself to sleep while Paul quietly prayed in the Spirit beside her.

"So the masks weren't a rumor after all," Priscilla remarked, but Hadassah remembered nothing else until they arrived at the Lighthouse.

Hadassah felt Priscilla shake her gently awake.

"We're here." The girl was entirely gracious about the line of drool extending from the corner of Hadassah's mouth to her shoulder. She didn't even wipe it off.

Thoroughly embarrassed, Hadassah could hardly look Priscilla in the eye. "I'm so sorry."

"There's no need." She smiled a second time. "It happens to everyone."

Part 2

I do not run like someone running aimlessly; I do not fight like a boxer beating the air. No, I strike a blow to my body and make it my slave so that after I have preached to others, I myself will not be disqualified for the prize.

~ the Apostle Paul
1 Corinthians 9:26-27

Chapter 20:

The Lighthouse

Hadassah stumbled and staggered out of the van, still half asleep, and gathered with everyone else around the new guy. The man looked forty-five or fifty years old and stood like a general waiting for his army in front of this camp called the Lighthouse. His dog, a chocolate Labrador, sat alert beside him.

"Everyone, I'd like you to meet Lawrence Murray," Mr. Cooper said. "Some of you may have met him already, but for those who have not, I'm Mr. Murray's right hand man. He's the real deal. While I've been rounding you up and going over the basics, Mr. Murray has been cleaning the campgrounds, finishing the electrical and bathing this place in prayer. He's at least half the brains and more than half the brawn behind R.S.O., and now that we're here, I'll let him take charge. Murray?"

Unlike many military or paramilitary personnel, Mr. Murray was overshadowed by the presence of the Lord; he seemed to have a glow about him. When he started off with prayer, Hadassah felt strong conviction, especially about her anger and jealousy. She knew instinctively these emotions were unhealthy, and now she knew why. They needed teamwork at R.S.O. for the safety of everyone. Her jealousy undermined the whole ethos of the organization.

Mr. Murray surveyed everyone's faces with both scrutiny and compassion. "The first thing I'm going to ask of you is to help with the cleaning. We purchased this camp at a really good price because no one wanted it. You'll see why in a few minutes, but first I want to show you where the rubber boots, overalls, and shovels are. Now, I'm sure I don't have everyone's sizes right, and you're welcome to use your own boots if you'd like, but I wouldn't. By the way, the dog's Boaz. If you introduce yourself to him slowly, he'll be your friend for life. If you move too quick when he's meeting you he'll be suspicious of you from here on out and will bark when you approach. For now, he stays with me. The rest of you can follow me too."

He led them over to the tool shed set on a hill from which they could survey the buildings below. There were two rows of log cabins, none more than 250 square feet, with twelve cabins altogether; a large, green dumpster sat in between the rows of cabins.

At the end of rows there was a two story building, also built from logs. It was lined with wide decks and porches and boasted a chimney with the inviting sight of smoke rising and wisping through the delicate breeze. The lampposts on each side of the entry path added to the welcome this building exuded. Mr. Murray had even hung a 'Welcome to the Lighthouse' banner between the lampposts.

Hadassah began to get 'camp' excitement, remembering those summer weeks away from her parents as a child. The Lighthouse looked slightly littered, but compared with her expectations, it wasn't so bad. Everyone turned to Mr. Murray again for the next directions.

"Now I know you want rest after a long week and several hours in a van, but I can't promise you rest. But I will promise, after you've cleaned your respective cabins, you'll have new mattresses for your cots and a hot dinner in the Lodge. I've cleaned the kitchen already, and I cleaned the cook's quarters."

"Um," Amelia broke in, raising her hand.

"Yes?" Mr. Murray asked.

"First of all, thanks for cleaning my quarters, and secondly, can I go by 'chef' instead of 'cook'?"

Mr. Murray narrowed his eyes at her. "Are you ready for that weight of expectation? If we give you the title 'chef', we'll expect delicious."

Amelia grinned in return. "I went to culinary school for that weight of expectation, sir. I look forward to the challenge."

"Then we look forward to being the guinea pigs," he said, with a quick half smile. "Especially those of us who ate what the army cooks prepared."

Loud laughs burst from the former military personnel.

"Seriously though, Chef, your cabin mates will assist you in the kitchen tonight. That will be…" he paused to check the clipboard, "Lisa and Hannah. You'll have a lot of setting up to do in the kitchen, but you'll find ingredients in the fridge and on the counter. You three can go ahead now.

"And for the rest of you—as soon as I call your name, and the name of your cabin mate, step over here, choose your boots, shovel and overalls and Mr. Cooper will give you your cabin key. Ezekiel and Paul; Maleek, Pedro and Zacharias; David and Matthew; Hadassah and Rose; Christina, Andrea and Priscilla; Robert and Adam; Hyun and Tameka. That's everyone. I recommend you be white glove meticulous. I'll come around with cleaning supplies as soon as you're done with the shovels."

On the porch of Hadassah and Rose's cabin there were four pairs of gloves: two pairs of thick work gloves and two pairs of yellow rubber gloves. There were also face masks, but Hadassah doubted she needed one—until she and Rose opened the door. Even in the cold the stench was pungent; she wondered if it wouldn't be better to burn the place down and rebuild. It was a smell somewhere between dead rodents and rotten bananas. *Did I gripe yesterday?*

Rose's eyes welled up. "I don't think I can do this, Hadassah."

Holding her breath, Hadassah surveyed the cabin again. She quickly closed the door. Her brief glance had revealed to her a two-foot thick pile of everything from candy wrappers and rotting food to animal droppings and campfire ashes. There had to be ten to twelve touristy t-shirts mixed into the heap, decomposing at the same rate as the banana peels. She looked at Rose as soon as she caught her breath. "We'll do it together. I'll fill the trash bags if you run them to the dumpster."

"Are you sure you want to?" Rose asked.

"*Want?* No, but I don't mind the gross jobs. I have a tough stomach."

"You must have a stomach of steel. But thank you. I really, truly owe you one."

"There will be lots of opportunity over the next few months, I'm sure." She lifted the latch but held the door closed a moment more. "I'll need one of those face masks."

The persistent jealousy regarding Matthew provided fuel for her work. By the time she had filled the fifteenth bag, the sun shone through the bare branches of trees at the west of the campgrounds. She had taken off her sweater and continued to sweat in just a long-sleeve t-shirt, but she was well over halfway through and didn't want to stop. Meanwhile, Rose scrubbed the outside, ran bags to the dumpster, and brought refills of drinking water back. Hadassah wondered if she had even an hour of daylight left, but didn't dare take a break long enough to remove her gloves and look at her watch.

Even in the cool January air, sweat dripped down her brow and along her face until she could taste it. Her hair fell out of its ponytail and wisped into her eyelashes more than a few times. But the rancid smell was diminishing, finally.

Mr. Murray came by to check on their progress when she had finished her eighteenth bag. "You weren't planning on sleeping on your porch, were you?"

"I might enjoy the fresh air." Hadassah donned her best smile. Even if Mr. Murray couldn't see the smile behind the mask, he might be able to hear it. "But it's a little cold outside so I'm going to have to keep going."

"I like your determination, but David and Matthew are coming to help you. They need some help sanitizing their cabin, and it looks like you need a change of pace."

Hadassah took off her gloves and mopped her forehead with the back of her forearm before looking at her hands. Two of her five blisters had popped. "Wow. That's gonna hurt tomorrow."

"Andrea, the nurse, is with Mrs. Cooper at the first aid station near the dumpster," Mr. Murray said. "Make sure you drink some more water before you start cleaning."

"Yes, sir." She leaned her shovel against the wall and staggered out toward the porch stairs, trying to leave before Matthew got there. The breeze was so refreshing. And what invigorating smell rode on it? Perhaps the surrounding forest? A river?

Matthew stood at the foot of the porch stairs with his hand extended toward her. She stared at it as if he offered a live electrical wire.

"Can I help you down the stairs?" Matthew was grinning at her.

She shook her head no, but said, "Sure, thanks," convincing herself it was merely a gentlemanly gesture, and she was trembling too much to refuse. He was so gentle with her blistered hand. And his smile lit up the sunset.

"We'll make sure you have a place to sleep tonight. Somewhere the bears won't get you."

Hadassah stepped down gingerly. "Are there really bears here?"

Dave laughed loudly. "We wouldn't want to chance it. Well, actually, *I* would, but we wouldn't want to chance you young ladies. You can prove to us you're tough in other ways."

As soon as she stepped down, she let go of Matthew's hand quickly. Too quickly. One more of her blisters popped and smeared his hand, mortifying her almost to silence. "I'm so sorry!"

Matthew looked at his hand, then hers, then laughed rapturously. "Aww, I'm the one who's sorry, girl." He shrugged his shoulders then winked. "I hear it's the best way to become friends."

She lingered with Mrs. Cooper and Andrea at the first aid station longer than she intended, trying to shake off the embarrassment of her encounter with Matthew while Andrea covered all the blisters.

Rose had already been cleaning the other cabin for half an hour before Hadassah joined her. She must have wanted to make up for not helping with the shoveling; the place smelled like a swimming pool and resembled sanitary.

"The bathroom is done." Rose didn't even pause as she scrubbed a desk. "I'm cleaning the bureaus and desks. Do you want to wash the bed frames before we wash the floor? Hey, what happened to your hands?"

Hadassah looked at her bandages. "Just a few burst blisters. It'll callous before I know it."

"I hope so. Thanks, by the way. It was kind of you not to say anything."

"Don't mention it."

"I was thinking—why don't we pray for Dave and Matt while we clean their cabin?"

"Sure. Why don't you start?"

While she wondered the whole time whether or not this was appropriate, Hadassah scrubbed the thick wooden bed frames and prayed with Rose for the men who would sleep there. But Rose's prayers were hard to disagree with:

"Lord, keep them pure, both in heart and in mind, and keep them under the shadow of Your wing. Give them each a greater love for You and for Your word, and a deeper revelation of Your heart."

By the time Hadassah and Rose turned back to their own cabin, Christina and Priscilla had joined Matthew and Dave. All four of them were scrubbing the place on their hands and knees: walls, floor, furniture and the small bathroom. How thoroughly the cabin was transformed from when Hadassah had first opened the door—from even an hour before.

"I hope this pays the debt for the maggoty trash cans." Christina beamed at her.

"Thanks." Hadassah fought another swell of jealousy toward her friend. "You didn't owe me."

Matthew looked up from scrubbing one of the bureaus. "Wait, what maggoty trash cans?"

"On Thursday's workday she cleaned three trash cans with maggots crawling in them because I couldn't stomach it. And she did it without getting sick once. I was impressed."

Hadassah's face grew red. "It was nothing, really. Hey, how did all of you have time to help us?"

Priscilla looked up, her face glowing with a quiet joy. "Mr. Murray said you two were the most behind. We finished ours almost an hour ago."

"Are you unpacked, too?" Rose asked.

Christina stopped scrubbing and wiped her brow on her arm. "Mr. Cooper didn't want anyone to get bags from the van until we could all get them together."

"Well, thanks so much," Rose said. "I'm glad Hadassah didn't say it, but it's mostly my fault we were so behind."

Mr. Cooper stood at the door carrying one mattress while Mr. Murray held the other. "Are you ready for the mattresses yet? I suspect we're going to hear the dinner bell any moment now, since Amelia was almost done when we looked in on her. Yup, there it is."

With a glance around the cabin Mr. Murray sniffed the air twice.

"It smells so much better in here. I think you two got the worst of the cabins."

Hadassah laughed nervously. "We suspected so, but didn't want to say it first."

Mr. Cooper set the mattress into the frame. "Just so none of you thinks Mr. Murray lazy, the dining hall and offices in the Lodge looked twice as bad when we first bought the place."

***

Amelia had proved her culinary skills when they all sat to dinner in the Lodge. Each plate had liver and onions sautéed to perfection, with a side of mashed potatoes that melted in Hadassah's mouth. On the table was a salad of romaine, spinach and dried cranberries with a strawberry vinaigrette—a perfect melding of light, sweet and tart with the rich main course.

Most everyone was too hungry and the food too good for there to be conversation. Christina, however, laughed loudly after the first bite and exclaimed, "Worth it! Thank you, Amelia!"

This produced laughter from Amelia and "Thank you!" from everyone else.

"Tonight, everyone washes their own dishes so we can all get some sleep," Mr. Cooper announced. "In the morning we'll meet here for breakfast and worship. Then you'll have a free day before we begin on Monday."

***

Hadassah slept most of the free day. Her arms ached and her

blistered hands throbbed unless she was sound asleep. Having church at the dining hall with this group was delightful, but none of the sore recruits expressed themselves too wildly. Tameka sang an old song, one of Misty Edwards's—"Beautiful Heart," all about Jesus' humility and meekness. Her version was just as ethereal as the original. Hadassah sang it in her dreams.

When she woke from a nap in the late afternoon, she opened the large box of parting gifts from Mom. Three wool hats, four pairs of wool-lined leather gloves, three coats fit for Siberian winters, a pair of snow boots, an all-in-one pocket tool kit, a deck of cards (*They fold out into maps of different cities*, the accompanying note said), the slim LED flashlight that fit in the little pocket of her new boots, and a set of mirrors and magnifying glasses of varying strength which fit into a case no larger than a compact (*Because you never know*, the note said). She missed Mom so much already. She packed the gifts away under her bed with the rest of her belongings and went back to sleep again.

***

The whistle to wake everyone came earlier than expected on Monday morning, and Mr. Murray's voice rang loud and clear over the megaphone:

"Ten minutes to roll call! Everyone up! Greet the day. Remember, His mercies are new."

The jackhammer pounding of Hadassah's heart made waking even more painful. *I could use some of that new mercy, Abba.* She felt sorer than the day before.

Rose had already turned the light on and was stretching. "Mind if I use the bathroom first?"

Hadassah marveled at Rose's cheerfulness. "Go ahead." She propped herself up on her elbows and smiled at her cabin-mate. "I like what you've done with the place."

Rose had decorated the walls with tasteful and beautiful art, and the accompanying scripture verses were poignant. The one over her dresser read, 'You shall love the Lord your God with all of your heart, all of your mind, all of your soul and all of your strength.' She remembered one of Dad's sermons. This verse was prophecy as much as command; she would be given power to love the Lord as much as she desired to love Him. As quickly as she thought this, it transported her back to her usual seat in the Brooklyn church, watching Dad give his sermon. In her mind's eye he looked so handsome, so confident, so thankful for the ability to love the Lord. She longed, suddenly, to be able to love God with the same devotion. She lowered her aching body to her knees beside her bed and asked the Lord to fill her with this love.

A vision, brief but thorough, streamed through her. Children all across the globe trapped in gross slavery, women kidnapped, men held hostage, and Jews, her own flesh and blood, sold for a kilo of coke, a bottle of ecstasy or even a loaf of bread. "Love Me," she heard in the vision. "Love Me. Love Me."

"Yes, Lord, I will," she replied aloud, and wept. She suddenly knew why He could ask her for this. *Because He loves me with all of His heart, all of His mind, all of His soul, all of His strength.*

When the door of the bathroom opened again, Hadassah pushed herself to her feet and pulled her newly issued fatigues into the bathroom, wiping her cheeks of tears along the way. By the time she stood under the stream from the shower, she had set her resolve to her Abba Father's will. Her Abba Father's will! Where Saturday's anger and jealousy jolted her then left her exhausted, this proved to strengthen and awaken every weary muscle and sinew.

Chapter 21:

Classified Lessons

Hadassah opened her eyes and looked around the empty cabin on yet another Monday morning. Three months had slipped by like a spy plane over Russia.

At least Rose left the decorations on the walls when she moved back home, a pleasant reminder of the sweet girl. She understood why Rose had to go. That bout of the flu was terrible. Her own fever took three days to leave.

Three months in and Hadassah still awoke sore every morning. Mr. Murray seemed to want their limits pushed as much as possible. Stretching her stiff muscles, she glanced at the pile of clean fatigues that needed to last the week. She determined to get to the shower before Mr. Murray's voice sounded through the megaphone, but her weary body employed every Monday morning excuse.

Too late.

"Rise and shine, morning glories! Roll call in ten minutes."

Another quick shower, but this became second nature two months ago.

She stepped down from the porch and into line between Tameka and Hyun before the first hints of sunrise kissed the sky. The routine push-ups and pull-ups were much easier without blisters covering her hands. Those first few days were unforgettable with throbbing, soreness and stabbing pain threatening all her steadfastness. Now there was just a constant dull ache in her refining muscles.

"How'd you sleep?" Tameka asked, panting during the pause between the 1,020 sit-ups. She spoke in Tagalog, their language for the month.

"I slept well. How about you?" Last month's Italian was much easier, but she was starting to get the gist of this language. At least Priscilla tutored her. But all this talking was agony when her abs groaned.

"Pretty well. Hyun and I had the last laundry tickets last night, so we were up late." Tameka gave a genuine smile. How she could produce it at this hour, Hadassah simply could not fathom; remembering to speak in Tagalog was as much as she could manage.

"Staying up gave me a chance to finish the homework for this week," Hyun said.

Hadassah wished she had the same eagerness on Sunday nights. "Have you guys noticed that there are no earthquakes here?"

Tameka winked at Hyun before answering. "Coming from Pasadena, I noticed it pretty quickly."

"I think that's why Mr. Murray and Mr. Cooper chose these campgrounds," Hadassah wondered aloud. "Don't you?"

Hyun smiled at her knowingly. "Come on, girls, we want to get to breakfast before 8:00am, and we still have our hike."

Hadassah's body resisted the hike. Mr. Murray had increased her pack weight another five pounds since Friday, bringing the total to forty-five. After the flu last week, she had little endurance and slept every extra minute, which put her behind on her homework. Then she remembered Dad's question all those months ago: would she have enough stamina for this program?

There had been no word from Mom about Dad, and every thought of him weighed upon her heart worse than the backpack weighed upon her shoulders.

For the eleventh morning in a row—or was it the twelfth?—Matthew walked up beside her. She smiled for the first time since yesterday morning.

"You alright this morning, Tsigele?"

"Goodness sakes!" She tried not to smile too wide. She tried not to like him walking so close, or all those accidental times of hands brushing against each other. "Whoever taught you Yiddish needs to teach you a better term of endearment than the word for 'little goat,' Matthew."

"And I keep telling you to call me Matt. My mom calls me Matthew."

"There was this pot-head in my school back in Brooklyn who called me Tsigele. Every time he said it I wanted to expose his stash of weed which would have landed him in juvie for a few years."

"Good thing I don't have a stash of weed, eh?"

Mr. Murray tromped by on his way to the front of the line. "Speak in Tagalog if you're going to talk."

"Yo, Mr. Murray, how do you say 'dude' in Tagalog?" Matthew called out to him.

Mr. Murray glanced back briefly. "Don't lag, either."

"I didn't mean to upset you," Matthew told Hadassah in Tagalog as soon as Mr. Murray passed. "You're just one of the coolest girls I ever met." He smiled shyly. "And your hair looks really nice today. Like a flock of little goats on the hills of Gilead." He jogged along to catch up with the larger group ahead.

How dare he say a compliment like that! Hadassah stopped briefly to glare at him before jogging to the larger group. "I've noticed you've let your hair grow."

Matthew smiled in return and turned his gaze to the ground as they ran.

Zeke, who had been walking beside Priscilla at the tail end of the large group, caught up to them and glanced at Matthew, then Hadassah. "Did you know that he took the Nazarite vow?"

He flashed an awkward grin at her. "No more grapes or raisins. But I'm sure you could teach me all about the Nazarite vow, Hadassah."

"I think it's great." What could she say to get him to say her name again? Especially with that Tagalog accent. Her stare lasted far too long. She dropped her gaze and her pace to walk beside Priscilla at the end of the line.

"We're almost done with a month of Tagalog." Priscilla's countenance brightened. "Do you think this means we'll be doing a mission to the Philippines by this spring?"

"Mr. Cooper said we'd be training for a year first, but I'm with you—I'd rather go sooner than later."

"I hope I can handle the operations when we go. I mean, Mr. Murray only has my pack at thirty pounds, and I know it's lighter than anyone else. What does he have yours at?"

"Forty-five."

Priscilla watched her feet as she hiked through a denser area. "What did Zeke say when you talked to him?"

"Just something about Matthew."

"Oh. Thanks for walking with me. I know I'm always at the back of the line."

"I like your company. Besides, you've helped me so much with the language this last month. And who else have I hung out with these last three months?"

"Did you do your homework for Mr. Cooper's Countries class?"

"You mean memorizing the major blood types in the black market cities in China? I found it easier when I memorized facts and didn't think about the implications of the perfectly healthy organ donors."

"Did it scare you as much as it scared me?"

"Especially when I heard Vladimir Therion's name attached to one of the cities." Hadassah shrugged, then thought of the Tuesday afternoon class. "I'm still trying to calm my heart rate over Explosives with Mr. Murray. I'm sure once I calm down I can tell the difference between the Russian and Italian land mines. Or remember how to dismantle a simple C4 fuse." She didn't want to tell how much she enjoyed this class for fear of boasting. She loved the thrill of it.

"Maybe we aren't as ready as we need to be, but I want to be ready to go soon." Priscilla's countenance fell again.

"Let's pray for your sister again at Wednesday's cell group meeting." It felt trite as soon as Hadassah said it, but all other words seemed just as threadbare.

***

As soon as she arrived in the Lodge for Tuesday evening's class on Song of Solomon, and found a seat as far away from Matthew as she could, she noticed that something about the classroom was different, but couldn't put her finger on what it was.

This was by far her favorite class. At first she hesitated liking Song of Solomon, with all of its potentially sensual poetry, but Mr. and Mrs. Cooper tag-teamed the class and stretched all of Hadassah's paradigms about how she could draw near to Yeshua and Abba Father.

But tonight, Robert and Hannah stood at the front of the class holding hands. Holding hands? What had she missed? Granted, there had been enough to occupy her attention, but she should have noticed a blooming relationship. All of her training was about learning how to notice. Maybe she needed to get out of her cabin more often.

Mrs. Cooper grinned from ear to ear. She stood beside Hannah while her husband stood beside Robert. "Okay, y'all, we figured this would be the best time to announce this."

"This is both sad and exciting for us," Mr. Cooper added with his same stoic expression. "Tomorrow, Robert and Hannah will be packing up and leaving the Lighthouse to get married. We wanted to bring them forward to express that this is the way we want it done. They came to us and told us plainly without sneaking around. We planned together, and they remained pure. If they decide to come back in a year the decision will be up to them, but we heartily invite them.

"Tonight, I want all of you to stretch out your hands to Robert and Hannah, and let's pray a blessing over them and the next stage of their lives."

Stretching out her hand, Hadassah pulled her glance away from Matthew and had to close her eyes not to see him in her peripheral vision, not to wonder whether he glanced back at her. She had been looking forward to the distraction of learning tonight, whereas praying for Robert and Hannah reminded her about Matthew and the way her pulse quickened under his gaze.

While she prayed her blessing over the couple, she thought about the homework for Wednesday's Cultures class. What was the proper response to a compliment when in Manila? Maybe these thoughts would help her ignore this swell of emotion. But extending her hand toward her friends without focusing on the Lord struck a bell toll of guilt within her heart.

The next day, as soon as she bid farewell to Robert and Hannah, she poured all her thoughts into her studies.

***

"I'm sure all of you have noticed our new guest speaker, Captain Roper," Mr. Murray began the following Monday afternoon. "He and I will be tag-teaming a class on handling torture."

Maybe Hadassah imagined it, but it seemed as if everyone in the room began to breathe just as shallowly as she did. Did Mr. Murray's words pull the oxygen from the room?

"Your work will be twofold," Mr. Murray continued, "to release captives who are in physical and spiritual chains, and to pray for their captors who are in deep spiritual bondage. So every team we send out will have two components: the reconnaissance team, which will do the search and rescue, and the intercessory team. You'll go in together; you'll come out together.

"Now, we told you that you must not have deception on your lips, but neither do you need to tell people anything. If you get caught, protect the lives of your teammates and don't release names, places or missions unless you're instructed to by Mr. Cooper or myself. Be as wise as serpents and as innocent as doves. Don't betray your brothers and sisters in Christ because you're afraid of a momentary affliction. Is there grace and mercy if you falter? Of course there is. But don't sell your brother or sister to avoid pain. If any of us military folk did that while in service, we'd face court-martial, would we not?"

This first guest speaker, Captain Roper, had been a POW in Afghanistan. Hearing the captain's gravelly voice and seeing his scarred face etched his words into Hadassah's memory while he taught about preparing their hearts for torture.

"People will say and do whatever they can to get you to talk. I remember waterboarding one week, and having all of my fingernails removed another week, among the more savory tortures my fellow servicemen and I endured. But I won't use threats to motivate you the way the army did with me. No, I want you to learn from the words of Christ, who spoke with real power, real authority and real encouragement. He told His disciples that if they identified themselves as His followers, people would beat, torture and kill them. If you say, 'I do what I do because I love the Lord,' you will be persecuted. During these days, while you are in training, deal with your fear and tell it to go in the name of Jesus.

"So, am I going to tell you what to say when you're dragged in for questioning? No. Why not? Because Jesus didn't. He said the Spirit would give us the right words in that hour.

"I want to put this in context for you now," Captain Roper continued. "Jesus is telling His disciples this when? During the discourse on the End Times. The Day of the Lord is coming, my friends. Strengthen yourselves, watch, pray, encourage one another, for the days are dark and they are only getting darker.

"Read the trials of Paul in 2 Corinthians chapter 11; read what happened to Stephen, to James, to Peter and to John in Acts. While you read these things, ask God to fill you with the same courage and resolve these men had. Read Hebrews, especially chapter 11. And think upon Jesus—He suffered immensely but never faltered once.

"Lastly, grow confident in love. God is love. Grow confident in the fact God loves you and you love Him. How do you do this? Memorize the scripture verses about His love for you, then pray these scriptures to God by the Holy Spirit. And grow in love toward one another. Serve each other in love *now,* when the days are easy. Serve, serve, serve. Give this amazing chef of yours a break for a day or two, although she raises the bar rather high. Do the dishes for someone else. Mop when it's not your turn. The least among you will become the greatest.

"What does this have to do with how to handle torture? Everything. If you grow in love, you learn to love even those who hate you. And if you pray for those who persecute you, your trial becomes easier. Trust me. I was a POW seven months before I began to pray for those who tortured me. Those were the worst seven months of my life. The following two years of captivity were some of the most glorious times of my life. Although the torture increased, I had amazing encounters with the Lord during my solitude. It all started when I began to forgive the Talibani who tortured me, and to pray for them, and to genuinely love them."

Chapter 22:

Jumps

After breakfast on the morning Captain Roper left, Mr. Murray called a meeting to tell them the schedule was changing, and there would be a shuffling of cabin arrangements.

"Hadassah, you'll move into Hyun and Tameka's cabin to make space for other guest teachers. You can go ahead, ladies. Meet back here by 1100 hours to hear the new schedule."

"I've been really proud of you," Hyun said as she helped Hadassah carry her bags, "how you pushed yourself through these last three months."

"Thanks for saying so, but I'm sure I can't take credit for the perseverance."

"I hear you. Can I give some advice, though?"

"Sure."

Hyun set Hadassah's belongings down in front of her bed. "You need to be more of an extrovert or this life will eat away at you. I'm not naturally an extrovert. Someone had this talk with me, and I forced myself to be more outgoing."

"My mom had this talk with me, too. But whatever she says, I'm sure she was born with spy-worthy social skills; she didn't have too much advice on how to change." Hadassah paused to stack the rest of her clothes into drawers. "No, I take that back, she did give me advice, and I practiced for a while."

"You were outgoing in the beginning. Did something happen to discourage you?"

Her frown was so deep she didn't want to turn and face Hyun. "You could say that. But I don't really want to talk about it."

"Did you talk to Mrs. Cooper?"

"I did right away, but after a while I decided to deal with it on my own."

"Tonight, let me teach you some of what I learned."

***

When they gathered again to hear about their new schedule, Mr. Murray and Mr. Cooper told them life would change on Monday. They would wake at 5:00am instead of 4:45—there were hoots and hollers of delight over the extra fifteen minutes of sleep—and there would be classroom teachings after breakfast rather than in the afternoons. Also, they would be leaving in groups of seven to practice jumps for anyone who was interested.

Hadassah raised her hand. "What do you mean by jumps, sir?"

"From an airplane, Ms. Michelman."

Her face lit up. "Where do we sign up?"

"Consider yourself signed up, Ms. Michelman."

Mom would definitely understand her excitement. She felt like a kid again for the first time in a long time. Then again, how many kids are allowed to jump out of airplanes?

Mr. Murray's voice broke her daydream as he continued to explain their schedule. "While some of you are away practicing jumps, the rest of you will be helping to do maintenance work around here. Mr. Cooper will be in the plane, so it'll be Mrs. Cooper and me who assign detail for those two weeks. We don't want anyone to miss classes, so we'll be holding off on them until everyone returns."

The first night with Hyun and Tameka as her cabin mates, Hadassah stayed up later than she had since Greensboro, but Tameka was fast asleep before 8:30pm.

What Hyun shared that night was something Hadassah had never heard before. "Most women are like a casserole—everything intertwined and mixed together. This is not bad. In fact, it's great for some aspects of life. Women, on the whole, tend to see interconnectedness better than men because of the way our minds work, and oftentimes this makes us better spies. But sometimes in clandestine work, the casserole thinking can be dangerous. Some of us women have to train ourselves to compartmentalize in order to make it in this line of work. In the field, every aspect of your internal life, except your relationship with God, needs a box so we can focus on the mission."

"That makes a ton of sense." Hadassah scraped at her fingertips. "How do I do it?"

"You don't want to deny your emotions, but you tell them they have a time and a place, and they can only come out at those certain times. If left to run at will, your emotions will distract and control you. And if you have feelings toward—"

"Wait, who told you I have feelings toward Matthew?"

"You just did." The smile in Hyun's eyes cooled the flush rising up Hadassah's cheeks. "So if you have feelings toward someone, or anger at a friend, you tell your emotion it can come out later—at the cell groups or prayer meetings, during your quiet time with God or talking with Mrs. Cooper. The rest of the time you've got to jump past it."

"How can you do that?"

"First, realize everyone gets offended, even when feeling offended runs contrary to wisdom. I cannot tell you how many times I've been offended at others because they rejected me or even corrected me. Now, I hardly notice. It's a habit of forgiveness."

There were so many people to forgive, where would she begin? Maybe with herself.

**

Hadassah's heart and mind exploded into prayer during the entire van ride to the airfield where she'd practice the jumps. More recruits had signed up; Mr. Cooper separated them into two groups.

Hadassah was in the second group, along with Matthew, Pedro, Paul, Hyun, Priscilla and Tameka.

As soon as she arrived at the airfield, Hadassah found her cot quickly in the girls' dorm, which was in one of two unused hangars, and was the first to return to the main hangar to hear instructions. They would all do five jumps before the week was out: three during the day, two of which would be with gear, and two jumps at night. Their instructor, Will, had been a Navy Seal, but no one would have guessed when they first saw him or heard his soft Boston accent. He had a fatherly manner, a twinkle in his eyes, and, as she could see by his bulging belly, a love for food.

"Make sure you listen to each word I say very carefully," Will told them directly, hardly pronouncing his 'r's. "I don't need you to be a punctuation mark in the middle of my air field. I haven't lost anyone yet, and I don't plan to this week."

He told them, with unexpected gentleness, what would be required for them to pass the course and what would be considered failure. Then came the five hours of training, and the multiple exercises in body positioning and controlling the parachute. By the end of the day, Hadassah collapsed onto her cot filled with confidence, but devoid of all the initial excitement.

The next morning, her excitement returned. The first thing she did was send a text to Mom, not even knowing where in the world her mother would be, or if she'd be able to reply.

The air was warm and clear when Hadassah donned the jumpsuit for the first time. Her heart raced as she suddenly remembered all the horror stories people told about parachutes not opening. She pushed those thoughts to the back of her mind, behind all the recent training, then spun around and skipped out of the girls' hangar. Her cell phone beeped, and she turned back one last time. Mom.

U'LL DO FABULOUS. ENJOY! PRAYING 4 U. SO PROUD OF U, HADDY. LUV.

Anxiety turned to exhilaration as the C130 plane rose to 2,500 feet.

When she first unhooked herself from the static line and leaped from the plane, the whoosh of the wind and thinness of the air almost took her breath away. She was afraid again for a moment, but the ground seemed surreal racing toward her, as if it was too far away to be a threat. The brief free-fall was amazing—the sense of flying, the heart pounding. She had understood the allure of thrill-seeking beforehand, but never so much as in this moment. Was Pastor Ronny Gibbons right about people flying on the new earth? She hoped so.

When she pulled the ripcord and the parachute opened, it jerked her body less than she expected; the slow float down was even more gratifying than the free-fall, albeit less thrilling.

She spotted the circle below her and steered the parachute to where she was supposed to land, where Tameka just dropped and rolled, and where Priscilla would soon follow. Would she keep proper form? Would her body absorb the impact well? *Please don't let me be the first to break a bone.*

Her landing was exactly what had been asked for: a drop to the ground then a roll, all the while remaining within the circle. She couldn't keep the shout of joy from escaping her lips, nor her arms from making an elated V. Gathering up the parachute quickly, she moved out of the way for Priscilla.

The next four jumps were equally exhilarating, especially the night jumps when she could see the Milky Way as she flew through the air, and the ground looked like a black hole beneath her. Her excitement always outweighed the anxiety. On the fifth day, during the fifth jump, she thought of Dad. Would he be angry if she parachuted in to release him from his captors? She pushed the daydream away before it distracted her from observing the other recruits in the air.

***

On the way back, Hadassah's heart leaped when Matthew sat next to her in the van. What was it Hyun had said about compartmentalizing? Somehow that whole conversation became as muddled as a smoothie with Matthew in such close proximity. With shaky hands she took the ear buds out and put her music on pause.

"You did a good job this week, yo. I was impressed watching you." He stared into her eyes as he spoke.

"You, too." *Don't smile. Especially not so ingratiatingly. It was just a complement, nothing more.*

"When I first met you I didn't think you'd be the type of girl who'd want to jump out of an airplane. But I guess most of the girls at the Lighthouse are that type of girl."

"I loved it." She bit at the side of her lip. "I'd stay another week if I could. Do you think we'll really parachute into places?"

He winked at her. "It doesn't hurt to hope, does it?"

Her whole body twitched as she sighed. *Sometimes it does hurt to hope.* She put the ear buds back in her ears, trying to drown out this hope. There must have been hours of unanswered prayer, begging God to let her either forget about Matthew or not let her heart bother about him anymore. Or, more often than she ever admitted, hoping they could be together and it would be okay.

And then she thought about Dad. All those fleeces she threw out, imploring the Lord for confirmation that Dad would be rescued before the year was out. She glanced around the van again, then prayed more. *And Matthew's dad. And Priscilla's sister. And Pedro's uncle. And Hyun's mom. And Paul's dad. And Christina's dad.*

Chapter 23:

Bridal Paradigm

Hadassah huddled in the stifling cardboard box, her bladder screaming, her sweat soaking the flimsy material. Except for crickets and owls, it had been quiet for far too long. The darkness had grown so thick she couldn't see the edges of the box anymore; her breathing grew shallow and terse. She had never struggled with claustrophobia before this. Two hours must have passed. No wonder Mr. Murray recommended leaving the watch behind—she would have been glancing at it every two seconds by now. And where was that rescue team?

Then it dawned on her. How many thousands around the world suffered much worse? A large contingent of the Lord's Bride remained in captivity across the globe. At least this was only role-playing tonight. She was still in the nature reserve, and she had a team coming to rescue her. In the pervasive silence, she prayed for her brothers and sisters in Christ around the world, tears mingling with sweat on the floor of the box.

"Lord, please be with them. Please let them encounter your glory so they would find comfort instead of terror, love instead of bitterness and joy instead of hardness of heart."

Another half hour passed, wherein she fell asleep. The rescue team was intercepted and the operation was a failure, but Mr. Cooper let her out to breathe the fresh air (and relieve her bladder) before she hid once more so they could practice the search and rescue again. Then there would be three more nights of this. After two weeks this had been only the fourth failure—if only Hyun, Matthew and Dave were on her team instead. Then she smiled, because in the end they would be.

May and June would have zoomed by if she hadn't been counting the seconds before rescues.

***

The last half of June was by far her favorite part of the training. Mr. Cooper called a ten-day corporate fast; they ate only fruits and vegetables, cut the morning exercise to half and studied the theme of the Bride of Christ intensely.

"Notice what it says at the end of Revelation," Hyun said at one Wednesday cell group meeting during the fast. "'The Spirit and the Bride say come.' The Father wants the Church to rise up as a Bride."

"But what does that really mean?" Priscilla asked. "What does it look like to be the Bride? Do we sit passively waiting for the Bridegroom?"

"It talks in the book of Esther about the preparation of the bride," Hadassah added. "She goes through a year of beauty treatments before she can come before the King."

Priscilla shook her head. "But it's still rather passive, don't you think?"

"For us, these treatments are figurative rather than literal."

"But what does the figurative look like?"

Before Hadassah opened her mouth to answer, Hyun began. "The Bridal Paradigm is about the commitment Jesus has for us, and ours to him. The more we have a revelation of His commitment to us and attach our faith to this revelation, the more our commitment to Him grows. As to what this will look like, it's up to one's personal walk with Jesus. We need to open our hearts fully to the Holy Spirit's examination."

Priscilla's eyes glistened with tears. "Sometimes I'm afraid of this Bridal Paradigm."

"Why?" Hyun asked.

"Well, nothing is hidden. Everything is laid open to His scrutiny."

"It's the same in every paradigm of the Kingdom."

"I know, but the Bridal Paradigm deals with our emotions, and sometimes it hurts to have those exposed." Priscilla began to cry openly.

Hyun reached her hand toward the young woman. "Look at the second half of chapter 3 in the Song. God is our safe Savior. He surrounds us with warriors who fight on our behalf. So we need to run to Him with our broken emotions instead of from Him in fear, because He alone can sanctify us."

"But what if they don't change right away?"

Hadassah looked up at her. "You mean the emotions?" she asked, suddenly gripped with the fact that this addressed her own struggle.

"Yeah."

Hadassah didn't have the answer either.

Hyun looked back and forth between Hadassah and Priscilla. "Even if your heart doesn't change right away, it doesn't mean He won't change you. Keep bringing everything to the Lord. Also, sometimes the Lord is trying to show us something through these emotions that we wouldn't understand otherwise."

Walking back to her cabin, Hadassah dragged her feet and prayed the Lord would teach her something through these emotions she couldn't shake. He did. He showed her His desire for her. A passage from the Song of Solomon rang in Hadassah's heart like sympathetic strings on a sitar, "I am my Beloved's and His desire is for me." In the middle of those ten days of fasting, the cycle of obsessive thoughts stopped. Now, whenever she prayed for Matthew, the Lord flooded her heart with peace and the knowledge of His desire for her.

Knowing how difficult emotional trials were, she prayed for Priscilla as well. What a mountain of emotion her friend must have.

Chapter 24:

A Visit from Mom

On the last Sunday in June, during a rare afternoon nap, a strange buzz and beep roused Hadassah from sleep. She lay still, staring up at the wood beams on the ceiling and trying to remember where she had heard that sound before.

"My phone!" She couldn't believe that in two short months she forgot what a text notification sounded like. She rolled over and checked her phone. Mom.

I'M COMING 2 A NEARBY HOTEL ON THE BEACH 2 SPEND 10 DAYS W/U. YITZ WILL B COMING 2. HE'LL INTERVIEW W/MR. COOPER 4 A POSITION W/R.S.O.

Hadassah received another text just before midnight on the third of July.

Mom again.

I'M HERE.

All the other recruits headed home the night before, so she was glad for the company.

As soon as Hadassah walked through the door of the hotel room on the morning of the fourth, Mom took her phone and handed it to Yitzak. "He's got an upgrade you'll love."

"Are you going to tell me what it is?"

Mom flashed a smile. "I'll let him explain it when he's done. You're going to jump on that right away, aren't you, Yitz?"

Yitzak nodded at her and smiled at the phone as he turned on his heals and left.

She turned toward her daughter. "Let's have breakfast while it's still hot."

Hadassah sat on the balcony and stared out at the waves pounding the beach below. "I had no idea I was so close to the ocean all this time."

"I take it Mr. Murray doesn't let you explore the area much."

"There isn't time. I do an insane number of sit-ups and push-ups before breakfast, and afterward I don't think about the surrounding area. But you've got to tell me what you know about Dad. And where you've been."

"Need-to-know basis, Haddy, that's how I've got to tell it right now."

Hadassah gritted her teeth and pushed the omelet away. "I need to know a lot right now, Mom, beginning with whether or not he's alive."

"I've had strong intel to prove he's alive."

"Have you seen a picture, or talked to him?"

"We've had video evidence." The corner of Mom's mouth twitched as if she'd cry, but she wasn't the crying type, then her expression turned stoic again. "And as for where I've been—Jordan, Syria even Russia, but I can't get into Iraq yet. The security around Babylon is tighter than you can imagine."

"Why? What are they hiding?"

Mom mimicked a stone again. "Tell me about your training."

Knowing she'd get no further answers, Hadassah yielded. "I wish I had MP3s of some of the teachings we've had. You'd love them, Mom."

"Like what?"

As she shared her new paradigms, she sensed for the first time she was teaching Mom about the scriptures and about the End Times. "I know most of this is similar to what Dad taught. I don't know why I didn't listen to him better. But these teachings hit so much closer to home now."

"What's your favorite part of the training so far?"

"I loved skydiving. And I love how strong I'm getting." A facetious expression crept across her face. "I bet I could even arm wrestle you."

Mom moved plates and glasses of grapefruit juice aside then put an elbow on the table with her hand extended toward Hadassah. "Show me your stuff."

"You better not let me win. Because you probably won't anyway."

Mom did win, but barely. "Six more months and I'll probably be embarrassed."

Hadassah breathed a laugh. "When will Yitzak have my phone ready?"

"A few days at least. But tell me more about R.S.O."

She fixed her gaze on Mom. "Tell me more about Dad."

Mom continued as if she hadn't heard Hadassah. "Any parts of your training you don't like?"

"Not being in the field yet." She stared at a group of girls frolicking in the surf below and prayed for them.

Mom smiled empathetically. "Of course, Haddy. You're my daughter."

***

Four days later, when Hadassah knocked on the door of Yitzak's hotel room, he emerged slowly, stretched, then shook his lanky limbs before hugging her.

"How's the super-spy?" he asked with a chuckle. "Are you ready for your upgrade?"

"Always ready. Whatcha got for me?"

Yitzak held up her phone and a set of ear buds. "Sonogram. Look at this." He connected the ear buds and turned on the phone. After pressing the screen in a few places he put the ear buds up to the wall. "I made it strong enough to work through steel." He chuckled as the outline of a person in the elevator across the hall appeared on the screen. "And then this." He slid his finger quickly across the screen. The image changed into colors, with the person's body glowing red and orange, while the rest of the area showed green and blue. "Heat sensor. Then last but not least..." He pressed the screen with his thumb and forefinger then placed the ear bud on his arm. The image appeared of his radius and ulna. "X-ray. Neat, huh?"

"I like." She grinned.

"There are also some fun new apps, including mapping and map interfacing. So here, have fun. Explore. Yada yada."

"Thanks so much." She stared at the back of the phone looking for any sign of his tampering. No sign—the thing looked brand new.

"You look really healthy, Haddy. I think this R.S.O. program has done you good. I'm glad I'm moving down here."

"You'll fit right in." She didn't want to show him her excitement over his move. The longer she'd been at R.S.O., the more stoic she'd become. Like Mom. And that didn't upset her at all. Then she chuckled. "And you might even see sunshine twice a week."

He nudged her with a pale and bony elbow. "Yeah, I might even put my desk near a window."

***

With Yitzak wandering the campgrounds, homecoming at the Lighthouse felt different. Most of the students were still away, and those at the campgrounds wanted to socialize most of the time. Lisa arrived at Hadassah's door every morning and urged her to join in the fun and discussions in the Lodge. Even Priscilla was in the lodge every day.

***

After all the recruits returned to the Lighthouse in August, Mr. Murray brought them to a remote beach for a few days of training.

"Safar!" Mr. Murray shouted to Zacharias on the third day. "I want you to touch the buoy next time you swim out there. You too, Michelman!" He stood where the highest waves would just hit his shoulders with a megaphone to his mouth and twelve of the recruits swimming around him.

Hadassah had spent the summer between her sophomore and junior years in high school as a lifeguard, and Mr. Murray's training reminded her of that. Except this was no cozy indoor pool, this was the Atlantic, which was cold even in the dog days of summer.

Her eighteenth birthday passed almost without notice as she swam laps through the salty waves. When twilight descended and every muscle in her body yearned for those easy days back in the beginning of January, she collapsed on the sand, licked her salty lips and stared vacantly at the strange activity Matthew, Dave, Zach and Zeke had taken up. Collecting sticks and stacking them up seemed an odd way to wait for the van, especially after an exhausting day battling waves. Then it occurred to her—they were building a bonfire. Mr. Murray must have obtained special permission for this. Once the blaze got going, Hadassah revived. She laid on her back beside her friends and watched shooting stars while a party bloomed around her.

It turned out that five of them had birthdays in the same week: Hadassah, Hyun, Zach, Paul and Matthew. The whole team celebrated that night on the beach with pizza followed by several rounds of s'mores and songs until well after midnight. At least Tameka was there to keep the awkward rendition of Happy Birthday in tune.

When Hadassah woke early the next morning, with sand in every strand of hair, stars still graced the sky and two silhouettes of her friends sat at the last hill of dry sand before the crashing waves hit the shore. She ambled over and plopped her tired body beside Hyun who was pointing out constellations to Priscilla.

"Good morning, Haddy," Hyun whispered. "You should see this."

"The Perseid meteors?" Hadassah asked.

"Better than that. See there and there, it looks like a woman. The woman with twelve stars around her head like a crown. If you notice, there's the half moon under her feet like a pedestal—before this month, no one has ever seen that."

"But she doesn't look pregnant." Hadassah had memorized that portion of Revelation 12.

"Look at these stars here. Planets, actually. There, there and there."

Hadassah followed the direction of Hyun's pointing finger. "I see it now, like a half circle in her middle. Wow."

Suddenly a whole pocket of meteors shot through the constellation as if they came from the woman's face.

Priscilla gasped. "She looks like she's crying."

Hadassah agreed. "But she's supposed to be clothed with the sun."

Even as she spoke the horizon grew brighter and brighter. The light sprayed across the stars concealing them in a robe of the sun's new rays.

A tingle ran from the tip of Hadassah's toes to her scalp. "Do you think anyone else sees this?"

"I have a few friends who are keeping their eyes on the skies." Hyun sighed. "Most of the people watching this, though, will misinterpret it into some twisted and self-serving astrology."

"But what do you think it means?" Priscilla asked.

"That we are being trained for such a time as this."

**

At the end of August, Mrs. Cooper signed up Hadassah, Priscilla and Lisa for an eight-week self-defense course taught by Hyun, Christina and Tameka.

"This isn't meant to hurt anyone," Mrs. Cooper explained on the first day. "This is to protect you in dire circumstances so you can escape from unspeakable harm."

From day one to the end of the course, Hadassah's jaw dropped open every time she saw Hyun give a demonstration. This woman was as limber and swift as a hummingbird when she began sparring with anyone. By the end of the eight weeks, Hadassah could give a roundhouse kick almost as high as hers but nowhere near as fast. *A goal to work toward,* she told herself on the last day.

***

The heat finally subsided, and every morning Hadassah observed the trees fading from green to golden brown. In November, when the recruits celebrated Thanksgiving together, Dave and Pedro talked Mr. Murray into renting a television for the weekend so they could watch the football games; those not interested in football played board games. Hadassah lost miserably in Monopoly, took Asia before utter defeat in Risk and ended up with a bruised knuckle after playing the card game Spoons, but fun and general mirth healed all wounds.

Staying at the Lighthouse for Hanukkah and Christmas meant Hadassah missed the lights and the hustle bustle of New York. Not nearly as much as she missed Dad and Mom. Mr. Murray, Yitzak and Hyun stayed with her; Hyun's company was the most comforting of the three. Both Mr. Murray and Yitzak kept to their cabins, Yitzak to work on gadgets and Mr. Murray to do the work he always kept secret.

Andrea, Lisa and Priscilla arrived back at the Lighthouse just before a blizzard shut down the airports. The girls enjoyed foraging for themselves and having girl time. Hadassah, Hyun and Priscilla encouraged one another to stay fit, while Lisa and Andrea tried their hands in the kitchen. With Amelia still in Georgia the cooking wasn't as spectacular, but no one complained. Until their stores ran thin and the campgrounds lost power. An ice storm following the blizzard forced them to cook over the fire pit in the dining hall, and to sleep in the lodge rather than their own cabins.

With the power outage lasting a full week even Boaz needed more food, so a trip to the grocery store became a necessity. Mr. Murray turned this opportunity into cold-weather survival training.

Hadassah doled out the extra wool clothes and Siberian-like winter coats from Mom to Hyun and Priscilla. Using broken chairs and flat boards they had found in the storage shed, they made snow shoes and hiked the twelve and a half miles to the nearest open store. Mr. Murray led. Lisa, Andrea and Yitzak stayed at the Lodge with Boaz, tending the fire and hot soup until the group returned.

It was dusk when they finally arrived back at the campgrounds, cold, starving and full of laughter and stories to tell. The milk had frozen, some of the eggs had cracked, and the bag of coffee got a hole in it, spilling some of the grounds onto the snow.

"Oh goody," Lisa remarked. "I love iced coffee."

The ice storm gave Hadassah time to study what she wanted to through the scriptures and books in the library. The revelations she received were meteoric infusions into her heart, especially regarding events leading up to the Lord's return.

More than ever, Hadassah grew desperate to know where Dad was.

Chapter 25:

Preparing for the Philippines

When everyone returned from Christmas break, Mr. Murray and Mr. Cooper called a meeting of those chosen to go to Manila for Operation Double-edged Sword: Hadassah, Hyun, Matthew, Paul, Christina Priscilla, Zach and Zeke.

Mr. Cooper passed out packets on the operation details while Mr. Murray gave the run down. "One of our sister organizations in Manila, a group of people who love Jesus and work to rescue women and children enslaved as prostitutes, are setting up an underground railroad. They need some extra people to come in and spy out the land. Our board approves the expense, especially since one of you has a family member over there, so the eight of you will be leaving in March. I'll sort out visas, but I want you to make sure to give me your passports.

"Your tasks until then will be to get your vaccines and attend a conference, the details of which you will see on page two of your packet. You'll need to introduce yourselves to those teaching about trafficking in South East Asia. I will have a speaker here the last week of February, but I want every one of you to be familiar with this issue before he gets here. Yes, Paul?" He pointed to the raised hand.

"Do the people at the conference know we'll be going on a mission to the Philippines?"

"Some of the conference organizers are friends of mine, but they don't know your names. Part of your training is to seek *them* out. Zeke?"

"Who's coming in February to give the talk?" Zeke asked.

"Mack MacArthur."

Eyes grew wide all around. For over two decades Mack MacArthur had been the foremost voice on trafficking. His work toward justice had sparked cells of abolitionists in every corner of the world. Hadassah smiled, remembering Mack MacArthur's teaching nearly two years ago.

Before he dismissed everyone, Mr. Murray told Priscilla to see him up at the front after the meeting.

Hadassah channeled her excitement about the trip into this next phase of training. Knowing as much as she did about human trafficking and forced prostitution, submitting to a year of training without rescuing another girl had frustrated her. Now she felt useful and empowered again—enough to comfort Priscilla during the conference.

"I can't believe what some of the girls go through." Priscilla's body gave a tremor as she spoke. "More than twice this week I thought I'd be sick listening to the stories of what people do to children. Those are *children*. Children should be playing and having fun."

Hadassah looked up at her friend, and a flood of empathy made her knees weak. How hard it must be for Priscilla to restrain from mention her sister outright. "I saw you get up at one point and go toward the bathroom."

"I didn't get sick, but I didn't want to cry during the lady's story. I guess I could have handled myself better."

"I don't think there was a dry eye in the room when she shared how she was freed. I wish you had stayed."

"Mr. Murray told me something after the meeting a few weeks ago. He told me that the organization in Manila located someone who matched my sister's picture and description. All during the lady's talk I just couldn't stop thinking about Filipa."

Hadassah held Priscilla until the girl's tears ebbed. What could she even say? "Learning what happens in these brothels made me want Yeshua to come sooner rather than later. Until that day, I'll do whatever I can to help you find your sister."

***

The day Mack MacArthur arrived, he shared on Psalm 27 and about how Yeshua must be the One Thing they sought. "A heart devoted to Jesus partners with Him, with hands of tender love, to liberate the crushed spirit of a child. No amount of therapeutic training can substitute for the healing power of the Holy Spirit."

Just like they had two years ago, his statistics stunned her. "Every year, 27 million children are trafficked. This is the conservative estimate; the real number might be devastatingly higher. The average age of a trafficked victim is seven years old. This should break our hearts, folks, but don't be afraid of your heart breaking. Having a broken heart prompts us to pray for them, to remember them, and to fight for justice on their behalf.

"This crime of human trafficking generates as much as $32 billion annually around the world. Some pockets in the governments are quite padded by this money. In some countries you can't even trust the authorities to work for justice for their own children. Be as wise as serpents out there, and as innocent as doves.

"As you go into the streets of the red light districts, remember individuals. Each one of the 27 million children is an individual who was made in the image of God. Please don't forget this out there. The sheer numbers can be daunting, but don't forget the one. Look at her, really look at her, and remember Jesus loves her. He gave His life for her. Her life may look like a charred and black stone, but Jesus will redeem all of that and turn her life into a white and living stone. Even if no one else in this world shows her love, love her as Christ loves her."

Hadassah found she was nodding by the end of his teaching, and so was every other head in the room.

Part 3

"...Lord, when did we ever see You hungry and feed You? Or thirsty and give You something to drink? Or a stranger and show You hospitality? Or naked and give You clothing? ..." The King will reply, "Truly I tell you, whatever you did for one of the least of these brothers and sisters of Mine, you did for Me."

~ Yeshua

Matt. 24:37-40 (NIV)

One week later

Chapter 26:

Operation Double-edged Sword

As she stepped onto the plane, Hadassah recalled why Mr. Cooper gave the mission this name.

"Edge one of the sword will be collecting evidence of the abuse," he had reminded them while driving the van to the airport. "Edge two will be searching out possible escape routes for these girls, like an underground railroad from the brothels to the safe homes. In this way you'll help my friend Rafael and his team in Manila."

Hadassah found her seat on the plane and pulled the belt across her lap, meditating on this operation name and something Matthew had said so many months ago. "Bringing God's justice and freedom to those who don't have it." For a moment she imagined that double-edged sword coming from Yeshua's mouth, the one St. John saw in the vision in that first chapter of Revelation. She was an agent of God's justice at last. She could feel her heartbeat in her fingertips.

The plane ride to the Philippines was the longest and most excruciating she had ever experienced; the jarring turbulence throughout the flight threatened to make her sick. Priscilla and Zeke did get sick after the layover in Alaska, and stayed sick the entire way to Manila; flight attendants ran up and down the aisle with a steady stream of paper bags.

"I've never been so embarrassed in my life," Zeke said as they collected their luggage and after he finished heaving for the last time in the men's room. "And I had no idea I'd have so much in my stomach."

"Yeah." Priscilla gave a half smile. "That was the worst trip across the Pacific I could have imagined. I've never thrown up on a plane before."

"Let's not forget to pray for this aspect of the trip on the way back," Hyun said.

"I know, right dude?" Matthew said. "I almost got sick watching the barf buddies here."

"I like that name, Zeke." Priscilla giggled and pinched him playfully on the arm. "You'll be my barf buddy forever now."

Zeke wiped the corners of his mouth and laughed. "Will you be ready for round two on the return flight?"

Priscilla giggled again. Hadassah loved watching Zeke put her at ease.

Humid, smog-filled air enveloped them as they strolled out of the airport terminal and turned toward their meeting point, a fast food restaurant less than a mile away. The Philippines struck Hadassah as wildly different from Africa. Manila in March seemed like New York City in August—bustling, stiflingly hot, unfriendly. But the trucks—Jeepneys, Priscilla had told them—were almost cartoonish with their vibrant paint-jobs. Some Jeepneys carried so many workers that sad faces and tired limbs spilled out the sides and back.

On the way to the restaurant, they crossed a river that reminded Hadassah she wasn't in New York. If ever she'd accuse the Hudson of being polluted again, she'd think of this river. Across its twenty-five foot span there was so much garbage that the water ran a vibrant green flecked with brown foam. The garbage created a dam further upstream. Beyond the dam, a few water rafts ferried people and goods from one riverbank to the next.

Reclaiming her appetite took an act of will after the stink of the river dissipated into the general smog smell of the city. Once they crossed the river she saw market stalls with fresh fruits and vegetables on display. Although the colors looked appetizing, the stall's proximity to the river revived her queasiness.

Soaked in sweat from her walk, Hadassah remained quiet as the team met their field liaison, Roberto, at the fast food joint. He was a lithe and intelligent Filipino with somber character; even his laughter sounded serious.

"I could easily pick your team out of a crowd. I'm glad we'll be splitting you up into twos while you're here; it'll make you far less conspicuous."

"This is a first trip for most of us," Hyun explained.

"And I want you to go home from it alive," Roberto replied. "You're really not as sore thumb as all that, but most of you are different nationalities from each other. Like you, Paul, you look Italian."

"I'm Irish," Paul replied with a gracious smile.

Roberto flushed. "Beautiful people."

"Thanks," Paul replied.

"Pair off however you like. It's quite a walk to the church and you'll be going to different homes from there, so you'll have plenty of time to choose your partner. You'll rest today, but we have a meeting at our headquarters tomorrow night."

Hadassah and Hyun settled into the tiny apartment belonging to Julia Ferdinand, one of the undercover agents with the organization. She only had a small patch of carpet to offer them, where Hadassah and Hyun could sleep with their backs to one another. Hardly noticing the floor after her flight, Hadassah slept until the following afternoon. She awoke refreshed, ready for whatever their meeting entailed.

Julia had made macaroni and cheese for their dinner. "I thought you might like it better than some of our native foods. I followed the directions exactly, so it should be tasty."

Hadassah stared at the over-cooked noodles and clumps of powdered cheese in front of her. She smiled. The woman had given a concerted effort, but cooking obviously wasn't her specialty. She silently vowed to eat it and complimented the chef after the first bite.

"You two enjoy." Julia beamed. "I have to change before the meeting begins."

And change she did. Julia had utterly transformed. Before, the woman was dressed in business attire, with bright eyes and tasteful make-up. Now, the layers of rags draped on her body made her look like a beggar. The dark circles under her eyes and the bruises on her face looked real enough, too. And even though the warts were fake, Hadassah would have been taken in if she hadn't seen Julia earlier.

"I should have warned you," Julia said as they prepared to leave. "This is my cover in the red light district. If I was to wear any less warts or clothing I could end up in a brothel or in jail."

"How long have you been doing this?" Hadassah asked.

"Five months. We're really close to bringing down one of the largest strings of brothels in Manila, where we believe they are holding and torturing more than 150 girls and young women. But I guess you know this, since that's why you're here."

Hyun forced down another bite of the macaroni. "We just know the broad details."

"I'll let Rafaelo explain the fine details to you, but I hope you will be able to meet up with us tonight. Tuesday night is when they let a few of the older girls wander the streets and we were hoping you'd bring that promised camera with you."

"It's with one of our teammates." Hadassah's heart warmed as she thought of Matthew.

They arrived at the headquarters of the organization shortly before 8:30pm. The concrete block building was around the corner from the Holy Spirit College, a nice reminder of why they were all here.

The walls of the offices, decorated with rescue stories, reminded Hadassah of Mom's office in New York, except here the ledges had candles aglow to light the room whenever the power cut out.

"Power's been unpredictable since the last earthquake here in January." Matthew took the seat beside her. "That's what Roberto told Paul and me yesterday."

"I hope we don't have any quakes while we're here," she replied.

Rafaelo called the meeting into session as soon as the rest of the team was seated. "I'll be sending you off in different directions tonight with different objectives." The electric lighting flickered out, and only the light from the candles remained. "Matthew, you and Paul will bring the camera and accompany our undercover team, since we're hoping to get photographic evidence of bruises on the girls' legs to show the authorities the torture these young women endure. Julia and Roberto have been able to gain the trust of three of the girls and they know you'll be coming tonight. We can't bring any of the girls out of the red light district and into hotels anymore, so you'll have to work fast.

"Hadassah, Priscilla and Ezekiel, you will follow Matthew and Paul to provide the necessary distraction if they draw attention. Also, I need you to survey this alley to see if there are any paths in the trash." As he gave instructions he pointed to the alley on a map.

"Zacharias, Christina and Hyun—am I pronouncing that right?—you'll be scouting proposed escape routes. Bring back details of any suspicious activity. You'll see a list on the last page of your packet covering what I consider suspicious activity. We'll meet back here at 3:00am for debriefing."

Unseasonable heat and humidity filled the night air as Hadassah walked toward the infamous red light district with Matthew, Paul, Priscilla, Zeke, Julia and Roberto. Although it was a Tuesday and they were told it would be much quieter than a Friday or Saturday, Hadassah and Priscilla were dressed to look like two guys, for everyone's safety. Hadassah prayed as she walked, for success, protection from both danger and temptation, and for courage.

While they were still two blocks away, they drifted into two groups. And as they approached the area, which was bustling with people and activity, Matthew and Paul separated from Julia and Roberto.

The streets of this red light district were narrow, almost claustrophobic. It reminded Hadassah of the markets she had passed earlier in the day, except this market had people for sale. Many of the girls were dressed in such a way that only those predisposed to lust would desire them, but Hadassah kept Matthew, Paul and Zeke in her prayers nonetheless. The enemy was so prominent and obvious here, the buildings like beasts with red windows for eyes.

Hadassah reminded herself of Mom's maxim, *Blend in, keep a secret, slip away unnoticed.* As long as people believed she and

Priscilla weren't girls this would work.

The first moment the security guards and johns looked distracted, Hadassah, Priscilla and Zeke ducked down the alley, as Rafaelo had instructed.

Zeke stopped and pressed a hand against the wall. "You two go further down. If I look like I'm relieving myself it'll be better for our cover."

Priscilla gasped. "You aren't really going to pee against the wall, are you?"

"No, not at all. It'll just look like it while you two survey the alley further down." Of their whole team he looked the most likely to be a tourist, with his bulging muscles, receding hair line and the tattoo wrapping his forearm. Thankfully, his tattoo of Psalm 8 was in Hebrew. Hadassah doubted anyone would question him about it.

So much trash littered the alley that Hadassah and Priscilla had to jump over one of the piles. Hadassah dared not imagine what she would see if she could see anything in this light.

"Be so careful," Priscilla whispered. "Any pinprick could have a drug laced with who knows what diseases."

"The kind they don't have vaccines for," Hadassah whispered back.

Within a minute Zeke caught up with them. He crept beyond them toward the end of the building and used one of Hadassah's mirrors to spy out the back entrances. After another few minutes, he crept back to them and described what he saw.

"Two guards on the left side, smoking and laughing as they hold their guns loosely, more as a threat than as if they actually knew how to use them. Three guards stand behind the right hand building, plus a fourth man who's smoking weed and expressing himself with lewd gestures. Those guards on the right look as if they'd shoot someone just for fun."

They backtracked into the shadows of the alley.

Matthew stood at the other end of the alley with the camera ready. Lisa and Yitzak had designed the camera, and it was one of their more expensive pieces of equipment; Matthew could take pictures in any light and have the subject show up as if she was in daylight. The camera drew light from all around the subject and highlighted whatever was in the center. Lisa had also designed the bag for them, which completely concealed the camera until it was ready for use, and Matthew could take pictures without removing the camera from the bag or the bag from his shoulder. Plus, it was black with a tasteful green design—a stylish touch which helped the bag pass customs without questions.

It seemed like a half hour or more had passed while Hadassah, Priscilla and Zeke crouched against the wall in a clearing amid the sea of trash and prayed in turns while they waited for Paul and Matthew to meet with the girls Julia and Roberto knew.

Techno and pop music pulsed through the walls of both buildings, colliding into an unholy union of sound.

When Priscilla began to pray, Hadassah heard a strange sound in a trash heap next to the dumpster, halfway between them and the head of the alley. She moved to say something, but remained silent when Julia and Roberto appeared in the alley's entrance with a girl. The girl talked to Paul and Matthew for a minute and then unzipped her right knee-high boot and showed her shin, calf and ankle to them. Her eyes shifted back and forth. Then, as quickly as she came, she darted away. After her, another girl came and showed Matthew and Paul bruises on her side. When Hadassah glanced over at them, she saw movement in the trash heap and heard another moan faintly over the sound of the music.

Zeke shot a glance her way. "You heard it too?"

"It could be a dog," Priscilla whispered, "or another animal trying to find food."

"It sounded human to me." He crouched down and proceeded to carefully remove plastic bags, rotten food, torn clothes, papers, and used needles away from the place where Hadassah had heard the sound. Even in that dim light they could see that the human form was a young girl shaking with fear.

Zeke tapped Priscilla's knee. "Tell her we won't hurt her."

Priscilla crouched down carefully beside the girl, then whispered, first in Tagalog then in English, "We won't hurt you, we are here to help, but we have to keep quiet."

The girl nodded.

"I'm going to talk to Matt and Paul." Zeke straightened up again and looked at Hadassah. "We have to get her out of here. We can't just let her die. Pris, find out if the girl can walk."

As Zeke crept carefully down the alley, Priscilla turned to Hadassah. "Three of us came in here; only three can walk out again, or people will suspect something."

"What do you think we should do?" Hadassah looked briefly at the girl buried in trash. She couldn't leave her here, even if she had to take her place.

"She and I will switch. I'm going to stay here while you and Zeke walk out with her."

"I can't let you do that, Pris." Hadassah scrambled to think of an excuse, but couldn't. "Let me stay here."

Priscilla asked the girl to stand. Her clothes were in shambles and her skin, where it was exposed, was covered in bruises.

"I'll have to give her my clothing," Priscilla said.

Hadassah looked down the alley again. Zeke was trying to explain to Paul and Matthew still, but Matthew shook his head and Paul signed, "Against protocol."

"Matt and Paul are not in," Hadassah whispered.

"Zeke's right, Haddy, we can't leave her here to die in this garbage heap."

"I'm wearing an extra shirt. I can give one to her."

"I don't know how to give my jeans to her."

"What will you wear?" Hadassah asked. Then she looked down. A long wrap skirt lay draped over the dumpster—it was in tatters, but it looked to be the only option. "What about this?" She held up the skirt for Priscilla.

"It'll work." Priscilla wrapped it around her waist over her jeans. "I'll need your arm to lean on while I slip these jeans off."

Zeke had come back by the time Priscilla finished dressing herself and then the girl.

"Here, wear my hat." Priscilla tucked the girl's thin hair into the baseball cap.

"What are you doing?" Zeke asked her.

"I'm taking her place," Priscilla said. "You and Haddy need to walk her out of here."

Zeke shook his head. Hadassah thought for a moment he might cry. "Why?"

"If the four of us leave someone will notice, especially if one looks like a worker. I know the language, I know people in this country—it's better this way."

"Both Paul and Matt said this is way outside of protocol," Zeke whispered loudly.

"I love Jesus," Priscilla whispered back. "How can I leave her here to die like an animal when Christ died for her?"

Chapter 27:

The Midnight Swim

Hadassah helped Priscilla find a hiding place amid the piles of trash, then handed over her cell phone.

"ICE contact number one is where you send a text if anything happens to you." Hadassah pressed a few places on the screen to demonstrate. "You only need to send a page—it'll give your coordinates then track your signal."

"Who will track the signal?" Priscilla's voice quivered as she spoke.

"My mom. And here, an all-in-one pocket tool kit if you need it, and a tiny LED flashlight light."

"Thank you." Priscilla looked up and tried to smile.

"I want the phone back when you're done." She winked at her friend. "And you, too."

Priscilla turned to the trembling and frail girl beside Hadassah. "Go with these people," she told her in Tagalog.

"I speak English," the girl whispered, her eyes downcast. "I heard what you said about Jesus. Thank you."

"You can't cry until they take you far away from here, okay?" Priscilla said.

"I know." The girl took hold of Hadassah's hand.

Hadassah squeezed her hand gently and smiled at her. "You'll need to walk more like a man than like a girl."

"I'll try." The girl gripped her hand tighter.

When Hadassah, Zeke and the girl reached the end of the alley, Paul and Matthew were gone.

"Where?" Hadassah asked.

"Turn right," Zeke scanned their surroundings. "Wait. Stand facing the wall for a moment because that guy is watching us a bit too closely."

Hadassah did as he suggested. She felt uneasy, though, as if she had crossed one too many lines of protocol.

"Okay, let's go, and don't forget to joke around as much as you can."

She tried, but didn't have a heart for it. She glanced one last time down the alley. Zeke did too.

As soon as they stepped outside of the red light district, they caught up with Matthew and Paul. The former had been dragging his feet.

When Hadassah explained what happened, Matthew frowned. "I can't believe you left Priscilla there."

She couldn't tell what tinged his voice more—anger or sadness.

"Priscilla decided to stay." She ground her teeth and stared hard at him. "I tried to talk her out of it, but she was convinced it'd be the best plan."

Matthew's frown deepened. "I'm not convinced. We told Julia and Roberto just before we left. They aren't happy, but they'll do what they can. I'm scared for her, yo."

"So am I." Zeke hung his head.

"Me too." Paul glared at his companions. "But can we get the girl back to the headquarters before we discuss this further?"

"Sure." Matthew turned to the girl. "Forgive me, friend, I'm Matt. What's your name?"

"Hi." The girl didn't say anything else until Hadassah held her hand again. "I'm Kiri."

Matthew looked at her and smiled, then suddenly stiffened. "Don't turn, any of you. We've got company." He fixed his gaze straight ahead as if to signal to the rest of them to do the same.

Hadassah could feel a tremble run through Kiri's fingers. "Whatever you do, don't turn around."

"We should break up our party," Zeke suggested.

Matthew growled. "Not happening, dude. I'm not letting these girls out of my sight."

Zeke shrugged. "Then Paul and I will go."

Paul nodded in agreement.

Hadassah slid one of her mirrors out of her pocket and angled it to catch sight of their pursuers. There were two. And what was that black thing when one lifted his shirt? "Looks like one's packing a 9mm, kids," she said as cheerfully as she could. "Remain calm, but then we've gotta act fast. I think Zeke suggested the best plan."

Matthew grunted, then handed the camera off to Paul. "Fine. This next street. You ready, Zeke? Paul? You take the left, we'll take the following right."

Zeke wrapped his arm around Paul's shoulder then pulled him close and toward the street on their left. Paul waved back at them and forced a laugh as if he was in on a joke.

"Wave friendly then look straight ahead again," Matthew instructed.

Even as angry as she was at him, Hadassah saw wisdom in this and waved.

They walked briskly along, past closed-up shops and dilapidated homes with barred windows. Every couple of feet, Hadassah checked a window beside her to see if she could catch a reflection of the men following them. All of the windows were too dirty to reflect anything.

Kiri squeezed her hand a bit tighter. "Can I cry yet? It hurts so bad."

Hadassah's eyes almost welled up as she considered the girl's question. "Just a little further. You can cry soon."

Matthew glanced her way. "Did they take the bait?"

After checking her mirror again she had to stifle a gasp. "We lost one, but not the one packing."

"Ten more feet, girl, then off to the right. And we've got to look less suspicious."

Her heartbeat pounded further up her throat with every step.

As soon as they turned down the street, Matthew gestured toward one of the bridges spanning the river. It was no more than four blocks up.

"As long as no one follows us, we'll head for that bridge."

Hadassah raised her eyebrows at him. "And if someone does follow?"

"Then head for one of those rafts." This time he angled his head toward a pier stretching into the murky river. "If I need to, I'll distract him. Here's my knife if you need it." He stiffened and his mouth drew tight. "He's behind us. Plan B. Run, girl—get Kiri on a raft."

Hadassah pulled Kiri as fast as the girl could go while, Matthew ran to the left, then to the right. Then he passed out of her peripheral vision altogether. A gunshot fired. Hadassah's heart jumped into her mouth and her legs felt like jelly as she pushed them along. *Come on, Matt! Please let him be okay, God!*

At the sound of the gunshot, Kiri sped alongside Hadassah all the way to the pier. Hadassah surveyed the various and primitive ferries, then jumped from the pier to the last raft in the line, hoping her splash would frighten off any of those water rats she saw in the flotsam. She tugged and pulled at the mooring rope that fastened the raft to the pier. It never budged. If only she could see where it was fastened on the raft. Too much trash covered the vessel.

"Come on, Kiri." Hadassah stretched her hand toward the girl. Kiri stood on the pier, frozen in place.

The next gunshot made the girl jump. Pieces of the pier ahead of her splintered, and flying debris hit her arm. She jumped again, this time toward Hadassah.

As soon as the girl landed on the raft, it began to sink. Kiri screamed.

"Get down!" Hadassah ordered the girl.

Suddenly, as if time slowed, Hadassah saw where the mooring rope was tied to the raft. When Kiri landed on the raft she had moved the piles enough to expose it.

She whipped out Matthew's blade and opened it. With one swipe against the rope she cut it free. And none too soon. Their pursuer stood on the pier aiming his black barrel at her face.

How am I not afraid? Her heart pounded adrenaline, and everything she needed to do appeared so clear. She shoved debris off the raft, throwing some of it toward the man.

Matthew jumped onto the pier and careened into the man as he squeezed the trigger. The bullet hit one of the branches overhead. The branch was small, but its crash onto the raft caused the vessel to sink faster. Kiri screamed again.

Matthew continued to wrestle the man on the pier; the two of them were sprawled across the wood, their arms and hands scrambling for the other's throat.

Hadassah, now paralyzed with fear, stared at them while water gathered at her ankles.

Suddenly, Matthew thrust against the man with both knees and arms, throwing him off the other side of the pier. As soon as she saw this, Hadassah began to toss junk off the side until the raft buoyed to the surface again. The vessel caught the river's current and began to float downstream.

"Come on, Matt!" she shouted in a hoarse whisper as she threw more items overboard.

Matthew dived toward the raft, missing it entirely and plunging into the murky, polluted water. Hadassah chewed hard on the sides of her tongue as she scanned the dark, rippling surface.

His arms appeared and then his head, his mouth gasping for air, his hands grasping for the edge of the vessel. Not much further behind him she saw the head of the man who'd been chasing them. He was swimming toward the raft instead of the shore.

"Matt!" She leaned over the side as much as she could without it tipping and reached for his hand. Kiri cried out; Hadassah longed to comfort the girl, but Matthew needed her first. His hand slapped against hers, then slid beneath the surface again. With his next stroke he grasped her forearm, but only enough to steady himself.

The man swam swiftly with the current toward them.

Hadassah pulled Matthew's body over the edge of the raft until only his feet dangled in the water. As she sat back panting, she saw the man reach for Matthew's foot. She picked up a sizable bag in the heap of trash and hurled it into the water at him. The force of her throw caused the bag's seam to break, and a rain of ripe mangoes pummeled both the water and the man. He cried out, then sank.

When the man emerged again, he was closer to the riverbank than the raft, and he scrambled ashore.

As the current continued to carry their vessel steadily downstream, Kiri trembled quietly under the last pile of nicknacks and fruit. Matthew panted, dirty water dripping from every inch of him. Knowing the task of getting this ferry to the other side remained up to her, Hadassah rifled through the pile around Kiri for an oar or pole.

"Did you see a stick or pole?" she asked Kiri.

The girl stared wide-eyed, then shook her head.

"You looking for this, girl?" Matthew rolled onto his back and sat up, holding up a pole the length of the raft. "It was getting a bit uncomfortable."

Hadassah used the pole to punt to the opposite shore.

"Are we safe now?" Kiri asked.

"Soon," Hadassah replied between punts.

"Are you taking me to the police?"

"We could." Matthew looked kindly on her. "Do you want us to?"

Kiri trembled again. "Please don't. Not at night. All the night police bring us back to the brothel."

Matt groaned as if he was trying to hide anger. "Do you want us to bring you home?"

"No." Kiri gulped as a tear rolled down her cheek. "Mother would be disappointed."

Hadassah turned to her. "What happened to you wasn't your fault. We can help explain that to her."

"I don't have enough money. She'll send me right back again." She curled up in a ball and stared at the garbage littering the raft.

All the reasons Hadassah decided to join R.S.O suddenly flooded her. "We're going to bring you to friends of ours who are working to shut down the brothels. They have a safe house you can go to."

"Yes. Okay." Her tremble calmed slightly.

Hadassah pushed the raft toward a pier, where Matthew caught hold of one of the stumps of wood and clung to it until both girls were safely off.

Once they reached the closest street, Matthew turned to Hadassah. "I don't suppose you have a map on you, do ya?"

"As a matter of fact." She pulled the playing card out of her pocket and handed it to him.

"Nine of diamonds? What is this?"

She took it from his hands, pulled the card apart at one of the corners, shook it, then handed an unfurled map of Manila to him.

"Okay, I want one of those."

"Present from my mom."

"Tell her I love her." He smiled. "Did she mark off the red light district?"

"I did it tonight before we left."

He looked up at the street signs then back at the map. "I see where we are. Good work steering the raft, girl. You got us within three blocks of the office."

"I wish I could say I did it on purpose. I don't suppose you have a phone to contact Paul and Zeke, do you?"

"It's soaked. I don't dare touch it."

"I left mine with Priscilla."

"As you should have. I guess we better pray for them."

"Good call, Matthew."

Even as they prayed, her heart pounded in her ears. Siren-clad police cars prowled the streets and Kiri shook at the sight of each one.

Matthew pointed to their right. "There's the Holy Spirit College. What a landmark, eh?"

"We're almost there," Hadassah assured Kiri, clasping the girl's hand again.

As soon as they turned the corner and saw the organization's headquarters, Hadassah caught sight of Paul and Zeke walking toward them.

"What happened to you?" Paul asked Matthew.

"Midnight pleasure swim, dude."

"I got a text from Pris," Zeke told them. "She says she's still okay."

Hadassah sighed then turned her gaze to Kiri. "Are you still okay?"

"Please, please take me to the safe house."

"In through this door, then you can cry."

As soon as they walked into the headquarters, Rafaelo met them and made sure Kiri was under good care in another room before he spoke with the rest of them. And he spoke harshly.

"I don't care what the story is, you don't *ever* rescue one of the girls until either there is a raid or we give the all clear. *Ever.*"

"We left one of our number behind to take her place until morning," Hadassah explained, ready to take the fall for her team.

"*What?* What is wrong with you people? Do you have any idea what those brothels are like? How could you even think of doing that?"

"Sir, we didn't leave Priscilla in a brothel." Hadassah fought nervousness. She certainly didn't need that on top of the heap of other emotions.

"Where did you leave her?"

"We left her—" Hadassah began.

Matthew raised his hand for her to stop. "We left her in the alley, sir, the same alley where we found Kiri. And it was Priscilla's idea to stay behind." Hadassah was thankful Matthew took over.

Rafaelo narrowed his eyes as he stared at Matthew. "Do Roberto and Julia know about Priscilla?"

"Yes, sir, they do." He kept eye contact with Rafaelo better than Hadassah would have been able to.

"Hopefully they will be able to do something for your friend. I really hope you haven't blown their cover. But what about the photos?"

"We were able to get the pictures, sir, and Paul can download them onto our laptop tonight so we can print them out for you."

The lights flickered out again, leaving them in candlelight. Hadassah prayed that the laptop's battery would last until power returned.

"Good." Rafaelo shook his head again. "Mr. Cooper and Mr. Murray spoke so highly of all of you. I never anticipated something like this."

"We're sorry we disappointed you, sir."

"And why are you all wet?"

Matthew looked at his clothes. "I had to dive in the river to lose some company."

"And if we didn't find Kiri in the place we did, if she was just on the street, we wouldn't have done what we did," Zeke added.

Rafaelo merely grunted in return.

The door Kiri had gone through opened again and one of the organization's volunteers came out.

"Rafaelo, if they have only one photo off their camera, we've got enough evidence between those and Kiri that bulldozers will follow the police and knock the brothel to its foundation," the worker told him. She whispered to him briefly.

"You," Rafaelo pointed to Paul, "get those photos. You," he pointed to Hadassah, Matthew and Zeke, "you'll accompany me to the police station in the morning if the police can obtain the warrant tonight. I think they can. Good work. I'm not pleased by your actions, but the outcome of this might be better than what we hoped for."

Matthew smiled. "We understand, sir."

"Don't expect much sleep for a few days. You'll find towels somewhere in this office. Go dry off."

Chapter 28:

First Reunion

The testimony from Kiri along with the photos off the camera ended up being enough evidence for the authorities to schedule an early morning raid. Hadassah, Matthew and Zeke accompanied the police so they could search the alley for their friend.

But there was no sign of Priscilla.

Then Hadassah found what looked like the wrap skirt Priscilla had worn. And carved into the dumpster beside where they left her was the second half of I Peter 2:9:

...declare the praises of Him who called you out of darkness into His wonderful light.

Hadassah breathed shallowly and her lip quivered as she stared at the empty spot next to the dumpster. She swallowed hard to fight the tears and looked at her friends. Matthew's arms hung limp. Zeke's face was streaked with tears and his shoulders slumped.

After a minute of staring up and down the alley in shock, Zeke's cell phone rang.

"Hello." Then he paused. "Really? Praise God! We were so

worried. Thanks." He closed the phone and turned to Hadassah and Matthew. "Let's go. Priscilla's with Hyun and Julia. Our work here is done."

Over the following three days, Hadassah, Priscilla, Paul, Matthew and Zeke rested, met together, cried together and prayed together.

"Mr. Cooper took me through a partial debrief over the phone," Matthew explained, "and even though we didn't do things exactly right, he said the most important thing right now is praying for one another, especially for you, Priscilla. Mr. Cooper was really worried about how you're doing after the fact."

Priscilla shrugged and looked at the carpet as she sat on the floor of Julia's apartment. "I was stiff and sore, because I was so scared to move an inch in that trash heap." She pulled at the plush piles beneath her fingers. "The Lord really met me there, though, and I prayed for all of you. I don't think I'd have the guts to do it again. But I knew if I died, I'd go to Jesus. I don't know if Kiri had the same assurance." She looked up again. "I had to take her place."

"We know you did, Pris." Zeke's face was streaked with tears again. "That was the most Christ-like thing I've ever seen someone do. But how did you get out?"

"I almost didn't. I hid inside Julia's cart and Roberto wheeled me out."

"I'm sorry I gave everyone trouble about Pris staying in the alley," Matthew said.

Zeke wiped his tears away. "You took leadership where leadership was needed and then you took the fall for all of us with Rafaelo. Thanks."

"I want to say the same, Matthew." Hadassah fought the tears scrambling up her throat. "We were all blessed by your leadership, even when we didn't agree."

"I'm glad you didn't agree with me, girl." He gave Hadassah his glowing smile.

***

Ten days after the raid, early on a Saturday morning, Rafaelo summoned the team to the headquarters for a meeting.

"Girls in two of our safe homes have requested your visit, so we've arranged it for today. You'll stop by the church on the way. They are having a donations party and you'll be taking toys, musical instruments and toiletries with you. Go have fun, and allow yourselves to be blessed by them."

At the first home, all the girls lined up to dance a traditional Filipino dance. The girls received the gifts and donations with a profound thankfulness.

At the second safe house, only the women were allowed in, since the girls weren't able to handle the sight of a man yet, even a godly man. The house itself was cheerful, beautifully decorated in pink, orange and a soft blue, but the girls themselves seemed joyless. Still, as the R.S.O. team members entered, the girls lined up single file and expressed their gratitude, half of them in English, half in Tagalog.

No matter how much pain creased the faces of these girls, their gratitude was genuine.

It was during this procession that Priscilla cried out.

"Filipa?" Priscilla shook when she whispered her sister's name, but Filipa shouted with delight. For five minutes, the sisters held each other on the steps at the edge of the common room and wept.

"I am so ashamed of myself," Filipa confessed to her sister.

"My sweet, sweet sister, Jesus has taken care of all of that," Priscilla said amid torrents of tears. "I'm going to ask them if you can come back to the States with me."

"Soon," one of the counselors replied when Priscilla asked her. "We need to get her a new passport from the American Embassy, which will take a few more weeks. Until then, she will be in restorative therapy with the other girls."

"I will come back for you, my sister," Priscilla told Filipa. "I'll be the one to bring you back to America again. I promise." She held her sister until it was time to leave.

Before they left, the R.S.O. team members asked the safe house counselors if they could pray a blessing over the girls.

"They may not all receive the blessing right away, but please pray, for I want to see their spirits whole again," the head counselor said.

Each one from the R.S.O. team prayed a blessing. When Hadassah prayed the last blessing, the tangible presence of the Lord filled the common room and a few of the girls even began to form smiles.

As Hadassah turned to leave, one of the girls pulled her aside. "Because of you I feel like I might have a future and be able to have my own business some day."

"I can't let you give me credit," Hadassah whispered back. "God loves you, and He alone gives us the strength."

She now understood Dad's teaching when he said the power to love is a reward from God in and of itself. When she looked at this girl, and all the other girls, her spirit swelled with love for them and their faces were imprinted on her heart.

***

On the plane ride home, the only strong turbulence was the bickering and complaining which sprang up within the team.

"Matthew Cho, you know better than to pull a stunt like that."

Apparently, Matthew had waited until 36,000 feet in the air before he told Hyun what happened on the pier.

Matthew rolled his eyes. "I lived through it, didn't I?"

"Your mother is like a sister to me. How do you expect me to look her in the eye? She made me promise to look after you, to make sure nothing like this happened." She grunted, closed her eyes and turned her face toward the window.

"Zeke," Priscilla whined, "I told you to wake me up when they came by with the dinner."

Zeke sighed and shook his head. "You looked so tired, I wanted to let you sleep."

"But I'm going to be starving before we land."

"You haven't eaten much for days. How was I supposed to know you'd want dinner tonight?"

Priscilla sulked and slumped her shoulders.

Zeke huffed and shook his head again. "Do you want me to ask the stewardess to get you something?"

"Don't worry about it."

Zeke frowned, unbuckled his seatbelt and stood. "I need to stretch anyway."

Hadassah watched quietly as more and more of her friends began to argue.

When they landed on US soil, Paul gathered everyone in a circle. He sounded just like his dad when he addressed them all. "We just experienced a great victory as a team; let's not sabotage our unity any more with bickering."

His words had a profound effect. Around the whole group, team members turned to one another to say, "I'm sorry." Then they gathered again to pray.

By the time Hadassah saw Mr. Murray in the airport terminal, everyone was laughing together, praying together and doing what they could to serve one another.

"You guys have demonstrated the full ethos of what we hoped the Lord would do through R.S.O.," Mr. Murray told them during the group debrief in the van on the way back to the Lighthouse. "Actually, in some ways, you have exceeded our hopes. We'll discuss any breach of protocol later—for now I want you to know how proud I am of all of you."

Somewhere in the skies over the jungle east of Puerto
Vallarta, Mexico

Three weeks later

Chapter 29:
Operation Patient Endurance

Three weeks after she arrived back at the Lighthouse, Hadassah
was strapped to a static line in the belly of a C130 plane. Dressed in
a jumpsuit and full gear, she was on her way to the coordinates in the
Mexican jungle east of Puerto Vallarta. They had left the East Coast
of the US early that morning and were on board the C130 in
Southeast California right after dinnertime. Now it was coming on
10:30pm as they approached their destination. She focused on every
one of Mr. Cooper's words.

"You will have five seconds between each jump," he shouted
over the whir of the plane engine. "Don't forget your order: Dave,
Maleek, Pedro, Matt, Hyun, Christina, Hadassah, Paul, Zeke,
Tameka, then me. Five, four, three, two, go, go, Go!"

As soon as Christina jumped Hadassah counted to five,
unhooked herself from the static line and jumped. She soared down
peacefully though the night air. Aside from the roaring breeze
against her ears, she enjoyed all the silence. Clouds in the distance

encroaching upon the stars filled her with more than a little consternation. Night jumps had always been her favorite, but she had never jumped with inclement weather on her heels.

She pulled the cord and released her parachute then spied out all of her teammates. Dave landed in the small clearing, with Maleek, Pedro and Matthew right behind him. There were scarcely fifty yards between them. Hyun and Christina had to maneuver to avoid colliding.

As concerned as Hadassah was for them, she had to concentrate; this was the first time she was parachuting into a jungle. And however much Mr. Cooper and Dave instructed her, she remembered little while in the air—the jump itself was too exhilarating.

Like everyone else, she made it to the ground with only a few scrapes and bruises. They all gathered at the edge of the clearing to pray together before beginning their hike to find their liaison then head to the drug lord's compound for Operation Patient Endurance.

This liaison, Pablo, had only recently given his life to Christ. He had spent a considerable amount of time at this compound before his conversion, so he knew where the kidnapped victims were held. Pedro's uncle, Pastor Jorgé, and his family were there, also several young girls and a young boy who was probably Maleek's brother.

The jungle, dark, thick and warm, was not at all quiet. Critters of all kinds scurried through underbrush or in treetops. Tree frogs, owls, crickets and other nocturnal creatures sang their night chorus with deafening resonance, even while the team slashed through the underbrush to make a pathway. Overhead, bats swooped back and forth through the darkness. Hadassah ducked more than once, cringing at the thought of another three mile hike through the jungle after they met up with Pablo.

Sometime past midnight, she heard a bird call in the trees ahead unlike any she had heard so far. Mr. Cooper halted the company immediately and repeated the call into the night. It was echoed back to him.

"Hola," Mr. Cooper called out in a loud whisper. "God bless you."

"Greetings in the name of our Lord Jesus," came the reply from up in the trees ahead. Two figures jumped to the ground and met up with them in a clearing. "You must be Aaron Cooper."

"Pablo?" Mr. Cooper asked. "I thought you'd be meeting us out here by yourself."

"Ah, forgive me, amigo, this is my friend José, from Pastor Jorgé's church. He came to keep me company. It's always safer out here to travel with a friend, in case one gets bit by a spider or snake. I know the Bible says snake bites won't hurt us, but I wanted to have a friend with me, just in case."

Mr. Cooper sighed. "He can come, but he will join the intercession team when we get to the compound."

"Before we go there, let me show you the blueprint drawings I made of the house." Pablo took a rolled up paper out of his shirt and pressed it flat on a tree stump.

As Mr. Cooper and Pablo poured over the amateur blueprints and the set Mr. Cooper brought with him, Hadassah hung back and strained to hear what she could of their conversation over the rumble of the distant thunder.

"You can cut the power here," Pablo said. "There will be about ten minutes before someone turns the generators on, since power cuts out all the time and then comes right back, and my old friend doesn't like to waste money unnecessarily on the fuel for the generators."

"Are you nervous?" Matthew whispered to Hadassah.

"Not really," she whispered back, "more excited. I'm glad to have the opportunity to work again. How about you?"

"I just want to make sure everyone gets out alive."

She looked over her shoulder and caught some of the conversation José began with Zeke and Paul. While the man chatted nervously, Paul looked at him intently, while Zeke appeared to be praying through the frustration seeping from his eyes.

"Even the Mexican Army is afraid of this man," José said. "He gunned down two of his own men during our church service simply because they gave their lives to Jesus; he also kidnapped several children along with Pastor Jorgé. If Pablo hadn't told us he saw Pastor Jorgé alive, we would've feared him dead. But we're thankful you've come. Some of these children were missionaries under our care, some of them were even orphans. And the ransom note asked for more than we'd be able to raise in a lifetime."

Hadassah hoped José would be able to control his nervousness when they neared the compound.

Within half an hour the team started their trek once more while Mr. Cooper silently put the plan together. The rain hadn't arrived, but the storm was close enough that they could see lightning all around them. Mr. Cooper had satellite footage of the house, provided by a friend in the CIA, and followed the GPS on his watch toward the location, over brambles, under overgrowth.

He stopped a half mile from the lights in a clearing ahead "Okay, everyone, I have formulated the plan changes. Pablo, Dave, Maleek, and Hyun, you're going to follow me into the house to find the hostages. The rest of you, I want you to stand here, and here." He spread out the blueprints again and pointed to the northeast and southwest corners of the compound, closest to where the master bedroom was on one side and what appeared to be the main office on the other side. "Divide yourselves as you like, but I want Christina at the head of one team and Matthew at the head of the other."

Matthew picked Hadassah, Paul and José to join him, while Zeke, Pedro and Tameka joined Christina.

"Christina, take the master bedroom in the northeast, Matthew, the office on the southwest," Mr. Cooper told them. "We'll be going into the basement. We'll meet at our first rendezvous point at 0400 hours. Radio silent until 0300, folks."

Although she was disappointed she wouldn't be part of the rescue, Hadassah looked forward to her role, praying in close proximity for the safety of the team and for the salvation of everyone who lived or worked in the house. José told them on the walk over that the man who owned the compound prided himself on being the wealthiest drug lord in all of Mexico and he shipped over thirty metric tons of heroin and coke each month to the United States through various channels.

"He's a mastermind, they say," José added. "But he hates to waste bullets."

"Shh," Matthew urged as they neared the southwest corner. The power to the compound cut out just as they gathered in a circle to pray. Matthew began to employ sign language, for instruction and then for prayer. Hadassah whispered the translation to José, and then began praying herself. She tapped her prayers in Morse code with two fingers against her wrist. José, who was visibly nervous, breathing quickly and shifting his gaze all about, began to whisper in tongues, despite urges from Matthew and Paul to stay silent.

"Pastor Jorgé always encouraged us to pray aloud," José whispered back. "He taught us that there's more power in spoken prayers than in silent ones."

"Nothing louder than the rain," Matthew commanded. "Not tonight." Rain fell in a light sprinkle, but grew heavier every minute.

José nodded in agreement, but when it came his turn to pray, he whispered much louder than the sound of the rain. Hadassah's heart pound harder and faster with each of José's crescendos. Would they remain unnoticed until Paul's turn? She urgently beseeched the Lord for the guards about the compound to have blind eyes and deaf ears toward their prayer meeting, toward their whole operation.

The thunder rolled in, and with it louder rain.

"Father," Paul prayed when his turn came around, not as if he wanted to show off, and not as if it was only the habitual way to begin a prayer, "we ask You to bring a miracle here tonight, we ask You to release the captives from their chains, both visible and invisible. We ask You to move on our behalf. Send Your angels to war for us. Help us make it back to America with reports of how You plundered the enemy." His whisper was quieter than the pounding rain, and Hadassah strained her ears to listen to him. "Lord, please protect us." At his last word a loud alarm sounded, red lights flashed, shouting began and dogs barked fiercely.

Hadassah jumped despite herself. *Ten minutes have not passed.*

"Run!" Matthew commanded them. "Run to the rendezvous point."

He grabbed Hadassah's hand and ran toward the trees, but Hadassah tripped on the uneven terrain and fell, landing four yards or more away from him. When she looked up, she saw three large Dobermans jumping toward Matthew. José was behind her, still within the compound, with one dog pulling him by the arm. One of the owners called the dog off José and held the frightened young man at gunpoint.

Without forethought, Hadassah grabbed one of the sticks beside her and ran toward the dogs attacking Matthew and Paul. Halfway there, she realized she held eighteen inches of iron rebar, the kind used to reinforce concrete tubes, and in a surge of fury and fear she swiped at the hind legs of one of the dogs attacking Matthew. At its yelp, the other two dogs turned on her. She was able to protect her face, and her jumpsuit protected her skin, but the pressure from the jaws of one dog clamped her forearm. The pain threatened to make her black out. Then she heard the gunshot, and her terror ran so deep she was unable to focus. "Jesus!" she screamed into the night. "Yeshua! Have mercy on us!"

The two dogs attacking her suddenly yelped. She looked up to see the dogs jumping upon the security guards, not to attack them but from sheer terror.

"Get off of me!" one of the guards yelled at the dogs. "Get the witch woman," he commanded another guard, "and that one there." He shined his light on the figure running toward Hadassah. It was Matthew, and he stopped in his tracks with his hands up in surrender.

"I paid more for those dogs than I ever would for you, witch woman," the guard sneered as he dragged her roughly through the corridors. "I ought to break your legs from under *you*. How would you like that, eh witch woman?"

"She isn't a witch," Matthew said as he was escorted just as roughly behind Hadassah.

"What did you say?" the guard asked.

"I said she's not a witch. She is a woman of God who loves Jesus," Matthew said.

"You want to contradict me?" the guard asked, and then pistol whipped Matthew on the side of the head, causing him to collapse. "You don't even deserve a bullet, you Jesus freak."

Chapter 30:

"Sir, are we in heaven?"

They were dragged to the second basement of the house and tied to chairs alongside the other hostages. Zeke was there along with Tameka, José and two others she didn't recognize—a girl about fourteen or fifteen years old, and a boy who looked twelve. Both of these kids' faces were tear-stained and their bodies gaunt. After a brief glance around, the guards left and took all the lights with them.

The room smelled dank and putrid and was filled with the sound of heavy breathing and groans.

"Is Matt okay?" Zeke asked.

"I don't know." Hadassah's eyes filled with tears. She swallowed them. "The guard hit him pretty hard."

Matthew moaned. "I'm okay, just really dizzy and a little sick."

"You don't sound okay," Zeke remarked.

"I'm Hadassah, by the way," Hadassah said to the children in Spanish. "We came because we love Jesus and He loves you."

"I'm Tameka," Tameka's voice was as steady as anyone could muster.

"I'm Ezekiel, or Zeke for short."

"I'm Matt."

"Hi. I'm Lucia. This is Carlos," the young girl said in perfect English.

Hadassah sighed. Then she took a chance—it might be the same Carlos. "Carlos, your brother, Maleek, came with us to look for you."

"My brother, Maleek?" The boy's voice was filled with shock. "He came for me? I thought he didn't love me. Where is he?"

Before anyone could answer the boy, Lucia began to sob. "Please help us get out of here."

"God can help you," Matthew mumbled. Coming from anyone else this may have sounded trite, but Hadassah could tell he still couldn't lift his chin from his chest. "Tameka, would you sing for us?"

"What shall I sing?" she asked with wavering voice.

"Sing the Hallelujah song, the one about the morning," Zeke suggested.

"Lord God, we ask you to give Tameka strength to sing," Matthew prayed.

As Tameka lifted up her voice, weakly at first, then increasing in strength, the others joined with her.

"Hallelujah, morning is coming... Hallelujah, we will yet see the dawn... Hallelujah, the sun of righteousness will rise with healing in its wings... Jesus, Jesus, You are the Morning Star, Hallelujah... Jesus, Jesus, You are coming again, Hallelujah!"

As she sang, Hadassah remembered she had her utility knife, the one for cutting herself from the parachute if she needed to, nestled between her sleeve and the side of her forearm. It was the arm the dog clamped his jaws around, and its pulsation made her feel nauseous. She continued to sing praises as she edged the knife toward her palm with the chair post. Her arm throbbed, but she worked at it none the less.

By the third chorus of the song, she had the blade out and began to slice through the ropes holding her. Once she freed her hands, she groped around the room to find the others.

"You're free?" Zeke asked her.

"Shh," she whispered in return, and then turned to Tameka, José, Lucia and Carlos.

"You're like the angel in the book of Acts," José said.

"I suspect there are many angels here tonight," Zeke said.

"How are you feeling?" Hadassah asked Matthew as she crouched close to his chair and began to cut the ropes binding him.

"Less dizzy. Ready to roll out of this joint."

"What happened to Paul?" she asked as she hid her knife again.

But she didn't get an answer. The door burst open and three of the guards strode in, accompanied by a bald man well dressed in pajamas. She knew immediately that this was the drug lord.

"Well, well, is this who woke me? A bunch of children. And all unbound. That one. He's much too old." The drug lord pointed to Zeke, and the guard he addressed shot Zeke at point blank range.

The children began screaming before Zeke's body hit the floor.

"Oh, be quiet. And don't try to escape, please, I don't like my men to waste bullets, and I'm not keen about blood on my new carpet upstairs. But we'll shoot you if we need to." The drug lord turned to one of the guards. "Lock the door again after us."

When the drug lord left the room with his guards, they were in the dark once more.

Tameka and Hadassah held one another in total shock while the children cried and Matthew prayed in the Spirit louder and louder.

"Jesus, you came so we may have life and have it more abundantly," José said over and over amid tears. Hadassah and Tameka joined in, though they hardly felt the faith for it. After ten minutes, everyone stopped and fell silent, for they heard a peculiar groan and rustle in the dark.

"He showed me the way to lead you out." There was no mistaking it—this was Zeke's voice.

"We saw you," Tameka said with a shiver. "You died. They shot you and... and you died."

"They nailed the Lord of glory to a cross," Zeke said, "but He rose to life again after three days. Surely He can raise this jar of clay. Carlos?"

"Yes," the boy said meekly.

"Carlos, go try the door."

"But they locked it, sir."

"Go ahead," Matthew urged.

The boy tried the handle. "It's locked."

"Try again," Zeke said.

"Okay," Carlos answered. He twisted once more and the door opened readily for him. "Sir, are we in heaven?" he asked.

"Heaven has come here, my friend," Zeke answered. He spoke with such assurance it filled Hadassah with sudden courage.

"What should we do?" she asked Zeke.

"Go right through that door, on up those stairs, and lead these children out of here."

"What about the guards?" Tameka asked.

"I'll go chat 'em up a bit first, tell them about heaven and why they need Jesus. At least it should distract them, and then I'll see you in heaven. The Lord told me I'd be back in a minute, and quite frankly, I can't wait to see Him again." In the dim light coming through the open door, Hadassah could see a smile beaming on Zeke's face. He had about him, like clothing for a wedding feast, the peace she longed for.

All the way up the stairs and out of the house, Hadassah thought of the words Jesus said, "Greater love has no man than this—that he lay down his life for his friends." And when she was back in the jungle again and heard the second gunshot, her tears had joy mixed with the sorrow.

Chapter 31:

Navigating the Way

Paul was okay," Matthew said to her as the two of them brought up the rear of the group while Tameka led the way. "He was shot in the back of the leg, his right leg not his left. I gave him into Dave's care before I turned back to find you."

"Thanks for coming back for me."

"We did it, Hadassah. We lost a man and suffered a few injuries, but Zeke's with Jesus and the hostages are free."

"Thanks for coming back for me."

The rain had stopped, but the lightning in the distance strobe-lit a passage through the jungle. Both Matthew and Hadassah checked their watches obsessively during the 3 o'clock hour. They didn't want to miss the window of time when they could contact Mr. Cooper before the team was picked up by people from Pastor Jorgé's church.

"Oh, my goodness, you guys are alive," Mr. Cooper exclaimed over the comlink. "How many of you have been hurt?"

"We're alright and we have children with us. But we lost Zeke."

The cheers at the other end of the comlink died.

"What do you mean you lost Zeke?" Mr. Cooper asked coolly.

"He's gone to be with Jesus, sir," Matthew said.

"Listen, get here as quickly as you can, but the van will be gone. We'll be leaving some supplies, and Dave, Maleek, Pedro and Hyun will wait for you. Pastor Jorgé said he would wait for the children, too. But we need to get Paul and Pastor Jorgé's wife to the hospital as quickly as we can: they've both been shot. Follow the coordinates exactly, because the forest gets pretty thick before the clearing."

Matthew turned to Hadassah and Tameka as soon as he finished speaking with Mr. Cooper. "We're going to have to carry these kids."

"Sure," Hadassah said. "I can put the pack on the front of me and carry one on my back. But are you up for it?"

"My head hurts, but I'm okay. I saw you favoring your arm."

"I think the dog fractured it, but I can use the other well enough," Hadassah replied.

They hobbled along at a quicker pace with the children on their backs. Hadassah and Tameka took turns holding Lucia. While on Hadassah's back, the girl clung to her neck a few times and fell asleep once.

Hadassah's knees threatened to buckle, not only from the weight of the girl, but under the weight of guilt for what she did to the dog. And how much she felt like a coward when she saw Zeke get shot.

She rehearsed different ways to phrase what she had to say during the debrief, scraping for something that wouldn't make her feel sick.

Dave contacted as soon as the sky began to brighten. "The others just left in the van, and it'll be another two hours until the next van comes. Give us your coordinates and we'll meet you."

Matthew read the coordinates off his watch, then paused to rest in the growing light. "We'll have to start again in a few minutes, but I'm as tired as I've ever felt."

Lucia looked up at him pleadingly. "Please, sir, we cannot stay in one place. The guards may be on our trail and all the animals..."

"I understand your concern, but if we're going to get you back, we need to rest for a minute," Matthew said. "Just long enough to catch our breath, then we'll go."

"We'll walk, won't we Carlos?" Lucia said.

"I don't want to stay here," Carlos said. "I want to see my brother."

"If you're okay to walk, then we'll go right away."

By the time they connected with the others, Hadassah's arm throbbed so intensely her vision began to blur and she felt nauseous. Although it was a joyous reunion when Carlos saw Maleek, Hadassah could do little more than feign a smile and hold her arm.

As they walked back to the rendezvous point, Lucia walked beside her rather than with the others.

"Thank you for risking your life to save us," Lucia said. "I've seen the power of God in ways I never have before tonight. But I'm afraid He's mad at me."

"Why, Lucia?"

"I don't want the pastor to hear. He'll be mad at me too. I'm afraid because of the drug lord. He... well, he did things to me, at night sometimes, and, um... I tried to enjoy it so it wouldn't hurt so bad, and I'm scared God's mad at me for that."

Hadassah's eyes welled up as she heard this confession. "Can I hold your hand, Lucia?" She stretched her good arm toward the girl.

"Yeah," Lucia replied.

"That man's sin toward you was horrible, and I'm so sorry you had to endure it, but I assure you God is not mad at you for trying to... to navigate your way through someone else's sin against you. What that drug lord did to you was not your fault. But you'll need to see a doctor."

"I don't want my family to find out," Lucia said, fighting back a sob. "Please don't tell them."

"I know you're scared to tell your family, but they'll be a lot less angry than you think. You need to tell them."

The girl cried. "He was getting ready to send us away."

"What do you mean?"

"I heard him on the phone one night. He was talking to Vladimir, Vladimir, oh, what was his name?"

"Vladimir Therion?" Hadassah asked.

"Do you know about him?

"Just bits and pieces."

"He said that there was room for Carlos and me on the next cargo ship. I think that's how the other children disappeared. I'm glad you came to get us."

"I'm glad too."

"I thought for so long that he loved me. Why would he want to send me away? What did I do wrong?" The young girl cried again.

Hadassah took hold of her hand. "You didn't do anything wrong, Lucia."

***

When they were all climbing into the van, and expressing relief over a mission accomplished, Hadassah knocked her arm against the door. She cried out in pain even with her best efforts to constrain herself.

"Come on, Haddy," Hyun urged when she heard the story of how the dog bit her. "You've got to get your jump suit off."

"It can wait," Hadassah insisted. "We should get these kids back to the city first."

"No, it can't wait," Dave said, "and I'll cut the sleeve right off of you if you can't pull it off. I can see how much it's swollen from here."

The van bumped down the dirt road as Hyun and Dave helped Hadassah get her arm out of the sleeve of the jumpsuit. She tried her best not to make a sound, but she groaned loudly as they pulled the fabric away from her swollen forearm. The sight made her weak in the knees—the broken bone pressing against her skin, the skin swollen and bruised to a deep purple.

"That's a break," Hyun said to Dave.

"Take my phone, Hyun." Hadassah pulled it out of her pocket, but in all her shaking she dropped it on the floor of the van.

"Whatchu want me to do with this?" Matthew asked as he caught up her phone.

"There's an x-ray app. But only I can access it—biometrics and all. Can you hold it for me?"

It must have been both concern and curiosity drawing everyone around Matthew while he held the phone over Hadassah's right arm. She accessed the x-ray application and waited for the image to appear. A full break of one bone, and a fracture in the other.

"Cool," Carlos said.

"This needs a splint," Dave remarked. "Is there anything in the van we could use?"

The driver said he had a few six inch one-by-fours and some strips of canvas in a bucket somewhere in the back.

"How tight are you going to make the splint?" Hadassah asked.

"Tight enough, girl." Dave handed her an extra plank of wood. "This is for your teeth if you need it."

"I should be okay without it." She didn't want to make a scene in front of Carlos and Lucia—they had been through enough.

As Dave and Hyun wrapped her arm in the splint, Hadassah

267

asked the Lord to help her bear the pain. At one point she thought she would cry, and a few of her tears did manage to escape, but she kept her composure.

"Part of me wishes you hadn't come," Pastor Jorgé said suddenly in the lull of conversation. "These guys are going to come looking for my church family and me because we left without paying the ransom they asked for."

"I think once you hear the whole story you'll feel differently," Matthew said.

"Si, Señor," Carlos said. "I don't think they'll be coming for us."

"Why don't you go ahead and tell him what happened after we met you," Matthew said.

So Carlos told the story, as only a twelve year old boy could, of how they had been worshiping the Lord and then were cut free from their bonds, and how Zeke had been shot right in front of them then came back to life again talking about Jesus and heaven and a way for them to escape.

"Wait," Pastor Jorgé said, "I thought you said your friend is dead."

"He is, Pastor Jorge," Matthew said. "He said he couldn't wait to get back to heaven and to Jesus' presence; he distracted the guards while we slipped away."

"They were probably so scared when they saw him," Carlos said.

Pastor Jorgé sat agape as if he was trying to process such a story. Hadassah cried silently at the retelling.

Even Dave was teary-eyed "That is the craziest thing I have ever heard."

"The Lord is going to be doing something special through all of you," Pastor Jorgé said, "something the world has never seen before."

***

Hadassah was admitted to the hospital in Puerto Vallarta to get a cast on her arm. She and Paul were released within an hour of each other.

"Here's some good news," Mr. Cooper announced as they all congregated outside the emergency room inspecting the cast and bandages. "We'll have our post-ops debriefing on the beach. Pastor Jorgé has a friend with a resort for Christians on furlough, and he offered us half price."

"Wow, so what's the bad news?" Christina asked.

"You guys will need to help me pay for it," Mr. Cooper confessed. "I'm over budget after these hospital bills."

There were more than a few blank faces in the crowd. Not many of them came from well-to-do families.

"I can pay for mine," Hadassah offered.

"I'll pay for two," Christina said.

"I think I can swing the same," Dave said.

"So do I," Hyun said.

"Thanks, everyone. I'll be contacting Mr. Murray after the debrief, and he'll let the board know what happened," Mr. Cooper said. "We may get reimbursed."

Chapter 32:

Resort

The resort was even more expansive than the drug lord's compound. It was an airy, cream and terra cotta mansion set on a hill jetting into a glistening sea. There was a Jacuzzi bath in every suite, soft towels, cool tile underfoot and sea views from every window. Many of those they rescued from the compound the night before also stayed at the vista and basked in the longed-for peace and presence of the Lord lingering here.

The debriefing had its tense moments, even in those pristine surroundings. For a while Mr. Cooper seemed angry, as if the operation had been a failure. When Hadassah recounted what she did to the dog, she felt as if she would throw up, especially as she glanced at the faces of her teammates. The desire to lie about the events wormed within her. She stopped, then closed her eyes and prayed. It took every ounce of strength not to break down crying, but she prayed for forgiveness and for grace even as she relayed details to the team.

"While I hate the idea of any of God's creatures being harmed," Mr. Cooper said, "that animal was trained to kill any one of you it could catch. It had been corrupted beyond its natural tendencies. Still, in the future, I want all of you to avoid retaliation. That's not our calling."

When it came time to tell about Zeke, Mr. Cooper asked Matthew, Hadassah and Tameka to give an account. With each version of the story more tears were shed, but Hadassah sensed a new, unshakable faith rising up in the group.

"So all three of you attest that Zeke was dead and then came back to life again," Mr. Cooper verified.

"Yes, sir," each of them said in turn.

"And then he went to distract the guards while you three walked up the stairs, out of the house and off the compound with José and the children?" Mr. Cooper asked.

"That's what happened," Matthew said.

"Did the alarm go off when you walked out of the house?"

Matthew shook his head. "No, sir."

"The only sound we heard after we left was the second gunshot," Hadassah added.

Then Mr. Cooper told them about the earlier portion of the operation.

"The alarm kicked in because of a failsafe. The storm cut the power, and then we cut the power, but the drug lord had one of the doors rigged, which triggered the generators and then the alarm. This was something Pablo didn't anticipate, nor could we have expected him to know, so we cannot hold him accountable. How was José?"

"The dude was inexperienced, but genuine," Matthew said. "I don't think he jeopardized us in any way."

"I'll be meeting each one of you for an individual debriefing over the next three days," Mr. Cooper said, "but no more meetings for today."

Hadassah decided to unwind along with everyone else on the long porch overlooking the ocean. A few socialized, but most, like her, had earphones in and Bibles, or other books, open.

Suddenly, Matthew's shadow blocked the blazing sun.

"Do you mind if I sit next to you?"

With quivering hands she removed her headphones. "Go ahead."

He sat on the adjacent sun chair and smiled at her. "I want to thank you again for saving my life."

As she smiled, guilt writhed within her heart again. "Yeah. I'm glad I was there at the right time."

He reclined and stared at her. "How are you doing about Zeke?"

"I should be asking you. You were closer to him than most of us."

Matthew shut his eyes much longer than a blink would require. "It hasn't hit me yet."

"Really?"

He sighed. "I feel like a coward. He was so fearless, so sure about heaven, and there I was, hardly able to lift my head."

"You had a concussion, Matthew. I think God gave Zeke grace to face what came. None of us could do what he did without God's grace."

He turned his face toward the sky. "You seem so strong about all this."

"I've struggled with feeling like a coward, too."

"At the same time, after seeing what happened with Zeke, my faith might actually be as big as a mustard seed now."

She smiled at him, even though he wasn't looking at her, and allowed a tear to slide down her temple and into her hair. She opened her mouth to tell him of all the emotions she held and hid for him, but her voice failed her. She closed her eyes and prayed.

Chapter 33:

Confessions

After the team returned to the Lighthouse, Pastor Gibbons arrived to lead the memorial service for Ezekiel. Tears were shed for Zeke, but not as many as Hadassah anticipated. Except for Priscilla. Priscilla cried as if her heart had shattered at the news. As Hadassah saw her friend's inconsolable tears, she realized what Priscilla had referenced several months before, during their cell group meeting. Or rather, who. She, too, had hidden love for another recruit in her heart. Priscilla had been in love with Zeke.

Mrs. Cooper accompanied Priscilla when she flew to the Philippines to pick up her sister. But instead of returning to the Lighthouse with Mrs. Cooper, Priscilla went home to Florida with Filipa.

Her leaving hit Hadassah like a fastball at Yankees' Stadium. The bravery Priscilla showed in Manila matched Zeke's in Puerto Vallarta, and Hadassah thought she really might stay.

The morning after Priscilla left, Hadassah sat on the porch of her cabin and rocked in the bench swing, staring blankly at the ants working busily in the bright sunlight. She sat and stared for so long she didn't notice Matthew standing at the pillar beside her.

"You want company?"

She smiled wider than she intended and stopped the swing.

"It's gonna kill me, yo, if I don't talk to you soon." He sat on the bench beside her.

Her smile quickly faded and she braced herself. He might know already. He might have come to let her down gently. "Go ahead."

"I am in love with you, Hadassah. I have been in love with you from the first week I met you. I've almost dropped out a dozen times because of the guidelines, except I believe so strongly in what we're doing. And I have never met someone who is as natural at this as you are, girl, except maybe Hyun or Dave. But please—tell me you hate me, tell me you wish I'd quit, tell me *something* in return. When you look at me like that, I wish I hadn't said anything."

Hadassah sat completely speechless for a full minute, hardly able to breathe, listening to the sound of work around the camp, of hammers, table saws, the emotions pounding her heart. "I think I need to talk to Mr. and Mrs. Cooper first." She couldn't understand why she would say this right off the bat.

His hands collapsed into his lap. "Oh."

"Wait. I meant to say I feel the same, and have since I met you in Greensboro, but it's been a struggle for me. I thought you had feelings for someone else; or at least I tried to convince myself of that when it was too painful to love you."

"You love me?" His hands flew into his conversation once more. "You mean you've been in love with me all this time and I didn't know it?" His face beamed, and Hadassah thought for a moment he might even shed a tear. "Just knowing this... everything makes sense now. This is why you've been avoiding me almost since we met."

She nodded, too embarrassed to answer out loud.

"I was trying to avoid you too, for a while. It didn't work."

"I know what you mean. We should talk to the Coopers, though," Hadassah said.

He stared into her eyes. "You saved my life, girl, first in Manila and then in the jungle. Thank you. I just... I couldn't die without telling you I love you. In a way, Puerto Vallarta scared me. I want to be ready to meet the Lord any time He calls me, like Zeke was ready. But I wanted you to know I love you, Hadassah. I'm so into you, girl."

The fullness of emotion in his eyes shook the last dusty places in her heart.

"But you're right," he continued, "we should talk with the Coopers. I'll talk to Mr. Cooper first."

"What would you like me to do, Matthew?"

"Maybe we can start being honest with each other," he said with a gleam. "And you can start calling me Matt."

"Okay, Matt." She stared at him for a long time without saying what she knew she had to. "I spoke with Mrs. Cooper a year and a half ago, when I started with R.S.O., and she prayed with me for several weeks so I wouldn't be distracted by my feelings toward you."

"Did it work?"

"It did for a while. I stopped having dreams about you for almost nine months. But then I fell for you all over again."

"In Manila?"

She nodded and hid her eyes. "The night Priscilla stayed in the alley, and I thought you'd been shot while we were running to the pier, then you took the blame for all of us with Rafaelo. All the while I thought you were mad at me."

"I wasn't mad at you."

She glanced at the wood slats beneath her feet. "I don't want to give up the search for my dad, not for anything."

"I won't ask you to. I don't want to give up searching for my dad either, especially since I'd probably find yours when I find mine."

She suppressed her smile, tried to hide her racing heart. "Do you think the Coopers would make an exception for us?"

"Do you think it would be wise of them?"

"I don't know. I want it to be." She looked up at him again. "I've wanted it to be okay for so long it's been hard to think straight. But I'm glad to talk to you plainly."

"I thought my feelings toward you were one-sided, except you did give hints here and there." He winked at her.

"I'm sorry, Matt, if I caused you to stumble."

He folded his hand over her fidgety hand and drew both her hand and her gaze his way. "I haven't stumbled. And you didn't cause me to stumble. When I look at you, Hadassah, I see the person I want to grow old with, who will challenge me to go deeper with God and to be conformed to the image of Christ. And the more I talk to you, the more I'm sure you feel the same."

Tears slid silently down her cheeks. "I do."

"I want to do something, girl, so we're not wandering around with shame over the way we feel toward one another. I'll be honest with you—you're my Eve."

"I'm not ready to move so fast, Matt."

"We've taken it slow already, yo. We waited over a year before even expressing our feelings for each other."

"But don't you think it would be good to get to know each other before declaring serious intentions?"

"We've already declared serious intentions. At least I have toward you, and I'm not ashamed of feeling this way. Are you?"

"I've fought these emotions for so long and built walls against them."

"Please don't do that to me, girl. Please don't lead me on one minute then dash my hopes the next. I have held this in for so long."

Even while he held her hand, she scraped at her fingertips with her thumbnail.

He brushed his thumb over her tensed hand.

"You didn't tell anyone?" she asked.

"I talked to Christina. You walked in on our conversation back at NoCaHoP, and I hated what you must have thought of me."

"I was so jealous I almost quit."

He hung his head. "Did you tell anyone?"

"Besides Mrs. Cooper, I told Hyun."

Matt's cheeks turned a peculiar hue akin to cherries. "Hyun? Really? You might as well have told my mom."

"Actually, Hyun pried it out of me one night, but she promised not to talk about it."

"Paul knows, but I tell him most things. Other than that I have held this secret so close, and I'm suffocating under your rejection."

"Matt, I'm not rejecting you. I'm just asking you to take it slow, until we get to know each other for real and we stop keeping this secret from one another. Are you okay with that?"

"I am." He stared at her for a long time, then smiled. "And I'm excited for the possibilities."

She allowed a smile to burst out of her again. "Me too."

***

Three days after Mrs. Cooper came back from the Philippines, Hadassah sat down with her to talk about Matt.

"Did Matthew share with Mr. Cooper what you just shared with me?" Mrs. Cooper asked.

"Yes, Mrs. Cooper, he did last week."

"My husband hasn't mentioned it to me yet, but I assume it's because so much has happened. How are you dealing with Zeke's death?"

"It hit me at one point the other day, and I cried in the bathroom for almost an hour, but then I felt the comfort of the Lord around me. Zeke wanted to be with Jesus more than anything, and that, above all else, gives me comfort. I'm just sad for Priscilla."

"We all are. But how is your arm?"

"It itches."

Mrs. Cooper nodded. "I bet it does. About Matt, I'm going to have a talk with my husband, and we'll pray together. In the meantime, why don't you read through Esther?"

"Sure, but why?"

"Because, Hadassah, you were born for such a time as this."

Later in the afternoon, when Hadassah read that passage of scripture, she tried to figure out what Mrs. Cooper had been insinuating. Was she supposed to prepare for marriage like Esther did in chapter 2? Would she leave Revelation Special Ops, like Robert and Hannah did the first year? Her prayers were open and honest, but she did more talking to God than listening, because it scared her to listen. She skipped dinner and remained in prayer, not wanting to see Matt and grow faint with emotion.

Chapter 34:

All the Options

Hadassah." Hyun woke her gently the following morning. "Matt is on the porch. He says the two of you have a meeting this morning with Mr. and Mrs. Cooper."

The disquiet crossing Hadassah's face must have prompted Hyun to ask, "Is everything okay?"

"I fasted and prayed all day yesterday, Hyun, and I think I know what the Lord has spoken to my heart, but I am afraid of what it will mean about my standing with R.S.O."

"Have you and Matt done something?"

Hadassah shook her head. "We've just talked. But I love him and he loves me."

Hyun's eyes widened and she smiled.

"Actually, he loved me before I loved him. A few days before, anyway. But I don't know if I'm ready."

"What are you afraid of?" Hyun asked.

"You know the rules. They'll let us go."

"But you said you didn't do anything to express your love other than talk to one another."

"I know, but Matt is talking about pursuing it and making it permanent. Remember Robert and Hannah?"

"They left because they wanted to get married right away," Hyun explained. "Also, both of them were in their twenties. You're still young, Haddy."

"I know."

"And I think Mr. Cooper will do what he can to keep you and Matt with R.S.O. You are two of the best."

"I've made so many mistakes here," Hadassah said. "What I did in Mexico, to the dog—that haunts me."

"You saved a man's life from an animal trained to kill. Furthermore, he's the man you love."

"And I dismissed protocol in the Philippines."

"Again, this was to save someone's life. If you remember, Matt, Pris, Zeke and Paul helped you."

"I know. Pris was amazing that night."

"God was amazing through all of you. Mr. Murray and Mr. Cooper said in the end that you guys did the right thing. You stayed with R.S.O. that time; I have a feeling you're going to stay this time. But you better go now, or you'll miss your meeting."

When Hadassah stepped out the door, Matt was sitting on the steps of the cabin porch looking as forlorn as she probably did. Boaz lay curled up at his feet, sighing and staring up at the two of them then stretching and falling back to sleep on the dirt.

"I'm sorry I took so long." Hadassah sat down beside Matt and stretched forward to rub the belly of the dog at his feet.

Matt scratched behind Boaz's ears and gave a sad smile. "I didn't know if you were having second thoughts."

It was a chilly morning for May, refreshing against the skin but causing muscles to ache. There was a strong ocean breeze.

"I don't have second thoughts about loving you." Hadassah looked at him. "I'm just weighing all the options. Shall we pray together?"

As they sat on the porch steps, he held her hand in the early morning sun.

As soon as Matt finished praying, Hadassah looked up at him. "I want to keep doing the work we're doing here."

"Me too."

"Am I being selfish?"

He shrugged his shoulders the way he always did, with his head cocked toward his right and the right shoulder raised higher than the left one. "Do you think so?" He stood before she gave an answer.

She slipped her hand into his and they walked toward the main building. So what if anyone noticed? "Do you think we'll ever go on a date like a normal couple? I mean, if we stay here at R.S.O."

Matt laughed loudly, putting her at ease. "What sort of date would you like to go on?"

"Not a movie, but somewhere I could spend more time with you."

"You mean where it's just me and you, instead of me and you and at least six other people?" He laughed again. "Fancy that."

"Well, I wasn't thinking completely alone, but around uninterested people."

"Walking on the beach?"

"That might be fun. Or rock climbing."

"Or bumper cars. What? What's that look for? Yeah, it's a total tourist trap, but I can guarantee there will be 300 uninterested strangers at any given time. And I haven't done bumper cars in years. Have you?"

"No." She giggled as they ascended the stairs to Mr. Cooper's office. "But I don't know if I want bumper cars to be my first date."

"Your first date ever?"

"Aside from sharing popcorn with a boy from my youth group when I was eleven, yes. I've been far too busy since then to notice boys."

"Until I came along," Matt said with a wink as he knocked on Mr. Cooper's door.

"You, sir, are not a boy but a man, and trust me, I noticed you." She smiled nervously as they waited and slipped her hand back to her side again.

Mrs. Cooper opened the door and welcomed them to sit at the couches. Matt and Hadassah sat on one couch, Mr. and Mrs. Cooper on the other. Hadassah scraped the tips of her fingers on one hand while her other hand entwined with Matt's.

"I have to say," Mrs. Cooper began, "that y'all make the cutest couple in the world. I loved hearing you laugh and giggle the entire way here."

Mr. Cooper smiled at his wife, and then turned toward Matt and Hadassah with a more serious expression. "I knew when Mr. Murray and I started Revelation Special Ops, and we'd have both guys and girls at the Lighthouse, a situation like yours would arise one day. And I gave a lot of thought as to how I would like to handle it. My actions are going to be different from my conclusions last year, because I've spent the last week praying about this. I gave Robert and Hannah the option to come back after a year of marriage, but the Lord had another plan for them. I could let the both of you leave right away and come back after a year of marriage. But I have two assignments coming up, and I was wondering if the two of you would be willing to do these first."

Hadassah and Matt both spoke at the same time.

"Sure," she said with her usual enthusiasm.

"What sort of assignment?" Matt asked with more reserve than usual.

"Mr. Murray and I would need you each in separate directions at the same time," Mr. Cooper answered. "Hadassah, you'd be going with Pedro, Zach, Tameka, Hyun and Christina to Rome. There are a number of aspects to this op including the search and rescue of Zach's sister in one of three possible nightclubs in the Trastevere district. This is the reason we'll be calling the mission Operation White Stone.

"You'll meet up with a friend of mine in Rome named Elisha who needs reconnaissance work done on some potential terrorists, and we believe his mission and ours are related. I'll have a side mission for the four of you ladies in Vatican City. It'll take half a day at most, but I'll need you to check up on something for us. All in all you'll be in Rome one month tops. You'd leave in two weeks."

He turned to Matt. "You'd be going to Iraq with Dave, Maleek, Adam and Paul. This is a more delicate operation, since you'll go right into Babylon to rescue some missionaries caught in the midst of a classified dispute between the countries involved. This may be the most dangerous operation to date, and I understand if you decline."

"I'd like to pray about it," Matt answered. "But tell me first why you'd want me in particular to go on this trip."

"My source says your dad's among the missionaries there."

Matt rubbed his eyes with his fingers before turning his gaze to Hadassah and then to Mr. Cooper. "What can I say? Of course I'll do it if that's the case."

"You'll be leaving in nine days." Then Mr. Cooper turned to Hadassah.

She spoke before he could say anything. "I'll be happy to be on assignment, sir. But why not in Babylon? If you have intel on Pastor Cho, then you have intel on my dad."

Mr. Cooper nodded. "I have information on that whole team. But I'm not sending any of you women into Iraq."

Hadassah growled quietly and stared at the floor. "Not even—"

"Not a chance. I won't risk any of you ladies."

Matt angled his head toward her ear and whispered. "I agree with Mr. Cooper. If half of the intel coming out of Iraq is true, then I don't want you near the place."

Hadassah closed her eyes to push back the tears of anger. "Okay."

"When you return, we'll get you two some premarital counseling and organize the wedding, but I want the two of you to have some time off afterward. Maybe not a year, but no less than six months."

Hadassah lifted her eyes again. "Can I call Matt while I'm in Rome?"

"As often as you like, but not with R.S.O. phones. I recommend the free internet calls, but you can do what you like on your own budget. Now, to the matter at hand, we love you, we trust you, don't go running off by yourselves or sneaking into cabins late at night."

"Yes, sir, Mr. Cooper," Hadassah replied.

"No problem, Mr. Cooper," Matt said. "But can I take her out on a date?"

"I'm not the one you need to be asking, Matt," Mr. Cooper said.

Matt laughed another of his contagious laughs. "We already talked about it on the way here."

Mr. Cooper smiled. "You tell us where you'd like to go and either my wife or I will drive you there."

"Maybe the beach, or a coffee shop, or the bumper cars and miniature golf place on 158," Hadassah said.

Mrs. Cooper chuckled, and Mr. Cooper let out the loudest deep belly laugh Hadassah had ever heard him give.

"Wow," Mr. Cooper said, "that is one huge leap from coffee shop to bumper cars."

"Weather contingency plan," Matt said. "And it all depends on how Hadassah's arm is doing."

"How is your arm doing?" Mr. Cooper asked her.

"The doctor in Puerto Vallarta said I'd be right as rain in by mid-May. I like the idea of bumper cars."

"Bumper cars it is, then," Mrs. Cooper said. She turned toward her husband "You talk with Mr. Murray, honey, and find out what day would be good with the schedule."

During dinner that night, Hadassah and Matt sat by themselves and ignored the stares of everyone. It was Matt's turn to wash up that night, along with Tameka and Paul, but Hadassah volunteered as well. The kitchen was cleaner than ever as Hadassah and Matt lingered in their duties, wiping down the spice cabinet and cleaning the inside of the oven.

Hadassah rinsed the paprika from her cloth. "So, I know you started training a year before I arrived, but I don't know your story. How did you meet Mr. Cooper?"

Matt pulled his head from the oven to peer up at her. "I don't know your story, either."

"I know, but I asked first."

"My dad and my mom, after hearing for years that I wanted to become a spy, took me seriously and asked Mr. Cooper to train me. Mr. Cooper said I was a natural, so my mom let me apprentice under him as soon as I graduated from homeschool, which was four years ago now. After my dad disappeared, my mom has been urging me to use my skills to find him."

"Your mom sounds a bit like my mom."

"Yeah, I remember your mom. I wonder what it would be like if the two of them got together and did miniature golf. Anyway, my mom told Mr. Cooper to train me, and so I was the first R.S.O. recruit. He taught me various forms of self-defense at first, and then taught me all about the underbelly of the world. What?"

Hadassah looked up from the dishes and smiled. "I'm imagining your training sessions. My first one was barbed wire."

"I'm jealous, girl. I had to wait three months before barbed wire. Tell me more about you. Did you have a job before you came to R.S.O.?

"Sort of," Hadassah said, "but it wasn't a normal one. My mom has a private detective agency in New York City, and I would do surveillance for her during my breaks from school."

"So, while everyone was opening Christmas presents, you were spying on people?"

"I only spied on the baddies. I was also a lifeguard for a summer, but that was when I was fifteen."

"But what about Africa? Did your mom send you there?"

"You know about Africa, do you?"

"Everybody does, I think. It was such a crazy story, with you being sixteen and all alone in the field."

"I was seventeen," Hadassah said, "and I wasn't alone, because God was with me. But I think I'll save that story for our first date."

"This is our first date." He paused in his scrubbing, wiped his brow and looked at her. His face glowed. She forgot to breathe.

"Okay, you two lovebirds, are we finished yet?" Tameka asked. "I want to go to sleep at some point tonight."

***

On the day of their date, mist and fog enveloped the whole campground. Mrs. Cooper drove them to a coffee shop a block from the beach and promised to pick them up in three hours. A first date at the seaside! A second date, rather. They took their tea out onto the beach and sat under one of the piers in the unseasonably cool mist. Her chai tasted better than she anticipated, but it went cold before she finished it. Matt had ordered her a chocolate chip cookie, but she was too engrossed with what he was saying to eat.

"My dad took me to South Korea when I was eight to visit the homeland and my grandparents. He was the main speaker at a conference, so we had all expenses paid. After the conference was done, he took me around to some fun places."

"Was that when you went spear fishing?" she asked.

"Yeah. You remembered."

"Yes, and I thought you were so arrogant when you said it."

"Do you still think so?"

"Go on."

"I love your diplomacy—I could just kiss you."

She scrunched her nose at him. "Not yet."

He chuckled nervously and stared at his feet again. "So, yeah, one day my dad told me my Korean was atrocious and I talked with an American accent. I tried to explain that I was American, but he didn't really go for my excuse. He dropped me off in the food court in one of the malls and hid in a toy shop. I had to ask around until I was given directions to this toy store. By the time I met him there I spoke without an accent, so he bought me something."

"Were you scared?"

"Not really; it was more like a game and I had fun. I also got some pretty sweet loot out of the deal. I was big into spy toys back then, and I got this whole set of gadgets."

She giggled. "Did you think you'd be doing this sort of work?"

"Are you kidding me? I was convinced of it! But what about you, girl, did you think you'd be doing this sort of work?"

"Not in the way we are now, but I was sure I'd be doing something in this field. My mom started training me the morning after my Bat Mitzvah."

"So you're into all the Jewish traditions, huh?"

"My mom's parents are Hasidic Jews from the Lower East Side in Manhattan. They live in Tel Aviv now. But my mom still eats kosher and keeps a lot of the traditions."

"Did you tell your mom about me?"

"I did."

"Would she disown you for marrying a Korean?" he asked.

"My dad wouldn't," she said, "but I can't read my mom when it comes to this sort of thing."

"My mom was upset at first when I told her you weren't Korean, then when she found out that you weren't just Jewish but are Pastor Michelman's daughter, she was ecstatic. She's gonna love you."

Hadassah smiled and sipped her cold chai, then stared off at the mist lingering over the waves.

Matt scraped the sand from under his fingernails. "Isn't it strange how our dads disappeared on the same trip to the Middle East but you and I haven't talked about it this whole year?"

Hadassah gazed at him, trying to draw his stare from his fingernails back to her eyes. "I didn't want to talk about it much, but mostly because I hate talking without putting together a strategy."

"Isn't that what we're doing here at R.S.O.? Besides, I think I know why they'd be alive still."

"Free labor." This time Hadassah averted her eyes and absently scraped the tips of her fingers.

"That's the reason for the cargo ships." His voice sounded hollow. After a minute he reached out his sandy hand and took hold of hers. "I remember this story my dad told me about these people called the Moravians."

"I heard my dad talk about the Moravians before."

"Yeah. There were two of them who actually sold themselves into slavery for the sake of reaching the West Indies' slaves with the gospel. They worked on a sugar plantation in St. Thomas in the Virgin Islands, and after several years as slaves, they formed a church."

"I don't know many people nowadays who would do something like that." Hadassah grimaced as she tried to imagine. "Most of the slaves... at least the women... Kiri..."

"I can't even think of suggesting that." He pressed his lips together and shut his eyes. "But our dads, if they are alive, have got to be serving the slaves and bringing them the gospel."

As they both stared out at the ocean's steady surf, Hadassah glided her thumb back and forth across the top of his hand the way Mom used to do with Dad whenever he looked overwhelmed.

"So, uh, are you going to take me to New York sometime?" Matt asked.

"Absolutely. And I'll take you to Coney Island where we'll have the best hot dogs on the planet."

"Wait, I thought you were kosher."

"Just my mom. You'll understand when you get to know her. And when do I get to meet your mom?"

"Probably as soon as we get back."

Chapter 35:

Operation White Stone

Their days of bliss were but a breath, with all their starry-eyed gazes at one another. Her cast came off the day Matt left and her bags were packed a few hours before she left with her team to catch her plane. She packed her phone in the hopes of seeing Matt's face through video while she was in Italy.

The air, when she landed in Rome, felt stiflingly hot after the cool weather back at the Lighthouse, but the heat didn't inhibit Hadassah's sense of impending adventure. She was on assignment again, even if the stay was to last a month, and even though she missed Matt.

Hadassah, Christina, Tameka, Hyun, Pedro, and Zach met in the café closest to the baggage claim and prayed together before meeting up with their driver outside the terminal. Everyone's face had a glow —the rest of them must have been just as excited as Hadassah.

She recognized Eli as soon as she saw him standing in front of the church. He looked no older than thirty, but he had a sternness to his face which would have looked more appropriate on a man of forty-five or fifty.

"I'm Elisha," the man said as they all piled out of the minivan. "But call me Eli. Shalom, Hadassah, you look just like your mother."

Sometimes Hadassah wished Mom filled her in more often. "Shalom, and thank you. How do you know my mom?"

"Eva and my mom served together when they were kids in the IDF. Your mother took you to visit us when you were younger, about three or four years old, and we played together a few afternoons." He would have been old enough to be the babysitter, but he was gracious enough not to say so. "Didn't she tell you she recommended you for this trip?"

"No, she's known to keep that sort of thing secret," Hadassah replied. She didn't know Mom had any connection to this operation at all.

After a light meal, Eli took them to one of the offices in the back of the church, where a conference table was set up and on the table, in front of each chair, was a folder labeled with each team member's name.

"Is this our assignment while we're here?" Pedro asked, thumbing through the folder.

Eli looked up briefly, as if a fly had bothered him. "The first two pages are rules of protocol and some suggestions to close the culture gap when you're following our suspects, who are mostly Arab. I don't want any of you to draw unwanted attention by inappropriate comments, dress or behavior. I sent all of this to Mr. Cooper and Mr.

Murray, but it seems some of you overlooked the memo." He glanced at Christina.

"We just got here." Christina pulled up the strap of her olive green tank top.

Eli continued as if he had never been interrupted. "Page three has your schedule for the meetings with me, and when you will have time for meetings among yourselves. Page four is the map to where you will be staying tonight. Also, notice the worship service times; I recommend trying to attend as many as you can. There is a house of prayer we participate with; you'll see it marked on the map. You are welcome to spend as much time at the prayer house as you need. I've communicated with the leaders, and they said you have special access there day or night.

"Turn to page five and you will see a map with circles. At the top of your map you will see the name of your teammate. I'm sending you out two by two, just like Yeshua did back in the day.

"You'll have tomorrow and the next day mostly free, so I recommend familiarizing yourself with Rome. You're free to go now and find your host home, but please, remember the first two pages on protocol and dress."

Christina rolled her eyes at him. "Are you for real?"

"If you think I'm hard to take, you should meet my friend Elijah."

"That's cute, Elijah and Elisha."

Eli glared at her briefly. "I guess it's good for you that he's in Kiryat Shmona."

Christina curled the edge of her lip and squinted. "Where?"

Hadassah stood from her chair. "In Israel. Northern border, next to Syria."

Every eye turned to her.

She shrugged. "I've always wanted to go back, so I studied the geography."

As everyone packed the folders into their bags and held out the page showing their host home, Zach stopped and said, "You never told us what our purpose and end game of this operation is."

"Those various locations you will survey and spy out hold the members of what we believe is a human trafficking ring stretching through Italy, Albania, Greece, Turkey, Syria, Egypt all the way to the Gaza Strip and even Israel. We believe their victims are mostly women and children and we don't trust their operations or businesses to be within the realm of the law—anyone's law—or of morality. I'm also convinced these guys are involved with some kind of terrorist activity. But we can't get the authorities to take us Jews seriously on what we've found. One of these guys has connections with the Mafia, but that intel won't leave this conference room. Also, the police and military have so many other concerns, they don't want to invest money and people power without some hard evidence. Over the next month, I hope each one of you will bring me back hard evidence."

The team filed out. All except for Hadassah, who stood at the conference table and tried hard to remember Eli from all those years ago.

"I'd love to catch up with you sometime this week, Hadassah," Eli said as he straightened up the room and pushed the chairs into place. His tone almost sounded pleasant.

"Maybe you can tell me what I was like at three," Hadassah said. "My mom never talks about it, and my dad only says I was cute."

He gave a smile. "You were. And you've grown into a beautiful woman."

"Um. Eli—"

Once more, his expression turned hard. "Do you have someone in your life?"

"I do." She scraped at her fingertips and thought of Matt. Was Mom upset about him? Did she arrange this? She decided she would e-mail Mom first thing when she got to the host home. She had a few questions for her about Eli. Then an e-mail to Matt.

***

"I was so excited when I saw you talking to Matt," Christina said when they were finally alone at the host home. "He told me a year and a half ago that he was in love with you. And you guys work so well together. If I was in love with someone at R.S.O. I don't think I could go on assignments with him and not buckle under the heartache."

They talked in low voices as they set up their sleeping arrangements in the spare bedroom of a family's home. It had been the father's office, but he took out his computer and most of the books. There was enough room to make a bed on the couch and a bed on the floor and they would need to sit on the desk to check e-mail. As for the sleeping arrangements, they decided to switch every few nights between the couch and the floor.

"You can take the couch tonight," Hadassah said. "I want to e-mail my mom and Matt, and I wouldn't want to step on you."

The next day, after sleeping off some of the jet lag, and while Pedro and Zach explored a few of the surveillance locations, Hadassah and Christina met with Hyun and Tameka for the side mission Mr. Cooper gave them.

After telling their driver about the drop off point in front of Vatican City, Hyun sat in the back seat of the van with Hadassah, Christina and Tameka. In a hushed voice she explained the nature of the mission. "There's an artifact from the ancient city of Pergamum that was excavated in the late 1800s and taken to the Pergamum Museum in Berlin, Germany in 1908. I saw the piece in person during an assignment with the CIA."

"What is it?" Christina asked.

"Satan's throne," Tameka stated as her jaw dropped.

Hyun nodded.

Hadassah's stomach somersaulted at the thought of it.

"You mean the throne spoken of in Revelation 2?" Christina grimaced.

Hyun pulled a paper from her back pocket and unfolded it. "This is what Mr. Cooper wants us to look for."

Hadassah stared at this picture of the massive structure built with steps, columns and statues that had to have been bigger than her whole apartment back in New York City. The steps led up to a columned platform covered with intricate carvings which were hard to make out in this picture.

Hyun continued. "An altar to Zeus from the second century B.C. That, among other artifacts, is what Mr. Cooper heard was delivered to the Vatican from Germany last month. We're going to confirm whether this is rumor or reality. It's pretty big so it shouldn't be hard to spot."

When Hadassah entered St. Peter's Square and walked past the immense obelisk, then under the shadow of the statues of saints, she immediately felt dwarfed by the antiquity of the place.

Hyun waited until they were at the far side of St. Peter's Basilica before she turned to them again. "You ready to split up?"

She waited for them to nod. "Tameka take the eastern side of the museum, Christina the western side of the museum, Hadassah explore the gardens, and I'll go through the administrative buildings."

The tickets Hyun had bought for each of them gave Hadassah almost unlimited access, at least for a tourist. But as much as she explored the stunning gardens of Vatican City, Hadassah couldn't locate this giant edifice Mr. Cooper had commissioned them to find. Her frustration burgeoned. After an hour of traipsing past the greenest grass she had ever seen, her phone buzzed with a text from Tameka.

I FOUND IT.

Hadassah headed toward the eastern side of the museum. As soon as she saw the huge altar a tingle of nausea went right down to her bones.

Tameka looked distressed. "It would have been better if they planted a bomb instead of bringing this awful thing here."

"Sometimes people don't know what they're playing with." Christina shrugged.

Giving them all a hard look, Hyun said, "And sometimes they do."

Hadassah stared at this altar to Zeus with an impending sense of doom filling her.

After a few minutes Hyun leaned toward her. "Would you take a picture with your phone and send it to Mr. Cooper?"

Hadassah pulled her hairpin out and handed her phone to Hyun. "I'll use this camera if you use that one."

With the pictures taken and the sense of doom shaken off, Hadassah followed her friends back through the Sistine Chapel and the Basilica to the square. Every cobblestone of St. Peter's Square was filled with tourists and pilgrims, packed like sardines under the afternoon sun. In the matter of a minute she saw why. There on a balcony stood a young man dressed in Pontiff garbs from head to foot, waving at the crowd. Hadassah pulled her phone out again and snapped pictures of him. She quickly zoomed in on a few of the shots. Just as she thought—his mouth formed a perfect smile, pushing up his sculptured cheeks until he looked like he was modeling for one of those men's magazines, but his eyes held a shivering coldness and contempt. For who? These people? Why?

They had to wait until Pope Leo XIV walked back inside before the crowds dispersed enough to let them leave.

A sadness crossed Hyun's face as they strolled among the crowds toward the gate. "Thanks ladies, you can count this as mission accomplished."

Christina fixed a level stare on her. "What's wrong, friend."

With a shake of her head, Hyun looked at them. "So many people adore him for his position without realizing the blackness of his heart."

Tameka looked as if she was about to cry. "I know. For half my life I thought we'd be raptured before we saw something like this. Now, I almost wish we were."

So did Hadassah, until she considered the work they set out to do. The idea of the Rapture before the tribulation suddenly felt like abandonment, like she was saying to the world, 'I'm goin' to paradise, I guess it sucks to be you.' She didn't want that, no matter how tempting.

On the afternoon of their third day the four of them shopped for the perfect blending-in look. When they gathered with the rest of their teammates for dinner and the meeting, even Eli approved of their apparel.

Christina sat down next to Eli at the conference table. "Glad to know I'm up to standard."

He nodded toward her without making eye contact. "Glad you know how to keep with protocol."

Christina gave an exaggerated roll of her eyes, then a flat smile, then a, "Thanks."

When the meeting started, Hadassah concentrated on every word that was said.

"We may need to shift surveillance locations each week, or every couple of days, so we don't arouse suspicion," Pedro told Eli.

"I have given some thought to that." Eli drummed his fingers on the conference table. "We'll also be shifting you to different host homes periodically to keep the families safe."

"What do you know so far about the people we're watching?" Zach asked.

"We think a few are Jordanian and Palestinian and at least one is from Syria, although this is still unconfirmed. The rest seem to be from Serbia, Albania, Macedonia, Italy and Egypt. Two or three of them are family men, but the rest are single."

"We followed one of the men last night right up until he went into a nightclub," Zach explained.

"Did he come out of one of the houses?" Eli asked.

"Yes, and he had a key to the place so we know he lived there," Pedro said.

"Did you catch the name of the nightclub?" Eli asked.

Zach and Pedro looked back and forth at each other, as if they hoped the other remembered.

"La Bestia Alata, I think it said," Zach told them.

"Hm. The Winged Beast." Eli grimaced and stayed quiet for a few minutes. "I don't suppose any of you speak Arabic, do you?"

"I do," Zach said.

"Good. I want you to go there and scope out the scene. Just don't take the ladies there."

"What do you know about the place?" Pedro asked.

"It's the sort of place you wouldn't bring your sister, or even your enemy's sister. All sorts of unsavories spend time there, young and middle aged men who border on what you Americans call, uh, gangsters."

"That's the strange thing," Pedro said. "Earlier in the day we saw our tango dressed as conservative as can be, like a proper Muslim man who prayed five times a day. But when he emerged later that evening, he looked like a regular thug. Am I right, Zach?"

"We followed him at first to make sure it was the same man," Zach said. "He was, just all thugged out. It was really strange."

Eli growled in a low tone. "I've heard they have a back room in the club where only members can go, but the use of that room is kept secret. I know of it because one of our brothers at the church used to frequent the club before he came to know Yeshua Ha'Mashiach. I can tell you he has no good words for the place. He calls it Il Ventre Della Bestia, or the Belly of the Beast."

"And you want us to go in there?" Zach asked.

"I want you to find out what goes on in that back room," Eli said. "But only if you don't sear your conscience or compromise your soul in the process."

The next evening, all six of the team members gathered for a meeting among themselves before heading out for more surveillance work. After much prayer and mutual decision, Zach and Pedro went to the club while Hadassah and Christina, and Tameka and Hyun agreed to pray at cafés just down the street.

"Then to the prayer room afterward," Tameka said, "because we'll all need it."

Hadassah and Christina stopped along the way to buy some new clothes so they'd blend into the club district in Trastevere.

While they prayed, open-eyed as if they were merely chatting at a café on the outskirts of this sketchy section of Rome, Hadassah noticed one of the men she and Christina had been investigating. He was dressed exactly the way Pedro had described his tango the night before. Thug. Stereotypical gangster. She motioned to Christina.

"Shall I follow him?" Hadassah asked.

"Let me do this," Christina suggested. "If anyone stops me, I'll look more like a lost tourist than you."

"Remember not to lie, though."

"I remember." Christina winked. "Still, I don't have to tell the whole truth."

Hadassah sat uncomfortably alone in front of those two cups of coffee. Christina was out of sight quickly, lost in the thick Saturday night crowds, but Hadassah still looked toward where she had last seen her, and prayed.

"You are so lovely, and I keep seeing your face everywhere I go."

The man standing beside her table, standing practically over her, was one of the men she had been surveying. He sat in Christina's seat.

Chapter 36:

The Recording

Her heart pounded but she smiled coolly at the Middle Eastern man sitting across from her. He was dressed just like the other two men, as if he was on his way to the Winged Beast club.

"I have seen you, too." She employed her normal Brooklyn accent. "Such a strange occurrence in such a large city." She switched on her watch's voice recorder.

"Or maybe not so strange," he replied. "How long will you be staying here?"

Hadassah shrugged. "A month."

"You may be looking for work while you are here," he said.

"I don't know. Perhaps. But I am waiting for my friend."

"Your boyfriend?"

"No, she's just a friend."

"Perhaps she would be interested as well in making some money while in this beautiful and ancient city."

"I don't think I'll speak for her. But tell me what sort of work so I can consider." She tried on her best innocent smile as she spoke.

"Waitressing, bartending, singing, dancing if you're any good. You look like you have the body of a dancer, if I may say so."

"Thank you, sir. But it's been years since I've had a lesson."

"Do you like to dance?" he asked.

"Sometimes I like to. Do you have ballet? I mean, that's a ridiculous question, ballet's just the only dance I know."

"Ballet would come in handy." His grin and glance made her even more uncomfortable. She tried her best not to cringe. "Would you like to come with me now and see for yourself?" he added.

"I have to wait for my friend."

"Are you sure? Because it's not far—just down the street. And I can buy you a drink as well while we discuss your possible employment. That is if you are old enough for a drink."

"I am in Rome. But I'll have to take a rain check."

"A rain what?" the man asked.

"Sorry," she said with a laugh, "American expression. It means I'll have to do it another time."

"You have the most exquisite laugh, young lady, if I may say so."

"Perhaps if you have a card with your phone number, I could give you a call."

He brought out a whole pile of business cards from his pocket and rifled through them before selecting a card for her. She noticed a few written in Greek, some in Arabic, a handful in English, but most of them in Hebrew.

"Here's my card. Please, call me for that, uh, rain check," he said, staring into her eyes and caressing the tips of her fingers as he handed her the card.

"Tell me, sir, how would I be able to work here if I'm a foreigner?" She stared at the card, noticing it only listed his first name, Junayd, and a cell phone number. No address.

"We'll help you take care of work permits. Once we decide to hire you, which I'm sure we would, we fill out the paperwork and submit the application on your behalf. It's simply a formality, really. Immigration is quite generous with us."

Hadassah thought he would never go, and she was sure she had crossed the line of R.S.O. regulations during the conversation before he finally did leave. She wanted to wash away the smell of his breath and the stench of his cologne, but instead she switched off the voice recorder on her watch and waited for Christina.

"Who was that?" Christina asked as she came from behind.

"You scared the beheebee's me!" Hadassah covered her racing heart with her hand until her breath calmed. "He's one of them, but I'll explain later. What kept you so long?"

"I was watching you from over there and taking a few pictures. Also I was ready with a text to send for help if he tried anything."

"Nice. Good thinking to take pictures. I got a voice recording. We need to stay here until we hear from the others, then we can talk about what to do next once we've reached the prayer room."

The night had grown cold when the team convened near the café and walked through the Piazza to the prayer house on the other side of the city. Not one of them was short on reconnaissance information, but they were all silent on the road.

Instead of gathering immediately into one of the side rooms for a meeting, they headed straight for the main prayer room. The room was painted in pastel hues of blue and green, with a huge mural of the tree of life on one side. Painted within the tree of life, darker brown than the trunk, was the cross and, even more subtly, a lamb. Instead of leaves painted on, there were prayer requests taped or tacked on. Instead of fruit, there were notes of praise to God.

When they stepped inside, Hyun rejoiced; Zach wept; Pedro, Tameka and Christina prayed over Zach; and Hadassah sat in quiet prayer as a vision descended upon her, a vision of leading the despised and lowly through the sewers of Rome.

"Wherever you call me, Lord, I will go," she whispered, with her arms raised high in the air.

The steady stream of prayers up front paused as someone made an announcement: the Messianic rabbi, Zebulon Hus, would be teaching on the End Times in five minutes in one of the side rooms. Pedro and Zach decided to stay in the main prayer room for a time of worship in the word while the ladies listened to Rabbi Hus's teaching.

"How important it is to take Yeshua at his word," Rabbi Hus preached. "He said we would have trouble in this world. He did not say to wait around for the rapture to take us up out of the tribulation

—no, He said to watch and to pray. Watch what? And pray what? Watch on the walls, stand in the gap, like it says in Ezekiel. We sing in that old song, 'These are the days of Ezekiel, dry bones becoming as flesh.' If these are the days of Ezekiel then I tremble, friends, because those were days of God's manifest wrath against sin. And many whom we stand in the gap for right now, those who refuse to repent from adultery, drug use, idol worship, murders and thefts, will be objects of His wrath. Pray you will not fall into offense when you see the wrath of God and of His Lamb against sin. Because I believe many in this room will see it.

"We are not going to be raptured out, Beloved of God, as if to watch the outpouring of His wrath from balcony seating—" at this the old man paused and wept. "No, my friends, we will be right in the midst of it; and if our eyes are not overflowing with tears like Jeremiah's were, then we need to get closer to the heart of God. We will be rejoicing and weeping all at once—rejoicing for the Day of the Lord is near, and it is *great;* weeping, because the Day of the Lord is near, and it is *terrible.* Oh, Beloved of God, what a great and terrible day it will be. And just as Moses witnessed the great and terrible day of God's wrath on Egypt, so you, too, will see, will pray, will partner with God, because now is the hour to ask God to open the seals."

Did she hear what she thought she heard? Hadassah wanted to linger longer than five minutes as people in the room began to pray this prayer at the end of the sermon. But the team had delayed their meeting long enough.

The office they met in belonged to one of the leaders of the prayer house, who gave the key to Pedro and hung the Do Not Disturb sign on the door before leaving.

Everyone was as anxious to speak as they were to hear, but Pedro and Zach went first.

"The place was vile," Pedro said. "I doubt those girls get paid a decent wage, if at all. I saw one smile, and it was forced, as if she knew what was expected of her. I spent most of the night observing without trying to look, if you know what I mean. And the mental attacks from the enemy were intense. I can't, and don't want to imagine, what it would have been like without your prayers."

"I second what Pedro said," Zach began. "I would have drowned in spiritual and fleshly filth without your prayers. But I found the door to the secret room. It was heavily guarded, and security packed semiautomatics. I found out the men's room is quite close, and there's a vent in one of the stalls."

"What are you thinking of?" Hyun asked.

"I'm thinking I want to go back there next Saturday and see if I can get into the vent. The music is so loud I doubt if anyone would be able to hear me. But first, I need to find a hall of records for buildings to see if there are copies of blueprints. I want to know where I'm going if I'm going to crawl through the vents."

Tameka and Hyun were the next to relay what they had learned.

"We saw one young man from our surveillance practically transform in front of our eyes," Tameka said. "It was strange to see him go from the devout Muslim look to the gangster look as he walked along. No one seemed to take notice, either, which was the odd thing about the whole episode."

"I waited until he was about fifteen yards ahead," Hyun said, "and then I started to shadow him—all the way to the club. I had no desire to go in, but it took time to backtrack to Tameka while avoiding attention of bouncers."

"I had about the same experience," Christina shared. "I actually saw you, Hyun, from a distance, but thought better than to say hello, given our circumstances."

Hadassah told them what had happened in the café and of the voice recording, although she didn't dare play the recording in the prayer house. "I've been totally compromised for the surveillance work, but I think I have an idea."

"The voice recording and pictures may be enough to blow their operation wide open," Pedro said.

Hadassah shook her head. "More hard evidence is necessary."

"I could take the camera into the club," Zach said, "but I don't know if it would pass the pat down on the way in."

"I have an idea I'd like to share," Hadassah said.

"What is it?" Hyun asked.

"I could try to get into the sewers, and survey from under the club."

"The sewers of Rome are crawling with all sorts of people," Hyun explained.

Hadassah nodded. "I know. But how do you guys feel about this plan?"

"Not too good about you being on your own," Christina said.

"But I'm not sure what our other options would be," Hadassah said.

"Me neither," Hyun said. "And if you've been recognized and identified, some of the rest of us may have been as well. We'll have to use far more caution. For now, Hadassah, help Zach find the building specs and investigate those sewers, but only in daylight. I'll be calling Mr. Murray and Mr. Cooper tonight. I'm glad we stopped to pray—thanks for the suggestion, Pedro. We should do this as often as possible."

"And make sure you catch one of Pastor Hus's teachings next time," Christina said.

"It was right on target." Tameka lifted her face to the ceiling and closed her eyes. "He said that it's the hour to pray for the Lord to open the seals."

Zach's mouth tightened, then he nodded his head. "Wow. I think I'm going to pray about that tonight."

"Me too," Hadassah added. "Rabbi Hus didn't seem like the sort of man who'd jump ahead of God. And I'll see you, Zach, first thing on Monday morning."

When she arrived at her host home, Hadassah called Mom to ask for a map of Rome's sewers.

"What do you mean I already have it?" Hadassah said. "Since when?"

"It's one of the apps on your phone. You can also interface the map of the underground tunnels and sewers with the map of the city."

"That'll come in handy. But why don't you tell me these things, Mom?"

"You know me, I only give out information on a need to know basis. I love you."

Hadassah hung up the phone. "Done."

"Did I hear you right?" Christina asked. "You already had maps of the sewers without knowing it?"

"My mom." Hadassah shrugged her shoulders.

After locating the application Mom talked about, she e-mailed Matt. He had been in Iraq for three days at this point, but still hadn't written her after the initial "I'm safe," e-mail. She was worried, but held back most of the worry in her letter. Within five minutes of sending it off, she received his reply.

"Mr. Cooper was right about the work here in Iraq — not the safest, but I have only seen the mere perimeters of the assignment so far. Four of us are in Babylon now: Adam, Maleek, Pedro and me. And what opulence surrounds us. I can barely think of words to describe it. The buildings are not only taller than most in America, but the architecture surpasses any elegance I have seen in any other

country. They employ color and texture here as if to please some heathen god. No one neglects to add what would be most pleasurable to the eye. A carving of a flower here, a statue of an animal there, but all tastefully done, and all covered with precious stones.

"This place feels like a museum, and I'm afraid to touch anything. Also, the people living here walk about as if they had to have dance lessons before they could live here. I've had to learn how to walk like this because there are police and soldiers everywhere, and people are stopped and searched frequently if they look like they don't belong here. Our contact says this won't last too much longer. He says it has to do with all the cargo ships coming up the Euphrates from the gulf. There have to be ten or more ships on any given day, and they operate with such precision.

"Now, about Eli trying to ask you out — why shouldn't he think you're gorgeous and extremely intelligent? You are. He should be jealous of me. I pray for you every day, even when I cannot write. I can't wait to see you again."

She searched the social networking sites to see if they could chat in real time. There he was, with the happy little on-line circle glowing green. Her face lit up when she saw the flashing screen—he had beaten her to the keyboard.

"Real time is always better than e-mail," he typed.

"Real close is even better than that," she typed back.

"*The connection at the hotel is spotty; it may cut out before we say goodnight.*"

"*What time is it there?*"

"*Three forty-five,*" he replied.

"*Are you up early or late?*"

"*Either. I can't sleep much. I'm worried about you. Write me as often as you can to let me know you're okay.*"

"*I will,*" she replied. "*I love you,*" she typed for the first time, but it came back with a message saying Matt was now off line and didn't receive it. She had the option to send it as an e-mail, and she stared at the screen for five full minutes, debating. She closed her laptop instead. She didn't want the first time she said it to be through e-mail.

Chapter 37:
Plans and Tunnels

Finding the building plans for the Winged Beast Nightclub was harder than Hadassah had anticipated. The manager of the records recommended searching by the club name, and when that failed, they looked up by the building's previous name. This search yielded the name of a possible builder, but the file only had a few permits for electrical and HVAC upgrades. No blueprints.

After another two hours, Zach found blueprints under the builder's name. There were two sketches: one of the bar and one of the dance floor, both with the building's previous name at the top. On one of the pages in the lower right hand corner was the architect's name, scrawled in Arabic. After searching files and asking the staff at the hall of records, they discovered that this man was retired, but his firm was still in the city, two streets up and a mile east.

"I'll take over from here," Zach said.

"Get copies if you can," Hadassah requested.

***

From the hall of records, Hadassah followed the maps on her phone to the closest entrances of the sewers and underground tunnels. Some entrances required tickets, and the tourist lines were long. Other entrances required cover of darkness and empty streets to conceal her activity.

As she walked down one of the streets, Hadassah did a double take. A man, surrounded by a whole crowd of official looking men, bore an uncanny resemblance to Liberia's Minister of Justice, Xavier Rhodes. For a brief moment, they made eye contact and she knew beyond a shadow of doubt: this was him. But why would he be in Rome? There wasn't enough time to stop and ask, and there was no way she'd give away her involvement with the operation that took down Augustus Lavo.

***

At the meeting with Eli after dinner, the team analyzed the maps from Hadassah's phone which she projected on the wall, then the rolls of blueprints Zach had secured.

"The architect who gave these to me said they were pretty old, and a lot of changes had been done since," Zach explained, "but he said the original architect took the newer blueprints with him when he retired. Apparently the man was quite secretive about his work, his clients and his pay."

Pedro raised his eyebrows. "Sounds like he's got a few connections in the Mafia."

"Ha—just like I thought." Zach tapped on another section of the blueprint.

"What is it?" Pedro asked.

"The air duct from the men's room goes right past the members' room," Zach said. "I'll go ahead and plant the listening device there on Saturday."

"Hold up, everybody," Hyun said. "Look at this."

Everyone looked close to where Hyun pointed. "It's a door from the lower level of the building," Hyun continued. "To where?"

Hadassah matched it up with her map of the sewers. "It looks like it goes right into some of the sewers."

"I'll investigate the door from the sewers this week," Hadassah said.

"Tell me before you try to go in," Eli said.

"Keep your phone on," she retorted.

***

Early on Thursday morning, when the sun's first rays tickled the cirrus clouds pink and the trash collectors attempted to wake everyone, she threaded her way through the alleys until she found the entrance to the sewer closest to the nightclub.

Just as Hyun suggested, a door stood in the murky walls right where the basement of the nightclub would be. It was locked on the outside with a padlock. A simple screwdriver would open this. Hadassah took out the bag of tools Eli had loaned her and began rifling through it with her flashlight in her teeth, admiring the strange assortment. When would she need a hand held welder and its tiny canister of propane?

Suddenly, Hadassah heard a clank, a rustle and a sharp cry down the corridor of the tunnel. Her limbs stiffened. Then she realized this cry belonged to a baby and the mother was gently shushing the child. But someone was walking toward her.

A round barrel of cold steel pressed against her temple. "Who are you?" the man beside her demanded. He spoke Italian with a very poor accent.

The flashlight dropped from between her teeth and rolled along the floor. She cringed and scrambled through her mind for a suitable response. One that wouldn't get her killed. "Please, sir," she replied in Italian, "I am looking for a friend."

"Leave my family alone, we mean no trouble," he told her gruffly.

"I mean you no trouble, sir." She fought the tremble hijacking her limbs.

The man lowered the steel barrel. "If she is behind that door, she is crying every night, just like all the girls. But I beg you, do not bring trouble to my family and me."

"I won't."

"Be quieter, please. Many of us are trying to sleep, and the police ignore us here if we're quiet."

"I'll be quiet."

Hadassah's hands were still shaking when she picked up her flashlight and took out the Philips head screw driver. It might not have been a gun he held, but after Manila she always expected a trigger to be pulled; it took more than a few deep breaths to calm herself.

Once the padlock was removed there was only a door handle with a simple lock. This door was locked as if to keep people inside.

She turned the lock, twisted the handle and pulled the door open. Its creak echoed throughout the tunnel. She winced, anticipating another threat. When silence resumed, she looked to the door again.

She turned her flashlight back on. There before her was a thick sheet of plywood nailed against the door frame, and beyond, the sharp, frightened voice of a woman speaking in Italian. "Who's there?" Her accent sounded remarkably Hebrew.

Hadassah took a chance with Mom's native tongue. "If you want to get out, I'm a friend."

Soft weeping lasted for a minute or longer. "Praise the Living One! You are Jewish," she replied in Hebrew. "I have waited so long. But it's not safe today. It's only safe on Fridays. Please come back tomorrow, if you are able, at noon."

"Is it just you?"

"There are seventeen of us."

Hadassah remembered the feature of her phone Yitzak showed her. She plugged in the ear buds and pressed them against the door to verify the count the woman gave. The screen of her phone showed warm bodies all over the small room, crammed in like sardines. "I can try to get this plywood off for you."

The woman whimpered. "Please, I cannot talk anymore. He may come back."

Hadassah closed the door again and reattached the padlock.

The next day, at lunchtime, she brought Christina with her into the tunnel leading to the door. They shined their flashlights down the corridors to make sure no one else was around. A young mom huddled in an alcove nursing her infant. Hadassah walked toward them and dropped a small gift bag a few feet away.

"Some diapers and a few cans of food," Hadassah chanced in Italian.

The woman looked up fearfully, then softened. "Thank you."

When Hadassah took the padlock off again, the girl she'd talked with the previous day spoke almost immediately.

"You came back!"

Hadassah smiled. "I did. And I brought a friend with me to see about getting this plywood off."

"I have worked away some of it." The girl spoke through a small hole at the bottom of the board. "Please come close with a light if you can, so I may see you."

Hadassah crouched low and put her face to the ground, holding her flashlight so it shone down on her.

"Are you an angel?" the girl asked.

"No, but we come in the Name of the Lord, Yeshua

Ha'Mashiach," Hadassah replied through the hole in the plywood.

There was a long pause on the other side, so long Hadassah began to push herself up from the filthy ground.

"Wait," the girl said. "Please don't go. I had a dream about your Yeshua two weeks ago, a dream where He said He would set me free. I thought I had the dream because I was crazy after... after being here for so long. But here you are. And blessed are you who comes in the Name of the Lord."

"We're going to try to pry off the plywood," Hadassah said. "After each pause tell us if it's safe to continue."

"I will."

Hadassah tried her hand with the crow bar.

The first pry was so loud it echoed through the sewers: the nails screeched through the wood like a warning alarm.

"Stop, please," the girl begged with tears in her voice. "I don't want anyone to come back."

After a long pause, Hadassah asked, "Do you want us to try once more?"

"Maybe."

"Do you want us to wait a minute?"

The girl remained quiet, but after another moment she replied, "Go ahead."

Hadassah handed the crow bar to Christina. The second pry was not quite as loud as the first, but it was loud enough.

"No more!" the girl begged. "Not today. Maybe we can try from our end when it's safe."

"We can come back next Friday," Hadassah told her.

"Please do," the girl said.

"And I can visit you every day during the week until then."

"Yes, please, but only early morning."

***

"Perhaps it was for the better we were unable to pry the wood off today," Christina said once they were out of the sewers again.

Hadassah shrugged her shoulders hard. "Maybe. My heart hurts for these girls."

"Mine too," Christina said.

The next evening, Saturday night, Hyun, Tameka, and Christina accompanied Pedro and Zach all the way to the edge of the club district to pray in proximity as the two men went to the club again. Hadassah stayed at the House of Prayer. A special session of prayer had been arranged on behalf of the mission.

Chapter 38:

La Bestia Alata

As soon as Zach and Pedro paid the €50 entrance fee into La Bestia Alata, they separated. Zach threaded through a thin aisle in the sea of people to the one empty slot at the bar.

"Seltz," Zach shouted to the bartender as he set three €2 pieces onto the dented wood. The bartender looked at him askance, then kept a watchful eye on him as he poured the soda.

"You saving your money up for one of them?" The bartender snickered as he gestured toward the waitresses and dancers.

No part of Zach wanted to look at them. He took a swig of the carbonated water to calm the rising nausea. But the bartender kept watching him with suspicious glances. Why would he be in this sort of club if he didn't want to look? He tried his best to think of reasons but they all made him look questionable. He glanced up, vowing to make this his final night.

That's when he saw her, dancing and parading herself on the stage with eyes full of lust so fake his heart broke.

"I see you found her." The bartender's sneer made Zach want to leap over the bar and leave that man with a permanent scar.

He prayed a desperate prayer in the last quiet place of his heart as he responded. "Excuse me?"

"You are young and nervous, I see. I will arrange a ticket for you. You will like that one, she is the favorite of everyone. But she will cost you."

Zach relaxed the tension in his jaw. Even now he couldn't give away the fact that this was his sister—it might spawn trouble for her. And for the rest of his team. He tried to smile. "How much?"

The bartender's chuckle riled him. "Six hundred for a half hour. But looks like you may only need fifteen minutes."

"I'll be right back." Zach's jaw tightened again as he stepped away from the bar. Where could he meet with Pedro in this crowd? He raised his wrist to his chin. "Meet me by the men's room."

"I'll be there in thirty seconds," Pedro replied through the comlink. "What's up?" he asked when they met up.

"I need as much money as you can give me."

"Do you think it's wise to exchange it here?"

"Please, man." He knew Pedro saw his desperation. "It's gotta be now."

Pedro slid his wallet out and slipped a folded purple bill into Zach's hand.

"What's this?"

Pedro quickly flashed five fingers.

Zach sighed. "Thank you. And pray for me. Please."

He acknowledged Pedro's nod before returning to the bar. Sliding into the last vacant space along the wooden slab, Zach pounded the bar with his fist and with his stare he bored a hole into the bartender, hoping to gain attention amid the techno, the catcalls, the yelling.

The bartender rubbed the €500 and €100 bills between his fingers before addressing Zach again. "Half hour ticket for you."

The muscles in Zach's arm ached with all the punches he restrained as he shouldered his way through the crowd toward the door he needed. A large man with shoulders even wider than his stood beside the door, towering over him and glaring down. As soon as Zach handed the man his ticket, the man opened the door and shut it quickly behind him. The room, dimly lit in various shades of red, was empty. There was a reeking bed and a fragile wooden chair, but no Ileyah. At least the room was a little quieter than the club; he might be able to think of what he'd say when he finally saw her.

End game, keep in mind the end game. His heart pounded.

The techno blared again as the door opened then closed.

Zach turned to face her.

The whole room filled with her gasp.

"Ileyah." He quivered.

The young woman threw her arms around her body as best she could and began to hyperventilate as she backed into a corner.

"Ileyah." He stooped to catch her glance, which shot all over the room.

"Please, Zach, don't kill me. Just pretend you never saw me and leave this place. You don't know what I have to do here to keep the others alive."

Zach sank to his knees. In his relief to have found her, he forgot how, the last time his sister saw him, he was hostile to her faith and trying to arrange a date with a nice Muslim man. He wept until his tears splashed on the grimy floor between his knees, then held his hands toward her.

Once their hands met, he stood again and pulled her close to rest her head between his shoulders. "I will never, never hurt you, Ileyah. I want to hurt those who have done this to you, but our Lord Jesus forbids retaliation like that."

At the mention of Jesus, she broke out in renewed sobs and wrapped her arms around him. "I wish Jesus would receive me again so I could share the joy of salvation with you."

Zach held her cheeks gently in his strong hands. "Do you want to leave here, Ileyah?"

"Everyday I look for a way to escape, but they post guards at the doors. Once, I got as far as the police station and a policeman escorted me back here, so I haven't tried again. I'm learning Italian —"

Zach laid his index finger against her lips. "You need to listen to me, okay? I need your help to get you out of here."

"What will you be able to do, Zach? You could pay the thousands to the owner for my so-called 'debt', but what about the rest of the girls here?"

"I have a team here with me, and we've come to blow the whole operation wide open."

A glimmer of hope crossed Ileyah's face. "Are you with Hadassah?"

"She is one of the team members with Operation White Stone."

"She's been talking to my friend, Channah, through the plywood in the basement."

"Does it look like you can get out that way?"

"We've started to pull the plywood away from the wall so we can get out through the sewers when Hadassah comes back next Friday. But what was your plan?"

"I need you to help me plant a listening device in their private back room."

"I can't. They never let the girls in there."

Zach sighed. "Then I'll have to go through the men's room after all."

"What good do you think a listening device will do?"

"We believe the ring leaders meet in there, and if we can prove it, then the police will have to raid the whole facility."

Ileyah let out a laugh of disbelief. "The ring leaders? You mean, of all the countries and clubs, they meet here? How is that possible?"

"Just trust me. They've been shadowed for a while."

Her glance shifted about the room again. "We'll have to go soon, or they'll come in. The half hour's almost up."

"If only I could get you out of here tonight. I can't leave you."

"You'll have to, Zach." She gave his cheek tear-soaked kisses. "You've gotta do this, or they'll hurt both of us. But please, I'm sure we have a minute or two left. Please pray with me, my brother."

Zach lifted his eyes to the heavens. "Lord of mercy, I plead for Your protection upon my sister, Ileyah. Please hide her under the shadow of Your wings."

When he finished praying, she wiped her cheeks of tears, smiled morosely at him and snapped back into character before opening the door again. He stumbled after her, melding once more into the crowds, hoping no one noticed the anger he couldn't hide. He walked up to the bartender again and slapped another €100 bill on the wood. "A tip." Maybe they'd treat her well for a few days. At least until the police raided.

He headed straight for the stall in the men's room which he had seen in the blueprints. "Pray for me, Pedro," he whispered into the comlink once he pulled himself into the air duct.

Chapter 39:

The Device

When the audio transmitter was in place, Hadassah received a text from Zach to let her know. That was the last any of them had heard from him.

The rest of the team gathered back at the House of Prayer late and forlorn. Tameka wept. Pedro hardly said a word.

***

"Any news about him through the transmitter?" Hyun asked Eli during their meeting the following Monday.

Eli straightened the papers in the file in front of him, then closed the file and placed his folded hands on top. "There was a reference made indicating he's alive, but nothing about where he is. They mostly talked about whether or not they will follow through with some plan, but the plan was discussed in coded speech."

Pedro narrowed his eyes. "Have you shared any of this with the authorities?"

"I did this morning."

Hyun cleared her throat. "I spoke with Mr. Murray and Mr.

Cooper about our situation. Mr. Cooper said he'll be here Wednesday morning."

Hadassah sighed and smiled at the prospect of seeing Mr. Cooper, who brought both stability and assurance, but her smile was small through the stiffness of uncertainty. "What are the authorities saying?"

"Quite frankly, they are angry and rather pleased at the same time." Eli gave a half smile. "They are pleased to have been alerted to possible criminal, even terrorist activity, and they are rather angry with us for discovering it first."

Christina threw her hands up in the air. "But I thought you said they wanted hard evidence from us."

"They did. All this means is they'll take credit for the work."

Leaning forward, Christina stared daggers at Eli. "We didn't come here to get credit for our work. We'd just like to leave with all of our teammates."

"Forgive us for our frustration concerning Zach," Tameka said. "We lost another teammate a month ago, and though we prepare ourselves for this, it's never easy to deal with."

***

On Monday, at lunch time, Hadassah went back through the sewer to speak with the girl from the nightclub.

"I'm glad you came back," the girl said. "I wanted to ask you a favor."

"Tell me," Hadassah said.

334

"When you come on Friday, are you able to bring clothes for us? We cannot walk through the streets in these clothes: it would bring shame on us."

"We will help you with that," Hadassah replied.

"I have written sizes for you." She slipped a paper through the hole in the plywood. "Also, I've been working at this wood, and I have it mostly dislodged."

"Do you want to try before Friday?"

"We can't." She stayed silent for a while. "My name's Channah, by the way."

"My name's Hadassah."

"Just like Esther's real name," Channah replied. "Have you read the story of Esther?"

"Many times. Will it bother you, Channah, if there are men with me on Friday?"

"Are they Israeli or American?"

"American."

"Are they coming in the Name of Yeshua as well?"

"Yes."

"It's okay, if you trust them."

***

On Wednesday, when Mr. Cooper arrived, everyone looked calmer, although there had been no word regarding Zach. Hadassah certainly felt more relaxed with Mr. Cooper around.

Friday morning, she rose earlier than Christina, a feat in and of itself, then dressed in the orange glow from the streetlights and sank to her knees in the small space between the suitcases and the plaster wall. So many requests to bring before Abba Father. And what grace! She soared into His presence and poured a torrent of prayers before Him, settling into an all consuming peace and assurance of answers. This assurance swung her resolve into full throttle.

He who dwells in the secret place of the Most High will rest in the shadow of the Almighty...

She opened her eyes in the light of dawn. Christina, awake and preparing for the day, caught her peripheral vision. She looked up and they smiled at one another.

"Shall we go shopping for those clothes?" Christina asked, finishing up the single braid in her hair.

Hadassah nodded, then sat on the edge of her bed. "You wanna pray together first?"

***

Mornings in Rome always saw cafes bustling, coffees sipped, newspapers leisurely read by tourists and sleepy conversations about nothing and everything. But these habits seemed only habits, as if they had lost their luster years ago and only clung to these pleasantries out of a desire to lay claim to someone else's memories from the golden era of black and white movies. This morning, even the sky looked old and dull from the thick air of nostalgia and vacancy of wonderment.

Hadassah and Christina met Hyun and Tameka in the Trastevere district just as vendors rolled out awnings, erected tents and set racks of clothing on enticing display as if retail therapy was the cure for all ailments.

"We have seventeen outfits to pick out," Hyun said. "Do you have the sizes, Haddy?"

Hadassah tore the paper with the clothing sizes into four strips and handed them out. "Since we have a two-hour window, let's try to find something nice for these girls."

Hyun handed €300 to each of them. "Don't go beyond this square. We need to meet back here by 1100 hours to get to the club by noon."

When they scattered, Tameka strode beside Hadassah to the shops along their right hand side. "You hear from our boys in Iraq?"

"Matt e-mailed me last night. Most of them are in Babylon right now. The city is beautiful from what he says, but a strange kind of beautiful, not at all what you'd expect."

"I kinda feel that way about Rome." Tameka shrugged. "And I have a weird feeling about today. Not a good feeling, either. I don't know how to shake it."

The edges of Hadassah's mouth curled. "I know what you mean, but I believe God will give us incredible grace through it. He spoke Psalm 91 to me this morning."

Smiling in return, Tameka quoted the passage as if in rap or song. Her musical annunciations added emphasis to their steps.

Rifling through the racks at the busy stores, the perfect outfits seemed to fall right off the hangers into Hadassah's hands and her selections ran under budget. Relieved to be finished early, with money to spare, she stepped into a quiet alley to fold clothes into her bag. There would be enough time to sit with a cup of tea and collect her thoughts before their noontime operation. She still couldn't bring herself to drink coffee, not even here in Rome.

Before she turned to leave the alley, she heard a groan behind her; immediately, she thought of Manila and of Kiri. Her body stiffened, knowing she had to see what or who this was. Her pulse quickened. She typed a quick text to Tameka, who was still shopping in the store she had just left.

MEET ME IN THE ALLEY TO THE NORTH.

Then she walked, hugging the wall and keeping her senses tuned.

Beyond a heap of cardboard boxes, she saw him curled in a ball and moaning as if each sound took every ounce of strength. On the upper half of Zach's body, someone had strapped a vest made of heavy metal, then chained and locked it into place. The metal vest looked like lead by its dull luster. Fastened to the front and back of the vest were two strange devices, each constructed of glass and a small aerosol can welded together. He grimaced as if every muscle in his body ached.

"Zach!" Her hushed whisper was like a lightning bolt to his limbs

—every inch of him twitched. His eyes blinked open, then he stared at her. His lips moved. "What was that?" she asked, then crouched at his side, angling her ear toward his lips.

"Ditch your cell phone." His breath, short and laborious, augmented his demand.

She obeyed immediately, sliding the phone worth untold thousands down toward the mouth of the alley. "Is that far enough?"

He nodded. "Please... help me reach the phone in my pocket."

"Left or right?"

"Right. Careful." He paused to catch his breath then sighed as she pulled the cell phone from his pocket.

"Shall I toss it?"

"Carefully. It's a..." He winced and a tremor rocked his hulking limbs. "It's a trigger."

She slid it away down the alley as if it was a live scorpion, then employed the most soothing and steady voice she could find. "A trigger to those?"

His body shook as he said, "Uh-huh."

She tried to smile. "Can I help you stand?"

"Don't. Stretching my limbs will set it off."

"What did they do to you?"

"The glass..." He paused and shivered despite the warmth. "The glass is filled with Ebola virus."

Ebola, she remembered immediately, was a fast-acting virus with no cure and a very slim survival rate. She had seen a picture of the virus in her AP biology class—the thing was shaped like a cobra ready to strike. Panic would definitely hinder her, so she fought against it with the loudest silent prayer she had ever prayed.

"It'll kill the ... whole city within ... a few days," he said through clenched teeth.

"But leave you distinguishable and make you the scapegoat." She paused, angry enough to vomit.

"Hadassah!" Tameka whispered from the head of the alley. "Is that Zach?"

"Take my phone and Zach's phone and find Hyun for me. And don't call anyone until you're at least ten feet away from the alley." She turned back to Zach. "Hyun will be here soon. She'll know what to do."

"You've got to do it, Haddy." His eyes fixed on hers, his shallow breaths shifting the vest only minimally. "If you can find something like ... metal bowls and weld it over ... the devices, we should be able to ... contain the viruses."

"I'm going to take that vest off you." She looked at the chains and locks. Wire cutters would work, but each would take several minutes, and there had to be fifteen locks. She could pick the padlocks, but that would be just as time consuming.

He shook his head. "Do you have anything like metal bowls? You can ... weld them to the vest."

Hadassah remembered seeing a vendor who sold kitchen supplies, and was glad she had money left over. Then it dawned on her. "If I weld anything to you the heat through the metal will scar you for life."

"Better than ... Ebola."

He gritted his teeth. He must have been beaten pretty badly, and she didn't have the heart to hurt him any more.

"I'll wait for Tameka and Hyun, then I'll get the bowls."

"Please. Help me get ... these covered."

Pretending nothing bothered her as she stepped back into the crowds of the market took serious compartmentalizing. Scenarios dominated every thought: the welder burning the lead to Zach's skin —she'd need something thin to shove between the vest and his chest; the devices triggering early—she had to move fast; the devices' eruptions blowing the metal bowls off—*the welding has to work, it just has to!*

The vendor of kitchen wares smiled at her choice of two black cast iron pans, each ten inches wide and three inches deep, as well as four pot holders with "As seen on TV" stickers—the Ove-glove.

"Black cast iron is the best for cooking," he explained in Italian as he took her money. "Everyone wants enamel coating, but those are the best of them all."

She smiled, waiting for her change.

"I could give you some good recipes to use for black cast iron if you wait a minute."

"Oh, no, I should be going." If she stayed a moment longer she might not be able to hide the shaking in her hands.

"It'll only take a minute. Special recipes from my family."

Smiling to hide her anger, she said, "I could come back for them later."

He hesitated handing her money back.

"Please, Signore, I'm in a hurry."

"Why? No one is in a hurry in Rome."

"Haddy, there you are!" Hyun said. And in the nick of time. Tameka and Christina were behind her. "We've been looking for you everywhere."

Hadassah's nerves calmed knowing Hyun would take charge.

"Tameka filled me in, but I can't guess your plan for those pans." Hyun and the others followed her as she walked briskly back to the alley.

"Zach suggested containment, and I think I agree with him. He has devices strapped to him filled with Ebola." Hadassah held up a pan in each hand. "We have to weld them in place, and call emergency services before we leave for the club."

"That means one of us has to stay with him," Hyun said. "Tameka, would you be willing?"

Tameka nodded. "Without a doubt. I could even give emergency services a call now."

"Do."

"Let me have my phone back," Hadassah said. "I'll need a few of the apps on it to help Zach."

Zach looked relieved at the sight of Hadassah, Hyun and Christina hovering around him, fitting the pans into place and sliding the pot holders under the lead vest.

"Did you buy a soldering iron?" he asked Hadassah.

"I had a welder in my bag. I just hope it's enough to secure the pans in place."

He shook and shivered. "It's our one shot."

Hyun smiled sadly at him. "This isn't going to feel pretty. You ready?"

He nodded.

Hadassah took the first turn, gripping the welder in two sweaty hands as Hyun held the pan in place and Christina clasped Zach's hand, stroking his hair with her other hand.

"How long until it sets?" Hadassah asked Hyun when she finished the first. She could feel his short breath against her shaky hand, and the cold sweat seeping from his pores. After all the pain she just had to inflict upon Zach she didn't want to look at him, but did anyway. His eyes stared off as if to block the pain. "Will you be okay?"

"Keep going." He didn't even look up at them.

"I'll do the next one," Hyun said.

Hadassah handed the welder over and wiped her hands on her shirt before grabbing the second pan to hold it against his back.

As Hyun manipulated the welder, affixing the pan over the device, Zach shed large, silent tears.

"Shh," Christina whispered soothingly.

"I think he needs a break," Hadassah said.

"No," he whispered hoarsely. "Keep going."

Before the pan was sealed all the way around, Zach began to cry aloud. Hadassah was glad Hyun had taken over—she wouldn't have been able to finish. Hyun kept steady to the end.

Hadassah took out her phone and pulled up the sonogram app to view inside the pan. "Completely sealed in the back. And the front."

Looking up to heaven, Zach stretched out his legs. Nothing happened.

"Tameka," Hyun called out. "Bring his phone here. Christina, use yours to call him."

Even as Tameka walked toward them, Zach's phone began to ring.

A muffled thud and shatter on the front of the vest set him coughing.

Hadassah held her phone over the pan. "It looks shattered but contained."

"What about the other side?" Hyun asked.

They waited during a heart-rending delay until the device on the back burst with a sickening thud. The four women laid their hands on Zach and prayed.

She saw Zach's lips move, but no sound came out. Hadassah drew her ear close. "What was that, friend?"

"Please, rescue my sister."

"It's after eleven, folks," Hyun said. "We've got to leave him with Tameka and run."

Hadassah, Christina and Hyun took turns giving Zach a kiss on the forehead.

"Here," Hadassah said to Tameka. "Wire cutters and lock picks. Hopefully you'll be able to get the vest off him."

"I'll do my best. Emergency services said they'd be here within five minutes."

"Then we've got to go, girls," Hyun said. "We can't be delayed. If those men did this to Zach, who knows what they'll do to those girls."

Chapter 40:

The Rescue

Y ou've all done excellent work here," Mr. Cooper said as he followed Hadassah and the others through the sewers. "Let's continue to pray for Zach. Don't be discouraged. God has given us great favor already today."

When they got to the basement door of the club they all set down their backpacks, which had clothes for seventeen girls and snacks to sustain them until they made it to the safe house.

Hadassah unscrewed the padlock plate and opened the door. The plywood stood slightly ajar with the girls gathered close around, eager to leave. Pedro and Mr. Cooper leaned their weight against the wood to try to give the girls more space to get out, and bent down the exposed nails so no one would be snagged trying to leave.

The girls filed out as soon as Pedro and Mr. Cooper turned up the steep stairs, out of the tunnel and back into the alley. They all appeared to be from various ethnic backgrounds. Hadassah tried not to stare at their waif-like appearance and scanty clothing.

With Hadassah, Hyun and Christina helping them, each of the

girls pulled the new clothes over their lean bodies. Everything they did was quieter than the sound of the cars on the streets overhead.

After they proceeded up the narrow, steep stairs and Mr. Cooper began to edge the large group cautiously down a narrow alley, they heard an explosion directly behind them, and the ground beneath them shook. The sound, sudden and deafening, set the girls screaming. A second explosion, much further away but just as loud, sent a ball of fire into the air above the skyline. There were six more explosions in quick succession, the last two shaking the walls of buildings around them. The girls screamed louder and clung to one another. Amid the chaos, Mr. Cooper and Hyun led them out of the alley and down other narrow streets while Hadassah, Christina and Pedro brought up the rear and tried to calm the rising panic in the crowd.

Pedro's phone rang. "It's Eli!"

Eli's shout could be heard through the phone. "Where are you?"

"We've just taken the girls out of the club," Pedro shouted back. "What happened?"

"Get as far away from the club as you can. A car bomb just went off outside it and the whole place is in flames."

"We got the girls out," Pedro shouted. "We're several streets away right now."

"Lead the way, Hadassah," Mr. Cooper shouted over the noise.

Hadassah raced through the labyrinth of narrow streets toward the bridge leading to the Ghetto. "Mr. Cooper, I'm leading them the only safe way I know."

"Lead on, Hadassah. We don't know if the safe house is even safe right now."

"What if we take them to Eli's church?" Hadassah asked.

Mr. Cooper paused and prayed aloud. "Father, please show us what to do." He turned again to Hadassah. "I'll call Eli again and tell him we're on our way there. Hyun, Pedro, Christina, take up the rear so the girls feel safe."

They raced over the two and a half miles through narrow streets to the church. Most of the girls cried as they walked, from a mixture of joy and fear. A few of them ate granola bars as they went; they looked as if they had hardly eaten for a year or more.

"Is this the safe house?" Channah asked as they stopped in front of the church.

"No, it's not," Hadassah said, "but it is *a* safe house, and you will be kept from harm until we can get you there."

"Turn around, everyone," Christina said. "Look!" She pointed with outstretched arm and mouth agape. Throughout the city, piles of rubble, smoke, fires and mayhem stacked nearly to heaven. One of the girls fainted, and Mr. Cooper caught her.

When they got to the church steps, a crowd from a prayer meeting had assembled outside, all of them just as shocked as the R.S.O. team.

"Get the girls inside," Mr. Cooper commanded.

They took the younger girls to the healing room and the older ones to the sanctuary, where women gathered near to tenderly wait on them and assess their needs.

All the while, the band and singers on the stage led sweet praise to Jesus. At some points the band looked as if they would stop, and they even slowed down, but they kept singing, and kept praying.

"How can it be so peaceful in here?" Channah asked Hadassah.

"His Name is Yeshua Ha'Mashiach, the Prince of Peace, and only He will bring peace," Hadassah said.

"I want what you have," Channah said in return. So did a few of the others.

"God our Father is planning a wedding feast for His Son and you're invited." Hadassah trembled with an unusual joy, especially given the circumstances. "To accept the invitation means you clothe yourselves with righteousness, clothing Yeshua Ha'Mashiach purchased for you with His own blood. When Yeshua dwells in your heart by faith, you have full access to the wedding ceremony, dressed in white and in righteousness alongside the King of the Universe. How many of you would like to come to the wedding?"

All seven of the girls raised their hands.

***

Eli set up a television in the lobby of the church and everyone watched as the Presidents of Italy and America, the Pope and the Prime Minister of Jordan urged people not to panic.

"The perpetrators will be found and brought to justice," Pope Leo XIV declared.

People watched with fixed expressions, ignoring their cell phones and breathing shallowly as events unfolded. Suddenly a woman called out from the sanctuary, "Turn that man off. He is evil."

Eli complied immediately.

"Let's return to prayer," the pastor said. "Prayer is the most important thing to do in this hour. Call out to God, Beloved, and let us continue to pray His heart back to Him, even in the midst of this great darkness."

Hadassah could smell the fire from the city as she turned to the prayer room again. She typed an e-mail to Matt on her phone:

"We're all okay. Zach 2. Please pray for us."

The music resumed as she sat beside Channah and held her hand while the young woman wept and wept. Her own heart and voice joined the trembling prayers uttered over the microphone:

"Abba, Father, we pray for peace and safety."

Chapter 41:

Aftermath

While Hadassah prayed, Hyun came and whispered into her ear, "Eli says we need to get the girls together soon and bring them to the safe house."

When Hadassah followed Hyun into the lobby, she saw Christina and Pedro. Mr. Cooper could be heard on the phone outside the prayer house.

"Mr. Cooper just got a call from the police." Pedro rolled his eyes and sighed. "We don't know why yet."

"I hope it's news about Zach," Christina said.

"One of the girls, Ileyah, is Zach's sister; she was taken from Cairo, Egypt."

Hadassah almost smiled when she heard this news. "Really?"

"Eli said it could take two hours before the bus gets here to bring the girls to the safe home," Hyun said

Just then, a voice came over the microphone in the sanctuary with an announcement. "Italian military and NATO have surrounded the Vatican after several bombs exploded there, as well." The sound of sobbing filled the sanctuary, yet on stage a quiet song about God's mercy began.

***

Traffic throughout the city was so snarled it took four hours to get the girls to the safe house. Then Hadassah, Christina and Hyun helped the counselors settle the frightened and traumatized girls, which took nearly three hours.

Traffic was even worse as the team headed back to their host homes; some people had abandoned cars where they were and walked home. But making one's way walking through the crowded streets was just as time consuming. A fight broke out down one street, and it nearly turned into a riot. All over the city, people had cell phones to their ears and were crying from grief or relief throughout the conversations.

It was close to 2:30am when Hadassah and Christina arrived at their host home. The family had left a basket of fruit and packs of clean socks for Hadassah and Christina, a gesture received with double gratitude after their day. They learned several facts from Mr. Cooper's text messages. Tameka was back at her host home. And Mr. Cooper was called in for questioning, but received no other information from the police.

When they awoke late on Saturday morning, Hadassah and Christina joined the host family around the television to watch the news and read the constant feed about the crisis in Rome. Then they saw a photo of Zach. The anchorman explained how the young man was either a suspect in the terrorist plot, so thought because of the devices he had strapped to his body when he was discovered, or a pawn of the terrorists, which would explain the signs of abuse found on him.

"All we know at this time is the devices found on this man held biological warfare compounds which were contained before authorities arrived on the scene," the anchorman said. "Also, authorities believe he is American. We don't know what connection this man had with the terrorists who destroyed our beautiful, ancient and peaceful Rome."

"I don't think I want to watch anymore," Christina said.

The anchorman moved on to a different story. "The reports of bombing within Vatican City have been a rumor. There is no indication of where this rumor began, but not a building or business around the Holy City has been hit. We have a reporter on the ground there live, to confirm this. Gillian?"

Christina lingered in the doorway. "Rumors of war..." she remarked.

The father at the host home looked over at her. "Exactly."

"In other news," the anchorman continued a few minutes later, "It has been confirmed that UN Secretary General Jenna Freedman was killed in the blasts in Rome. The UN is in a hasty closed session as they choose the new Secretary General. None of the names of the nominees have been released to the press. We will keep you informed as we learn of new developments."

Hadassah's phone rang.

"Tell Christina her phone is off." Mr. Cooper sounded exhausted. "I want it turned on. I've been allowed into the hospital to see Zach, but I want all of us to meet at the church when I'm done, so why don't you head on over there now."

***

When the team was assembled with Mr. Cooper at the church, Hyun was the first to speak up. "What's happening with Zach?"

Mr. Cooper sighed. "The officials are furious, but after the doctors saw Zach, no one is making him a scapegoat anymore."

"Will he be okay?" Tameka asked.

"The doctors say he will recover, but he'll need a few months."

Pedro's fist pounded the table. "A few *months*? What did they do to him?"

Mr. Cooper fixed a level gaze at Pedro, then at the rest of them. "The doctors are still running tests to make sure all his organs are okay. But the authorities will be deporting him once the tests are done and he's stable."

Folding her fidgety hands together in her lap, Hadassah looked up. "Don't the authorities realize we were trying to help bring those terrorists to justice?"

"They do, but it's complicated." Mr. Cooper sighed again. "They are unhappy with us publicly, but at the end of the day they're grateful to us. Because of your work they were able to respond to the crisis faster and more decisively."

"What about Zach's standing with R.S.O.?" Christina asked. "Is he going to be let go now that his face has been seen all over international news?"

"The authorities will be pulling Zach's image from the news feed today, and will not expose the rest of us at all. As for Zach's standing with R.S.O., that's something I'll be talking with him about directly once he's recovered. For now, let's be thankful he's okay."

"When will we be able to see him?" Pedro asked.

"Probably after he's back in the States," Mr. Cooper answered.

Much to everyone's surprise, Christina burst into tears. "I'm sorry," she sobbed, "I can't help it. First Zeke and now Zach... I don't know how much more I can bear."

Hadassah reached her hand over to hold Christina's hand. Seeing this strong woman cry like this brought tears Hadassah didn't want to release. She reeled them in, not wanting to eclipse her friend's sadness.

Mr. Cooper stood from the conference table and placed a firm but compassionate hand on Christina's shoulder. "I'm sorry this is so hard right now. But the authorities want to speak with each one of you. I tried my best to deflect them, but they want to talk to all of you, beginning with Pedro and Hyun tonight after sunset."

"Will they be detaining us?" Pedro asked.

"They said questioning," Mr. Cooper answered, "but I can't say what else they may do. The three of you ladies will be called in tomorrow."

"What would you like us to say, Mr. Cooper?" Tameka asked.

***

It was Pedro's turn to be interrogated first, while the rest of the team went back to their host homes. Hadassah defaulted to her laptop to keep from scraping away what was left of her fingertips. Matt's e-mail didn't help.

"They've closed off the roads into and out of Babylon after the attacks on Rome. Rumor has it they've done the same with Baghdad and Bozrah. This is particularly frustrating for the team since most of us are trapped in Babylon, investigating a lead, while Dave stayed in Tikrit to negotiate with a contact for additional resources. The good news is we have heard about the Korean group. I've spoken briefly with the man who saw them. The bad news is we've attracted attention and may find ourselves in the same predicament as those missionaries if we're not careful.

"Any news on Zach? We're all praying for him as well as the rest of you, especially after seeing his face all over Al Jazeer. They are definitely painting him as the scapegoat here. And how are the girls from the nightclub? I think of you constantly."

"Zach is at the hospital," Hadassah replied. *"The authorities are talking about deporting him as soon as he recovers, but they don't think he was involved, except as a pawn. Still, they won't let anyone but Mr. Cooper see him in the hospital. Security there is tight.*

"The girls we rescued are doing well and are settling into the safe home. Seven of them gave their lives to the Lord! It'll take time

for them to be whole again. Praise God the nightclub is a pile of rubble and the girls are all out safe.

"Now we wait for our turn to be interrogated. Hyun and Pedro are with the police tonight, then Tameka, Christina and I have our turns tomorrow. I hope I choose all the right words. Mr. Cooper drilled us pretty hard this afternoon, and I am thankful.

"I miss you. I miss you so much."

The next e-mail she wrote was to Mom, asking for help.

Chapter 42:

Interrogated

As she sat in the police station, Hadassah tried her best not to fidget or display any other nervous behavior as she waited for Christina's interrogation to be over. It was easier when the officers and citizens stopped staring at her. Papers littered every desk at the station in large piles, a testament of the chaos throughout Rome.

"Hadassah Michelman?" The woman who called her name had a strangely familiar face, and her voice made Hadassah think of her grandmother, her bobeshi from Tel Aviv. The woman's uniform, however, reminded her exactly where she was. "Please follow me."

Christina's smile, as they passed in the hall, carried a mixture of reassurance and perplexity.

"Have a seat, please," the woman said when they entered the interrogation room.

The room was as stark as any interrogation room she had seen, either on TV or in the New York Police Department: concrete walls, tepid temperature, buzzing florescent lights. It looked like they hadn't remodeled since the 1970's.

"You probably don't remember me," the woman continued, "but I'm your mother's cousin. Natalia's my name. Being a relative of yours, I'm not allowed to take part in the questioning, but I wanted to be the one to bring you in and reassure you no one is in trouble. We are trying to get the clearest picture possible so we can conduct a thorough investigation. Many lives have been lost, and the whole world is looking for answers. And the authorities are looking to you. But they've agreed to allow Colonel Schindler to speak with you first. Here he is with his team, and I must leave you."

Hadassah sat as instructed in the wooden, straight-back chair and started scraping her fingertips before the Colonel even opened his mouth.

With slow, calculated motion, Colonel Schindler took the seat across from her. "Ms. Hadassah Michelman, please tell us your intentions during your stay in Rome."

Lying would be so easy. Saying she came as a tourist could be justified by her visa and would save her from this incredibly uncomfortable interview. She stared at the grooves in the concrete walls and breathed past the temptation. "To investigate a possible human trafficking ring, sir, with the intention of exposing the perpetrators and rescuing those being exploited."

"Before you arrived in Rome, did you know these men you were investigating?"

"On the day we arrived, we were given the list of names."

"Who gave you this list of names?"

Eye contact, she reminded herself, *or he'll think I'm lying for sure.* "Elisha Rosin, sir. The man, I believe, is known to you."

The muscles in the Colonel's face twitched, but whether to form a frown or a smile Hadassah couldn't tell. "Mr. Rosin is known to us. Tell us the nature of your visa."

"I arrived on a tourist visa, with provisions for volunteer work."

"Do you feel you violated the conditions of your visa?"

"No, sir, since the work we did was volunteer."

"Who else assisted you while you volunteered?"

Hadassah suppressed a smile and decided to take a chance. "My mom."

"Please state the name of the woman you refer to." He looked intently at her, as if he would extract the information whether or not she wanted to give it. This look in his eyes must have been habit after years of interrogation, or maybe he did mean to use other methods if she withheld anything.

She fought the strange impulse to laugh. "Eva Michelman, sir."

"Eva Vishniac Michelman?"

"Yes, sir." She didn't stifle her smile in time.

He exhaled gruffly and his eye twitched.

"Did you know her, sir?"

"I'll ask the questions, if you don't mind." He glared. "Did you spend any time in the tunnels or sewers while here in Rome?"

"Yes, sir. Am I in trouble for this?"

"We will discuss that later. Did you also obtain a voice recording of a man named Junayd before exploring the sewers?"

"Yes, sir, I did, and submitted the recording to Mr. Rosin."

One of the other officers switched on a device and she heard the interview she had recorded in the café.

As soon as the recording was switched off, the Colonel turned to her again. "Were you instructed to make this sort of recording, Ms. Michelman?"

"We were encouraged to collect as much evidence as possible, sir. Since I was approached by Junayd, I thought it wise to make the most of the situation."

Before he continued, he flashed a brief smile as if he agreed. "When did you first make contact with the women who worked for La Bestia Alata nightclub?"

"Some of the *girls* are as young as fifteen," Hadassah clarified. "And to say they *worked* for the club implies wages. We have evidence saying no wages were given."

"Please answer the question, Ms. Michelman, and refrain from commentary."

"Yes, sir. I met Channah, a girl who was *enslaved* by the owners of La Bestia Alata, two weeks ago. When we freed Channah on Friday, I met the rest of the girls who were with her."

"Where did you take them after you freed them?"

"We took them to the church we used as our base while here in Rome. We intended to take them to the safe house on the far side of the Jewish Quarter, but we didn't know if there was a safe route through the city."

"Did you know La Bestia Alata would be a target?"

"We did not," Hadassah replied. "We had hints something was going to happen soon, but we didn't know when, what, or where. If we hadn't rescued those girls when we did, who knows what would have happened to them?"

"We have the recording from the listening device Zacharias Safar planted at the nightclub, and our analysts are reviewing the data as we speak. Did you assist Mr. Safar to plant the listening device in the nightclub?"

"I assisted him by helping to locate the blueprints and by praying for him."

"Was Mr. Safar seen after planting the device?"

Hadassah hesitated, then looked down. "Yes, sir." She tried to keep her composure while the image of his face alit in her mind. "I saw him Friday morning before rescuing the girls from La Bestia Alata. He was strapped with a device filled with Ebola. We secured the device and alerted the authorities."

"Tell me the nature of the organization you work for, this Revelation Special Ops."

She didn't want to say anything about R.S.O. She wanted him to acknowledge the trauma Zach must have undergone. He seemed immune. Maybe he needed to be.

Hadassah sighed. Then she explained R.S.O. exactly as Mr.

Cooper had instructed, switching around vocabulary and maintaining strong eye contact so it didn't sound as if she was reciting a cheat sheet. "We are a non-profit, religious NGO and the primary goal of our work is to free men, women and children from forced labor."

"How old are you, Ms. Michelman?" he asked.

"I'm eighteen, sir. I'll be nineteen in August."

"You're an Israeli citizen." He stated it as plain fact. It caught her off guard, and she tried her best not to stutter.

"This would explain why I have an Israeli colonel interrogating me in Rome instead of Italian police."

"Do you understand, Ms. Michelman, what it means to be an Israeli citizen?"

"I'll have to serve in the military."

"Two years with the Israeli Defense Force. But I want to give you a unique opportunity to serve your Eretz Israel. I can arrange a position for you with Israeli Intelligence, where your unique talents can be put to use defending our nation from similar terrorist attacks."

"So this interrogation wasn't about what happened here in Rome, but about recruiting me." She gripped the edge of the table and stared at him.

He ignored the stare even more thoroughly than Dad ever did. "Do you know what Sayeret Matkal is?"

"Yes, I know what Sayeret Matkal is. It's the anti-terrorism wing of the IDF." She smiled. "My mother is Eva Vishniac Michelman, sir, and she taught me about every branch of the Israeli Defense

Force. And I can tell you knew her. Your eye twitches every time I mention her name."

"You don't miss much, Ms. Michelman. Tell me what you think of my offer."

"You seem high ranking enough to put me in Sayeret Matkal if you wanted, but I want to work with R.S.O."

"More than protect your homeland? More than see Jerusalem?"

Hadassah fell silent.

"We are giving you a unique opportunity, Ms. Michelman. You will be off the watch lists, unlike the rest of your team."

Hadassah sank back in her seat and fought tears. "I thought we helped here."

"You did, but you must understand that your presence on the watch lists was necessary given the political environment these attacks created."

"But all anyone knows about is Zach. No one knows about the rest of the team except you, and we have given full disclosure of our activities." She was glad she remembered the phrase "full disclosure" from Mr. Cooper's drill the day before.

"After a full investigation, the authorities will review whether or not those affiliated with Revelation Special Ops will be allowed in the EU again. But you are being given a unique opportunity, Ms. Michelman. This is our expression of gratitude to you. If you accept, we may be able to clear your friends' names from the watch lists as well. And remember that if you step foot in Israel you will be required to serve your two years anyway, but your service to Sayeret Matkal could be in lieu of this."

"I am a Christian, sir, a follower of Yeshua Ha'Mashiach. I will not deny my faith."

"You won't be asked to deny your faith."

She let her shoulders relax slightly. "What if I don't accept your offer?"

"It would cost you your Israeli passport. And I cannot give assurance your friends' immunity if you refuse."

Hadassah reeled, her whole body atingle with a wave of anxiety. How could she face the team if she refused their offer? How could she say yes to such ultimatums? "You'll guarantee my friends' immunity?"

"Guarantee is a strong word, Ms. Michelman."

She cocked her head to one side and softened her gaze. "And you're a strong man with lots of influence, Colonel Schindler."

He gave his first real smile. "Flattery like that could get you far in this line of work."

Hadassah thought through his offer. No matter how much she tried, she couldn't compartmentalize her emotions about this. "Must I give an answer right now?"

"Your friends will be leaving Wednesday afternoon. Italian authorities have arranged a flight for them. I would need to know your answer by Tuesday afternoon. Any attempt to leave the country before then would be understood as refusal."

"I understand. You said my friends are leaving. Do you mean Zacharias as well?"

"I'm sure your injured friend will follow when his health returns."

"Is there anything else, sir?"

"Not unless you have more to tell me."

"No. Thank you, sir, and I'll contact you by Tuesday." She staggered out of the room after the accompanying officer.

***

The e-mail she wrote to Mom was the most difficult she had ever had to write. Between her tears and her reluctance, she hunted one key at a time. *"Please, Mom, please—what should I do?"*

She started an e-mail to Matt eleven times, but her eyes welled up too much after *Dear.*

Throughout the evening, Christina tried to gently pry a clue from her about the interrogation. Hadassah only cried until her throat was dry. All the sorrow she stuffed inside gushed forth: Zeke; Zach; the blast in Rome and so many lives lost; the possibility of being so far from Matt, the R.S.O. team, and Mom for two years; and the lack of leads about Dad. But maybe Sayeret Matkal would know something about Dad. The confusion overwhelmed her.

Chapter 43:

Separated

In the morning, when her well of tears had dried, Hadassah told Christina the details of the interrogation, pushing her words past the lump in her throat. Christina urged her to call a meeting and have everyone pray.

"Let me check my e-mail first," Hadassah said. There was nothing from Mom. But there was an e-mail from Matt.

"Mr. Cooper said you'll be returning to the States soon. And our work here is nearly done. I can't wait to see you again soon.

"This world looks so much like the days the Lord teaches will be the Last Days of this age. We must watch and we must pray, and eagerly await His coming. And we need to love His people more than ever. I can't bear to look at the newspapers anymore, and see the propaganda against the Jews. Why do they blame your people, my beautiful friend? The political cartoons break my heart and leave me feeling ill.

"All around here, through the streets of Babylon, the faces look cold. There is more wealth here than anywhere I've seen on earth,

opulence like I have never dreamed. But the faces are cold. The love of many has grown cold, and my heart aches because of it.

"But my love for you hasn't grown cold, and it will blaze like a bonfire in my heart, waiting to see your face again. I miss you, too."

Walking beside Christina to the church to meet with the R.S.O. team, Hadassah stared at the faces around her. The streets were filled with mourners. She prayed over them. In the distance, the smoke from Trastevere still trickled into the sky.

When they arrived at the church the rest of the team had already gathered in the conference room and she saw Mr. Cooper's face crisscrossed with concern. Although Hadassah thought of little beyond her own looming trials, this look in Mr. Cooper's eyes alarmed her.

"We're all here, now," Hyun said. "Will you tell us what happened?"

"Early this morning there was a raid on the hotel in Babylon where our team was staying," Mr. Cooper said. "Matt, Maleek, Adam and Paul were there. Only Paul made it out. He sent me a text twenty minutes ago. He doesn't know the fate of the others."

"But, but..." Hadassah could hardly get these words out. "I got an e-mail from Matt this morning, sir."

"He must have sent it before the raid," Mr. Cooper said. "I'm so sorry Hadassah. I'm so sorry."

"Who ordered the raid and why?" She couldn't even cry. Her throat felt dry.

"Paul doesn't know. He said the people who raided the hotel weren't dressed like police or military, but no one stopped the raid, no one paid any attention."

Pedro's mouth tightened. "Where is Paul now?"

"He sent a text saying he was hiding, but I don't know how long he can hold out." Mr. Cooper hung his head and sighed. He looked up at Hadassah. "I understand you have a separate issue to address, Hadassah, and we will address it. But I thought you'd want to hear this first. It would probably affect your decision."

Hadassah's throat tightened. "I'm unable to make a decision, Mr. Cooper. I wrote my mom, but I haven't heard back from her yet. Shall I tell you what the Colonel offered me?"

"Go ahead, and then we will pray for you."

After Hadassah told them the offer the Colonel made, she felt just as confused. She rested her forehead on her fist and thought about Matt, prayed for Matt, fought the tears sliding down her cheeks. Her teammates and friends gathered around her to pray. While they prayed earnestly on Hadassah's behalf, her phone beeped several times with incoming text alerts. She curbed her curiosity and prayed.

Wisdom, Lord! she cried in her heart. *You said to ask You for wisdom and You'd give it. Here I am. I need Your wisdom quickly.*

After five minutes of praying for Hadassah, the team sat quietly, everyone staring at the wall, or the table, or their fingernails. Hadassah's phone beeped again. She glanced at it under the table, unsure why she was keeping the text secret. The latest was from Mom, as well as the three before it. A whole e-mail sent as texts.

I'VE BEEN AWAKE ALL NITE PRAYING ABOUT THIS. U R A STRONG & CAPABLE WOMAN, HADDY, AND CAN MAKE A DECISION LIKE THIS 1 B4 U. THAT SAID, HERE IS MY HEART: WE MUST CONTINUE TO SEARCH FOR UR DAD AND THE OTHER MISSING MISSIONARIES. AND STAY CONNCTD TO R.S.O. U NEED A GROUP OF STRONG, UNCOMPROMISING CHRISTIANS AROUND. I LUV U WHTEVR U CHOOSE. LET ME KNOW ASAP & I'LL CATCH THE NEXT FLIGHT.

She sighed and checked her e-mail to see if there were any new developments. One e-mail stood out from the rest—Priscilla's.

"Over the last few weeks, I have given hours of thought and prayer as to why I left R.S.O. I left because Zeke died, or so I concluded. Now I realize I left because of my own fear. Zeke's actions should have inspired me, but I let them terrify me. I didn't understand why Zeke would throw his life away. But he didn't throw his life away. I'd believed it was important to preserve my own life at all cost — I believed this is what God wanted from me.

"Something you shared, Hadassah, about how Zeke laid his life down for his friends, struck me. But it's more than this. He laid his life down, yes, but it wasn't for just friendship, or an ideology or some vague concept of love. He laid his life down for Jesus. This is all about Jesus. It's not about our family members or loved ones. It's about Jesus receiving the reward for His suffering. Will we

complain about some light and momentary trials when we have such an excellent Friend? Or will we partner with Him to see His Kingdom come?

"God is so good! Even though Zeke is dead, and my sister suffered unspeakably, God is good. I'm going to ask Mr. Murray and Mr. Cooper if they'll have me back at R.S.O. I don't know where you are in the world, but I wanted to tell you first because you were there when God moved through me in the alleys of Manila. Do you think He will move through me again? I miss you, my friend. The world has gone crazy (did you hear what happened in Rome?), but at R.S.O., we were actually doing something rather than letting life drag us along."

Without hesitation, Hadassah sent a quick e-mail in return. "I look forward to seeing you sometime soon, Priscilla. And yes, I'm sure God will move through you again — He just did. Thank you so much for reminding me how everything we do is for Yeshua, Jesus of Nazareth."

After sending the reply, Hadassah longed to speak, but before she could set her unraveled heart on the table, Mr. Cooper broke the silence and set his tangled heart there first.

"I'm going to be fully honest with you, because I really don't know what to do, friends." He sunk his head into his hands for a full minute before he spoke again. "How can I tell the board of R.S.O. what has occurred? We expected our work to be difficult, but I don't think anyone anticipated this level of opposition. I don't know if we can go on."

"Are you suggesting we give up?" Hyun asked him plainly.

Mr. Cooper hung his head. "I don't know what I'm suggesting, but I think it's time we talk about things openly and begin to figure out where we *can* go from here. We've lost five of our best operatives, and we may lose another this afternoon." He looked up again and over at Hadassah.

"No," Hadassah said forthrightly. "I'm with R.S.O. Even if I decide to work with Israeli Intelligence for the next two years, I will not leave R.S.O.; I could work for you from anywhere."

"I will not ask you to compromise you commitment to Israel."

Hyun raised her hand to speak. "R.S.O. is not affiliated with a particular government, and nothing we do compromises the ethics or moral duties of an Israeli officer."

"It's the only circumstance where I could envision a totally honest dual operative," Christina remarked.

"Anyone who is in the military and a follower of Christ always is a dual operative," Pedro added.

Tameka stared at Hadassah. "If you go to Israel, Haddy, and enlist with Sayeret Matkal, all the while continuing to work with R.S.O., our every step will be tracked by the Israeli intelligence community."

"They're already tracking us," Mr. Cooper told them. "If you decide to do this, Hadassah, we'll be open to working with you, as long as you don't compromise the premise of R.S.O."

"I understand, sir," Hadassah said.

"When I get back to the Lighthouse," Mr. Cooper said, "I'm going to lay all the cards on the table, just like I am right now with all of you. But what I want to know from each of you is if you want to stay with R.S.O., or if you want to go."

Pedro lifted his head. "I'm staying, sir."

"I'm leaning toward that decision as well," Tameka said.

"I'm staying with R.S.O." Hyun seemed almost teary. "You have been my only family since my mother was taken, and I'll never forget that. I want to go to Babylon the next chance we get."

"I'd like to stay," Christina said. "I'd like to find my dad, and find our friends. I'll go with you to Babylon, Hyun."

"I wish I could go to Babylon with you," Hadassah said.

"You've made your decision?" Hyun asked.

"It'll be better for you if I'm with Sayeret Matkal. And who knows where God might lead me through them. I may end up in Babylon after all."

Hyun slid a folded piece of paper across the table to her. "Keep this in your pocket."

"What is it?"

"Friends of mine in Sayeret Maktal and the Mossad." Hyun winked. "Keep it hidden until you need it."

"Thank you." The sting of separation began to ease.

***

On Wednesday, Hadassah rode in the car while Eli drove Mr.

373

Cooper, Christina, Pedro, Hyun and Tameka to the airport. She vowed not to shed a tear as she watched them leave.

Eli waited with her in the three hours between the team's departure and Mom's arrival, but he hardly said a word since the television captivated their attention. Every few minutes Eli took another bite of his sandwich, but showed little interest in either food or his companion in light of the unfolding events. Hadassah had poked at the grilled cheese on rye in front of her, but her appetite plummeted as soon as the latest news report about the UN's new Secretary General appeared. The UN had chosen Liberia's Minister of Justice. Xavier Rhodes's face beamed from every screen throughout the restaurant.

"You can't be serious." She didn't remember opening her mouth when she heard herself speak.

"Do you know him?" Eli asked.

"I know of him. Enough to be disgusted."

The moment she saw Mom, Hadassah wrapped her arms around her and held her close.

Mom rented a car right away, ignoring Eli's pleas to escort them around. And as soon as mother and daughter were alone, Mom dived right in. "Haddy, I want you to know I haven't been sitting on my hands for the last year. I've been finding out why. Why was your dad taken? Why were the rest of the missionaries taken? Why cargo ships? The answers I've found are terrible, but they give clues as to where we should look next."

"And you are telling me now?"

"Need-to-know basis, Haddy."

Exhausted, she glared at Mom. "So, what do I *need* to know?"

"It's about economy. It's better for the Prime Minister's economy if he has slaves than if he has a bunch of dead bodies."

"Jordan's Prime Minister?"

"He now has control of Babylon. I acquired Echelon files on him —very unpleasant. But he's one of the people behind it along with his friend Vladimir Therion. They hope to kidnap and enslave so many Christians and Jews, particularly Messianic Jews, that Yeshua won't return."

"How can they be so ignorant and arrogant?"

"They've talked about branding or tattooing the workers and slaves. They want to run some sort of experiment."

Hadassah wanted to be sick as she tried to weigh which was worse: death, or slavery under this man. "You mean the mark of the beast?"

Mom closed her eyes as the car sat at the red light. "Therion is Greek for 'the beast', so I'm afraid this is probably the case."

"Matt wrote to me about cargo ships on the Euphrates, unloading in Babylon. He thinks that people are part of the cargo."

Mom's face darkened. "Bodies and souls of men. Just like the ancient prophecies." She stared at the sea of cars. "How did Colonel Schindler take the news about you joining Sayeret Matkal?"

***

The day before, in the morning, as Hadassah walked to the Colonel's private offices, tourists and Romans strolled all around her as if they yearned for normalcy and wanted life to be okay again. But every one of them watched the skies and their backs.

She watched her own back as she stepped off the street into the stylish building constructed of smooth stone. The windows of the building were so tinted she couldn't see past a foot inside.

The tinted glass doors opened to a pale yellow foyer. As soon as she entered a man in uniform emerged from one of the side doors and greeted her by name.

"This way, Ms. Michelman."

Sighing, she followed him. She'd have to get used to strangers knowing her name and friends not knowing her at all.

"Shalom, Colonel," Hadassah said as soon as she entered his office, and before he turned in his swivel chair.

"Shalom," he replied, then turned to face her.

"Hadassah Michelman, sir," the officer accompanying her said.

"You may go," the Colonel told the officer. "Now, Ms. Michelman, you look as if you have made a decision."

"I did, sir." She folded her hands to keep from fidgeting and looked at him with as much confidence as she had. "There has been a chain of events since I left the police station on Sunday evening, and those events cemented my decision. I will work for Israeli Intelligence, sir."

"Well, Ms. Michelman, I'm proud of you."

"And I'm expecting you to clear the names of everyone who works for R.S.O."

"I didn't promise to clear their names."

"You used this ultimatum to recruit me, sir; it would be decent of you to follow through with your end of the bargain." She had rehearsed this last part so many times in her head she couldn't understand why her bones shook as she spoke.

"Is that all?" His face twitched. She didn't know if he suppressed a sneer or a smile. "You are like your mother. We definitely look forward to your service with Sareyet Matkal."

"Can you get me into the hospital to see Zach, I mean, Mr. Safar?"

"All in good time, Ms. Michelman," he replied.

"Now is a good time, sir." Her bones might shake right out of her skin, but she began to enjoy this negotiation.

The Colonel frowned and stared at her. "For a girl of eighteen, you have chutzpah. We'll arrange something for you. Tell me, will we see anything of your mother?"

"All in good time," she said, suppressing her smile.

The Colonel's boisterous laugh startled her. "You are too much like her. I'll get you in to see Mr. Safar tomorrow evening. We'll leave for Jerusalem on Thursday so we arrive before Shabbat."

***

"So?" Mom said, snapping Hadassah from the memory of her meeting.

"He took it diplomatically."

"There's something I think you should know, since you'll be in Jerusalem. Something I doubt the Colonel will tell you."

Hadassah's ears pricked up, and a smile began to form. She knew whatever this was, coming from Mom it had to be interesting.

"The Ark of the Covenant was found."

The smile disappeared. Hadassah swallowed hard. "I didn't expect that."

"You know what this means, right?"

Her jaw felt strange and tingly. "Do the Temple Mount Advocates have it?"

"Yes, but no one knows outside the Advocates and the Mossad. I hope I can trust you with this secret."

"Yeah, definitely. Do you think they'll try to rebuild the Temple?"

"Not while the Dome of the Rock is there."

There was a long silence while they sat in traffic. A dozen or more scenarios buzzed through Hadassah's mind.

Mom cleared her throat as if she knew her daughter was trying to tie pieces together. "So, did the Colonel say anything else to you?"

"He said he'd like to see you."

"Oh, did he? The Colonel and I butted heads often while I worked for the Mossad."

"I can understand that. He's probably mellowed out by now. But why do you think he came to Rome?"

"The Pope. And intel about your tangos."

Hadassah stayed silent as she tried to make sense of it all.

"Tell me about Zacharias. Is he still in the hospital?"

"I'll be allowed to see him tonight."

"Shall we stop by the hospital first? I could walk up there with you."

Chapter 44:

Zach

Hadassah stepped passed the armed guards and into the room where Zach slept. The view from his window spanned the beautiful neighborhood around the Spanish Steps, where children played on the flagstones and mothers hung out laundry to dry in the beautiful sunshine. She continued to watch this domestic scene with a mix of sadness and longing until she heard Zach stir.

"Hadassah?" He coughed drily.

She turned from the window to grace him with a smile. "Hi, Zach."

"You look good."

"Thanks, you've looked better." He looked as pale as his sheet and scarred for life, but she couldn't bring herself to tell him all that.

"I know. The nurses keep threatening to put make-up on me to make me less appalling."

"You ready to leave yet?"

"I've been ready to leave for days, but he won't let me leave." Zach pointed to the armed security guard right outside the door.

"How did you get in?"

She rolled her eyes as she took the seat beside his bed. "I've got connections."

"Can you introduce me?"

"My mom."

"Ah." He chortled, then coughed.

"I was wondering, Zach—how did you know Ebola virus was in those devices?"

He gave a wry smile. "A little trick I learned from some hobbits in a book I obsessed over as a kid. I just pretended to be passed out so I could hear their whole plan." He coughed again.

She chuckled. "I'm glad you did."

"Me too." He laughed. Then he broke into a coughing fit which looked and sounded painful.

She rushed to get him a drink of water.

"Save your breath, friend," she said when he stopped coughing. "I wanted to let you know the rest of the team left for America today with Ileyah."

"Thank you for getting my sister out." He tried to smile, but could only cough more of those painful sounding coughs.

"Are they taking good care of you here?" Hadassah asked.

Zach motioned for the pencil and paper on the nearby end table. He wrote, *Doctors tolerable, nurses not. But I feel better.* "It's good to see your face, Haddy." Then the coughing started again.

"Save your energy for healing up quick. I'll be praying for you. And please pray for us while you have some time to spare."

He pulled the paper closer and wrote, *Help me find the men who did this.*

"I leave for Jerusalem tomorrow. I'll do what I can from there. I hope to see you soon." She gave him a kiss on the top of the head and left.

Thursday

Chapter 45:

Jerusalem

Once the plane reached 35,000 feet and the turbulence calmed, Hadassah took out her phone, angled it away from Colonel Schindler, who sat beside her, and switched it to plane mode. *What could I expect to find in my phone to comfort me now?* She opened up the Bible application and typed in "comfort." The first verse to pop up was from Psalm 23, "Your rod and your staff they comfort me."

Dad's teaching flooded her mind. Abba Father's rod and staff weren't intended to punish her, but to protect her from her enemies. What comfort she found in the knowledge of His protection turned bittersweet as her thoughts drifted to Dad. Would God protect him as well? Was he still alive?

With every limb tingling, she scrolled through the apps to her e-mail.

The Colonel turned toward her and scanned her face, but remained quiet as if he wouldn't know what to say even if he was the talking type. She looked up at him and neither one of them smiled.

The Colonel was impossible to read, and she hoped she compartmentalized enough to be just as difficult.

When she looked at her phone again, it took everything in her not to broadcast surprise. An e-mail from, of all people, Paul. Her fingers sweat and shook as she fumbled to open it. *Don't drop the phone.*

"Hadassah—I... I'm writing you at Matt's request. He knew, given the intelligence we unearthed, that we would be ferreted out by the authorities. I'm the only one who escaped the raid. I'm on the other side of Babylon now, hidden in a safe house with several of Dave's friends. But before I was separated from Matt, Adam and Maleek, Matt entrusted a letter to me to deliver to you. But I have no idea what address to send it to, and who knows how long it would take to get there or if it'd be intercepted along the way. So I typed it out:

"My beautiful Hadassah,

"I know that when you read this letter my fate will be unknown to all except the Lord and my captors, but even now, girl, don't fear, 'cause I'm not afraid anymore. Remember how we talked about having grace in this hour? I pray that God gives you the measure He has given me, or even greater grace.

"Very early yesterday morning I saw your dad. I saw him with my own eyes, and I saw my dad as well. They, among at least ten thousand others, are slaves here, mistreated but not badly abused. Some have suffered great abuse at the hands of their slave drivers,

but not your dad and not mine. They were working side by side building a stadium in Babylon. And what pretense keeps them, and so many others, here against their will? They have been deemed criminals. If you are reading this, then so have I. But don't despair, girl.

"Remember how we talked on the beach—becoming slaves to reach the slaves with the gospel? I will be a slave of Yeshua, just as Paul the Apostle was. So if they have my body and my freedom, they still don't own me because I belong to Yeshua, and am His slave first and foremost. It all makes sense to me now, as if the Holy Spirit gave a special revelation. And I hope it makes sense to you too, soon.

"Don't worry, though. This dude's not goin' down as a slave of Babylon. I'll be bustin' out of this joint the first real chance I get, and I'll have our dads with me. Until then, please pray for me, but don't cry. I'm yours forever, girl. Waiting on your sweet love, Matt."

Don't cry? What, was he serious? The tears began to roll silently by "My beautiful Hadassah" and torrented at his reminder of their conversation on the beach. She laughed out loud, even in the midst of her tears, when reading about him busting out of the joint. His voice rang so clearly in her mind.

She dropped the phone onto her lap, closed her eyes and willed her tears to stop. She couldn't bring herself to look at the Colonel, no matter how strongly she felt his gaze.

"News about your dad?" he asked.

She winced, both at the idea of him knowing about her dad and the prospect of answering this question. Without opening her eyes she nodded. A passing flight attendant tapped her on the shoulder and handed her a packet of tissues.

"On the house, sweetheart," she said with a wink.

The pity embarrassed Hadassah to silence again. She wiped her face of tears, refusing to look at the Colonel, who continued to stare at her.

"We're planning to send another recon team in come winter," Colonel Schindler explained.

She covered her eyes with her forearm. "He'll have been there two years." She gulped down fresh tears.

"I'm saying that if you're successful on your other missions, you may be included."

All at once her tears dried up and she faced him. "I won't let you down, sir." *Please, Abba Father,* she whispered in her heart, *please help me succeed.*

The plane landed at Ben Gurion airport, or, as Colonel Schindler called it, Natbag, which was southeast of Tel Aviv. Ignoring any nervousness, disquiet and general anxiety wracking her heart, Hadassah unbuckled her seat-belt before the captain turned off the fasten-seat-belts sign. She still hoped Mom would meet up with her in Jerusalem. But Mom had had that cryptic look during their farewell in Rome. If Hadassah knew anything she knew it meant more news about Dad. News Mom wouldn't share, but would be traversing the globe to learn more. Maybe it was better not to know.

She grabbed her luggage from the overhead compartment and squeezed past the lingering passengers crowding the aisle. Colonel Schindler followed behind her, eying her every move, poised to pursue her if she ran ahead of him. If she was supposed to be helping him, why did she feel like his prisoner?

But her lungs longed to breathe the air of Israel, to taste it as if for the first time. Her body twinged with delight, and if she had allowed herself she would have smiled.

The baggage carousel brought her luggage around first, as if the boys at El Al's baggage claim knew how much she wanted to see outside the airport. She wasn't in Jerusalem yet, but Tel Aviv put a bounce in her step. The thick, warm air enveloped her on the walk to the car, and she savored every breath.

Colonel Schindler drove to Jerusalem with the tinted windows rolled up, but she still studied many details of the landscape. Memories sprang to life as she saw neighborhoods, outdoor markets and museums. Memories of a simple life when the longings in her heart made sense.

Stepping outside the car in Jerusalem, and walking toward a nondescript building fashioned from Jerusalem stone, she tasted the air again. Hot. Humid. Holy. A torrid blast of this air pushed against her back and wisped her curls into her eyelashes; she blew the hair away while glancing up to the hill where Yeshua promised He would plant His feet—the Mount of Olives. On its slopes stood the resolute and relatively new neighborhood. And somewhere near that neighborhood, she was sure, sat a house of prayer, a promise of the Lord's presence and allies in the faith.

The gold dome on the Temple Mount caught her eye; to the west of it stood the Wailing Wall. She felt a bit like that wall, stuffed with the requests of others. If only the Colonel let her stop to think, she would hear Abba Father's plan in the midst of all this.

At least Paul was safe. And Matt knew what was going to happen before it did. That had to be some comfort. But it wasn't. She missed Mom, Dad, and her teammates who had become like family. Perhaps she could call for backup on the next assignment. Her thoughts were all over the globe, and she tried to reel them in.

However scattered her mind may have been, her heart knew this to be true: she was in Jerusalem, and Jerusalem was home.

Book 2

Preview

Revelation Special Ops Book 2

Pharmacia:

Those Magic Arts

East Jerusalem, Israel

Friday in June

Prologue

Don't back out on my now, Qamar." Junayd stared at his comrade as if he could impart courage, then sunk his head, hoping disappointment would be a greater persuasion.

But Qamar looked scared this time, as if he was more afraid of judgment from Allah than any repercussions from a friend.

"Are you sure we're doing the will of Allah?" Qamar pressed his back against the ragged couch as if he wanted to disappear into it. With the state of the furniture in this basement, the young man just might. But all of that would change once their plan succeeded. Jerusalem would belong to Palestine at last, a perfect capital for the rising state.

"I'm having my doubts too." But Hussein usually did.

Junayd's eyes flashed in anger as he stared at each one of his companions. He wasn't sure whether or not he would have chosen anger to persuade them. He nearly spit at Hussein's feet. "We always have doubts just before an assignment."

"I didn't in Rome." Fawsi wore a smirk across his face.

"That's because you enjoyed torturing the infidel too much."

"He still didn't repent."

"You still foiled his device."

Fawsi lowered his gaze.

"Next time you won't be given a budget for Ebola virus."

Fawsi sneered at Junayd. "If this plan goes awry, there won't be a next time."

Amin looked up at them. "Today is the day. Today or no other." He looked down again and stared at the plate of couscous and lamb that sat on the flimsy coffee table. Like everyone else, he didn't touch it. Must not have had an appetite. He flicked the ashes of his cigarette on the coffee stained carpet. Of all Junayd's friends, Amin showed contempt for everyone. But he reserved his greatest contempt for the Jews, which was why Junayd kept him around.

"I wish you wouldn't flick your ashes on my cousin's carpet." He knew Amin wouldn't heed the request, though.

Qamar peeled his back away from the couch. "What are your thoughts, Samad?"

Samad held his hands together against his mouth as if in prayer. Samad sincere in prayer? That would be more of a miracle than their entrance into Israel last week.

They had departed from Rome just before the first explosion, and no one said a word. No one suspected any of them as the masterminds. Except for that infidel who should have died. And that girl at the café in Trastevere. Here she was in Jerusalem—with

Colonel Schindler, of all people. Junayd would have to be more careful next time.

He raised his glance. "Samad, yes, what are your thoughts?"

"Just like you, Junayd—that we're wasting time here and allowing cowardice to rule our actions." Samad glared at Hussein who gritted his teeth and stared at the coffee table.

Someone's stomach growled.

"Shall we eat first?" Qamar asked.

Fawsi gave his strange grin again. "And miss our opportunity to plan a bomb on a Jew? The archeologist will visit his precious Temple Mount soon. No time for eating, brothers, this is our golden hour to protect our Haram Ash-Sharif."

After all, they wouldn't be destroying the Noble Sanctuary itself, just a few stones by the entrance. Allah should be pleased.

***

The June sun seemed brighter than usual as Junayd emerged from the basement into the alley behind his cousin's house. Eight minutes and they'd be at Bridge Street. Six minutes if he walked briskly. He picked up his pace. Maybe he'd make it in five. Carrying this many explosives always made him nervous, and all six of the men carried the same number. At least he had the only trigger and not Fawsi.

Fawsi couldn't be trusted with much these days. The young man had some dream or another of glory. Probably wanted to lead the charge that would end with driving the Jews into the sea. But wasn't that what they were doing today? Their work, if successful, would spark the Jihad to end all Jihads. It would usher in the Last Imam. Bring the new age. Their pockets would be well lined in the process. The Roman benefactor was especially generous for their last mission, but for this one they were promised Babylonian silver.

Was it the sun or his quickened pace that caused Junayd to sweat so much? His sudden dizziness overwhelmed him. They were almost there.

Their plan was flawless. Today, Avram Baruck, the highly acclaimed professor from the Institute of Archeology at the Hebrew University of Jerusalem, was making an unprecedented tour of Haram Ash-Sharif, or as he called it, the Temple Mount. He'd be surrounded by nearly twenty colleagues and at least as many members of the Israeli Defense Force. They had finally gained access to the holy grounds and were making a parade of it. It should never have been granted, especially on a Friday, the day of prayers, but this might have been arranged to make sure more eyes watched them. Make sure they behaved. And with such a pressing crowd, no one would notice Junayd's or his companions' activities.

Fawsi caught up to him, but walked beside him without a word.

"Yes, my brother?"

"I brought extra with me in case the first doesn't work."

"Extra explosives?"

Fawsi nodded and smirked again. "I thought I'd let you know. I have a separate trigger for these."

The excessive perspiration was definitely from nervousness now. He felt much better when he had all the triggers.

"Don't worry, I won't use mine unless I have to."

"Did Saifullah give it to you?" Saifullah had been their contact to their Roman benefactor.

"No, this came straight from Mr. Therion, our real benefactor. Or, I should say, King Therion. He took all contingencies into account."

"I see." Winded, Junayd passed through the entrance to Haram Ash-Sharif.

At the sight of the crowd of Jewish men filling the courtyard, indignation surged within him. He was suddenly thankful for the extra explosives. He nodded to Fawsi, who returned a look of agreement.

The beauty of these explosives was in their simplicity. The three-inch-by-three-inch clear plastic adhesives were primed by peeling away the protective papers and sticking them to a target. These adhesives wouldn't be noticeable for quite a while, giving Junayd and his friends the opportunity to seek cover before activating the trigger.

The six men pushed their way through the crowd of archeologists, plastering their adhesives as they went. Junayd stepped away, feeling sufficiently proud of himself. Either Saifullah or this Mr. Therion had planned so well.

Within the walls of the mosque, they'd all be at a safe distance.

They milled about, hardly acknowledging one another.

Junayd slipped behind a pillar and pulled a small bluish device from the folds of his garments. It looked like an old cell phone. He smiled and pressed the trigger. Nothing happened. His smile disappeared and his heart raced. He glanced at the red light that would come on if the device was working, then pressed the button again. The light came on, but nothing happened.

He spun around and nearly crashed into Fawsi, whose face was plastered with a mixture of fury and fear.

"Yours too?" Junayd asked him.

Fawsi nodded. They spun around to find their friends, but found instead a domino of explosions tearing life, limb and stone from the structures all across this sacred ground.

***

Hadassah gripped the desk as the building rattled. Her pen had completely marred the paper she was supposed to sign. But who cared about formalities at a time like this? And in Jerusalem of all places. Colonel Schindler's face grew deathly pale and he leaped for the outside door. In a single bound, he jumped to the street with Hadassah right at his heels.

Her mouth dropped open, as did every mouth in the gathering crowd. Where the Dome of the Rock had stood just minutes beforehand, a cloud of black smoke veiled a raging fire. Mount Moriah was aflame.

And to the north of that, two trails of exhaust announced the launch of missiles. Intercontinental ballistics. She prayed in her heart of hearts that they wouldn't be what her gut told her. Nuclear.

Whatever had begun was irrevocable.

ABOUT THE AUTHOR

Precarious Yates has lived in 8 different states of the Union and 3 different countries, but currently lives in Texas with her husband, her daughter and their mastiff. When she's not writing, she enjoys music, teaching, playing on jungle gyms, praying and reading. She holds a Masters in the art of making tea and coffee and a PhD in Slinky® disentangling.

You can learn more about Ms. Yates and about the issues discussed in this novel by visiting www.precariousyates.com

Book 2 of Revelation Special Ops, **Pharmacia: Those Magic Arts**, is due out in 2012.

10392261R00231

Made in the USA
Charleston, SC
01 December 2011